The _ʎ s Dream

Sara Alexi is the author of the Greek Village Series.

She divides her time between England and a small village in Greece.

http://facebook.com/authorsaraalexi

Sara Alexi

THE GYPSY'S DREAM

oneiro

Published by Oneiro Press 2013

ISBN-13: 978-1484873311

ISBN-10: 1484873319

For Alex

Chapter 1

The place looks nothing like the picture postcard image Abby had in her mind. The fountain in the middle of the square is broken and empty, skeletal leaves lining the bottom. The houses are low, grubby and crumbling, with sagging tiled roofs. A donkey stands motionless, eyes closed, tethered to a telegraph pole.

It is perfect! Abby grins.

Three people are hunched on a bench under the central palm tree by the dry fountain. In the pre-dawn light they are silhouetted against the whitewashed wall behind.

'Eight euro,' the driver says over the top of his muffled radio. He takes a cigarette from a crumpled pack on the dashboard and taps it on the steering wheel.

Abby fumbles for her purse. She clears her throat and fiddles with the coins. There aren't very many. She feels in the pockets of her shorts but there is only her boat ticket. Her heartbeat quickens. As the taxi drives away she comforts herself with the thought that at least she has enough money left to buy breakfast. She hasn't eaten since the plane. Abby wasn't impressed with her first experience of airline cuisine. Yiannis said he would pay her daily, cash in hand, so at most she will have to skip lunch. She turns her attention back to the village.

This is going to work.

She is still grinning. The possibilities! The sun is about to rise over the hill, its warmth promised by a clear sky, the dusty road, the scent of jasmine in the soft morning breeze. She hugs herself and breathes in this new world around her.

Abby searches for a word that will describe her feelings. The square, surrounded by single-storey whitewashed houses, made of stones piled one on top of the other, with blue shutters, feels safe, contained, unthreatening. 'Home' is the best word she can come up with. Her reaction surprises her as the place is foreign to her western eyes and her experience of 'home' is no longer such a joyful one. Especially since Dad married Sonia.

Her cardigan pulled around her shoulders, she arranges her tangled hair over her ears for warmth. Yawning, she looks towards the sun. She puts one foot on top of the other. Who knew Greece would be cold in the early summer? Trainers would have been warmer. So would jeans.

The flick of a light inside a shop lays a carpet of orange across the road. It is magical, and Abby feels a giggle rise in her throat. A cat runs across the glow into the shadows. The lit window now displays comfy sandals for old people, bottles of vitamins and suntan cream. Abby pulls her cardigan around her more tightly and wills the sun to rise.

There are no signs of café culture around the square, except a tall stack of white plastic chairs by a lamppost opposite. There are no neon lights, in fact hardly any shop signs at all. She swallows hard, she hugs herself tighter. It doesn't look quite right, although she has only seen rather grainy photos of the bar's interior on a web site that looked like it was designed in the mid-nineties.

A tractor grumbles its way into the square. The men sitting under the palm tree stand, backs straighten, hands come out of pockets. The tractor stops, the farmer points to one of the men who climbs onto the trailer behind, and stands holding the back of the tractor. The two remaining workers tuck their chins inside their jackets. Three more men wander into the square. Abby judges they are Indian, maybe Pakistani. Migrants, illegals probably. She has seen a program about it, eastern Europe a gateway to the west, how many die each year scrabbling to cross rivers to get into countries more wealthy than their own. The irony of her journey, also for work, in the opposite direction is not lost on her. The remaining men slouch and sit as the tractor rumbles away, hands back in warm pockets.

Abby shifts from foot to foot. The sun's first rays light up the dusky orange roofs opposite, the colours muted and warm. No wet, cold, greys anywhere. The sky, pale pink at the edges, seems endless. She takes a big breath in through her nose and releases it slowly. It's going to be a summer to remember.

A door off the square opens, an aisle of artificial light beckoning before the aroma of fresh bread reaches her. She takes a step towards it and rubs her hand across her empty stomach, the beginnings of hunger mixed with thrills of excitement. The aeroplane food feels a lifetime ago but she will wait to feel more settled before she eats. It will be the last of her money anyway, better to keep it until she finds Yiannis.

A cockerel screeches its morning call. A dog barks in return. She wants to stand somewhere high and shout 'I am here!' Looking to the blueing sky, she becomes aware of a strange background sound. Abby looks between the houses out towards the orange groves she passed in the taxi. There is a metal pylon, forty feet tall, with a fan on top. She wonders if it is a wind generator. There is no breeze but it turns, whirring. A working village, no pretence for tourists here.

She can hear another fan in the distance

somewhere. In the back of her mind is her old physics teacher, so tall his shirt was always pulling out of his trousers. Mr Rogers - Dodgy Roger - always walked with arms stiff by his sides, gliding with knees bent. The girls had decided he had worked out some equations to prove it was more energy-efficient to walk that way. What was the thing he said about fans and ecological farming? Something about 'heat flux density'. Or not. The thought will not come.

She feels a lump rising in her throat. The short summer will pass, and then what? Will she be able to stay on to do her 'A' levels? Sonia getting pregnant is not her problem. If she cannot deal with the baby she shouldn't be having one. Abby looks at her watch. Dad won't even be awake yet, so he won't have read her note. She yawns. Who would have thought travelling could be so tiring. Sleep on the plane was impossible, there was far too much to take in on the boat, now it feels like it is starting to catch up with her. She closes her eyes for a second and Rogers glides across her mind again, talking of mixing high-up warm air with lower cool air to avoid low ground temperatures.

'Against frost!' Abby crosses her cardigan over her chin when she realises she spoke aloud. She glances towards the men under the tree but they are silent, and still. They do not look over to her. A van draws up. The men stand stiffly on the edge of the pavement. Some take their hands out of their pockets.

The smaller one, Abby notices, stands taller. The taller ones slouch more, relaxed, assured. The driver does not hesitate; the taller ones are waved into the back of the van. As it pulls away the rest droop back onto the little wall.

In the advancing light a skirted woman with a headscarf strolls into the square towards a kiosk, which is dark and shuttered. She unlocks the door at the back of the booth.

The kiosk lights stammer their way to life, the central orange brilliance a sharp contrast with the dawn blues in the square. Metal shutters are unchained from the front of drinks fridges and the tops of ice-cream freezers. They clang as the woman stacks them on end by the wall, lifting them easily with unexpected strength. She returns to split bundles and hang newspapers on the line around the kiosk with clothes pegs. Her headscarf is pulled off to sit on her shoulders halfway through the task. Bottles chink as she pulls crates across her empire. Abby finds that she is smiling. She is in another world and the world feels good. She could not have imagined it just a few hours before at the airport in the English damp evening chill. England is two hours behind, they'll still be asleep. What will Dad think when he wakes up and finds she is not there? He won't expect her to get up till late morning; it is the holidays after all. Maybe he won't even notice and go off to work and not know till the evening. She doesn't want him to worry. Sonia will presume she is out. But this evening, what then? Maybe she should have left the note on the kitchen table instead of her bedside table. Actually it would have been more grown up to have told him, face to face. Has she over-reacted? She will ring him in an hour or two and face him.

The sun peeks over the hill and the tentacles of light bring heat down into the square. Abby stretches. She still hasn't moved from where the taxi dropped her. She is physically tired from her travels but she feels so alive.

A bitter aroma drifts from the kiosk. Abby thinks of Dad making his own coffee. Her breath quickens. She will not use the return flight in September unless he agrees she can continue at school. There's no point.

The coffee smells bad.

Abby takes a deep breath and looks around her. She is here now. Dad and Sonia will have to get on with it; he married her for better or for worse and all that.

She wonders if Rockie is missing her, will Dad think to take him for walks.

She lifts herself tall and sets off to find Yiannis of the emails and his 'Malibu' bar. She crosses the square.

Two old men with flat caps and shepherd's crooks stand outside a glass-fronted, very drab-looking café at the top of the square. So bare, so under-furnished. Abby cannot think why they would be waiting for it to open. No curtains, no tablecloths, bare bulbs. One sports an impressive moustache, the faces deeply lined and sun-scorched.

The sun rises high enough for its rays to touch her skin and the warmth flows through her veins, bringing euphoria. Her breath quickens at the realisation of her achievement. Dad will be waking up now. She bets that his first words will be 'overreaction' – that's what he always says of her. 'One life, live it!' she says to herself, and pulling her phrase book from her bag she walks up to the men, momentarily confident in her abilities..

'*Parakalo*. Bar. Malibu.' It does not even sound Greek to her own ears. The two men look at each other and shrug. She points to the words in the book but they seem happier to look at her face, the book does not register. She lifts the book higher, to eye level, but they only give it the briefest of glances.

'Thank you,' Abby says in English as she walks away, confused and just a little bit angry at their rudeness. The men call after her, 'Thank you, thank you.' Her hair flicks across her face and into her eyes as she turns back to smile at them. One grins toothlessly, his friend waves. Their animated and warm response brings her cheer. She re-evaluates why they did not respond to the book and the shocking possibility that they might be illiterate crosses her mind. She gives them a last sympathetic look, understanding, kind.

A lane leads out of the square, past a corner shop to a church, but there is no sign of a bar. The lane leads out of the village into the orange orchards, dotted with fans, which, one by one, are now slowing to a standstill. She watches them come to rest, the silence they leave soon filled with dogs barking, cockerels crowing. Unsure what else to do she slowly returns to the square and leans against the telegraph pole. The donkey has gone.

The palm tree is more dominant from this angle, the kiosk and the dry fountain crouching in its shade. The smell of bread mixes with the warming air.

It trickles into Abby's thoughts that if she does not find this bar, this promised job, she will not have enough money to eat for the day. She wonders if she has been really rather foolish. No, not foolish, stupid. Her stomach clenches and the bread smell is overpowering.

With a surge in her chest, and a huge welling of tears ready to fall, it smacks her. She has been absolutely ridiculous. What was she thinking? She has nothing in writing; well, there are the emails at home and the word of her friend Jackie who went out the week before. She pushes away these thoughts. It's done, she is here, she must focus, find the bar or figure out what she will do, like an equation. She needs logic, not over-emotional reaction. She doesn't overreact. Dad is wrong about that.

Drawing in a breath, she quells her panic. She thinks. She has the bar's phone number. She can call. It will cost a fortune to ring on her mobile, and she didn't remember to top up. She sighs.

Taking out her phone she flicks through her contacts until the number appears, the 0030 code distinguishing it. She should have just calmly done this when the taxi dropped her off instead off all that panicking.

It rings and Abby feels her spine straighten. How childish she has been.

'*Embros*?'

'Yes, hello, this is Abby. I am due to start work today and I cannot find your bar.'

'*Ti? Ti thelis?*'

Abby's heart quickens all over again. It sounds like an old lady at home, certainly not Yiannis.

'Abby, the job?'

'*Pios einai? O Yiannis den einai edo.*'

'Is Yiannis there? Ermm. There Yiannis?' Abby tucks the phone under her chin and flicks through the guide book for the word 'There'.

'Natos, Yiannis?'

'*Pou*?'

'Sorry!' The phone clicks off. Searching through the phrase book she find 'Pou' means 'Where'. It doesn't make sense. She opens the book to the page on telephone conversations and dials again. There is a bleep and a message tells her that her phone will switch off as the battery is dead.

She takes the battery out and shakes it and puts it in again, but there is no life in it.

A vein in her temple begins to throb. She sucks in her lips, chewing a little on the bottom one. Sweat runs down her back. She looks around the square, her eyes darting, unseeing. Her breath quickens. She takes out her purse and counts the change. The tears in her eyes begin to fall, their silence broken by her sucking of air. The sun's warmth, now full on her, is no longer a tender kiss. It is just heat that makes her sweat. The light is a nuisance in her eyes. The charm of the village turns to desolation. The excitement turns to fear. She can feel herself spiralling into despair and struggles to pull herself out.

Logic. She must use logic. The bar must be here. Abby throws her phone in her bag. Her shoulders are feeling hot, she should put some sunscreen on. But not now.

The woman in the kiosk is counting change.

'Excuse me, do you speak English?'

'English. Hello.' She pauses and then recites 'El'beeback' and laughs.

'Sorry?'

'El'beeback. Ter-min-a-tor. English. Welcome, welcome!' The woman laughs and offers a single wrapped chewing gum from her counter.

'Do you speak English?' Abby asks again, taking the gift without thought, hope binding her manners.

'Yes English.' The woman has a nice smile and, to a degree, it reassures Abby. Her perfect hair transports Abby into civilised salons. Everything will be fine, she breathes again.

'I have come for a job, at a bar. The Malibu?' Abby realises the woman's next words could quell all her panic, wipe out all her thoughts of her own stupidity, or not. She stares. Part of her wonders how much lacquer the woman must spray on to hold her halo so still.

Finally, 'Job', the woman says. She is still grinning as she leans out of her little window and points down the road to where the taxi had dropped Abby first thing.

Abby breathes again, exhales deeply, releases the tension from her chest and automatically says 'Thank you' in English and walks in the direction indicated, hoping, wishing. The shop the woman pointed to has opened its doors. It is not clear what it is from a distance. But there are no neon lights, no chairs and tables on the street. It is not the bar on the website. But maybe the owner speaks English and knows of The Malibu.

A donkey brays to remind Abby how far in the country she is. Maybe it's the wrong village. Maybe the right village is just a walk away.

A petite woman sits outside the shop, slid down in a plastic chair like a child, sucking her drink through a straw. She shields her eyes from the sun as Abby approaches.

'English?' Abby asks.

'No, I'm Greek.' The woman smiles.

'Ah, you speak English. I am here for a job. The Malibu.'

The woman stands, spilling her drink down the

front of her short dress in the process.

'What is this "The Malibu"?' Her accent is strong, she speaks slowly, wiping her dress with her hand.

Abby's hope dissolves. 'A bar.' Surely she must know it.

'Where this bar?'

'Here, Saros.'

'Here is no Saros.'

Abby can feel her shoulders droop. Her bag slips off and onto the pavement.

'Are we near Saros?' She feels she knows the answer before she hears it.

'The Saros an island.' The woman waves her arm, suggesting impossible distances.

'But the boat said Saros.' Abby blinks the tears away. She cannot stop her lip quivering.

The woman says kindly, 'I am thinking it say Soros.'

'But the taxi driver! He must have known this was not Saros.'

'Did you ask him? What you say to him?'

'The Malibu bar. I was told the bar was in a neighbouring village to the port, and everyone knew it.'

'What else you have said to him?'

'Well, he looked like he didn't understand so I said Yiannis' bar.'

'Ahhh!' The woman laughs and Abby feels herself relax a little, she seems to know of it. 'There is the Yiannis bar.' She points to the drab-looking kafenio on the square, where the metal-framed glass doors are now wide open and two old men, one with an impressive moustache, are playing an animated game of backgammon, slamming the pieces down, the noise echoing around the village. Abby puts her hand over her mouth and squeezes her nose in the crook of her thumb to stop herself crying. The woman continues, 'But Yiannis dead. Son Theo now has bar. But not Malibu, never Malibu. This not Saros.'

Abby sinks where she stands, next to her bag, and sits on the kerbside.

Her shoulders are burning.

Dad was right, she has overreacted. She wishes she was at home making his coffee, Rockie there to cuddle, for comfort and to be easily made happy with his marrowbone treats.

Chapter 2

Lighter fuel sprays cross the charcoals. A single match roars the grill into life. It will be hot in twenty minutes or so. The chickens are split and waiting, and a stack of thick sausages ready. By lunch-time the *ouzeri* will be full of farmers, stuffing down the food dripping in her lemon sauce, swilling it down with large measures of ouzo in glasses clinking with ice. Satisfied that another day has begun Stella mixes herself an iced coffee and strolls outside to watch the world go by. She'll peel the potatoes later.

It's early, but warm already.

She settles into the plastic chair and sucks her frappé through a straw. There aren't many people about. A girl stands in the shade leaning on the telegraph pole, a tourist. You don't see many of those here in the village. Shorts, sandals, strappy T-shirt, bag. Everything looks creased. Maybe English. Too blonde for English?

Distant sounds of morning echo around the village. Closer, from just across the square comes the grating sound of plastic against concrete as Vasso struggles with a stack of beer crates. It must be hard for her all day in the kiosk with no one to swap shifts with now. Not that Vasso will complain that she is alone. Her son's job in Athens is such a point of pride.

Stella stretches out her legs even further, luxuriating in the sun's touch relaxing her muscles. Child's legs, all skin and bone and no muscle. Stavros won't be here for hours. She didn't hear him come in last night but this morning the sickly sweet odour of sweated alcohol betrayed last night's excesses. She sighs and closes her eyes, the sun turning the insides of her eyelids pink.

When they first met he was an Adonis, with his charm, his flat stomach, his laugh. But mostly she likes to remember when he was still happy. When they were happy.

A sound of farmers laughing drifts across the square. The kafenio is starting to fill up. This is a good sign for Stella. All day she will be slicing meat turned on the upright spit, stuffing it into the folds of grilled pita bread with tomatoes, chips and garlic-yoghurt dip, wrapping it in greaseproof paper, handing these *giro* to hungry farmers, lazy wives and starving school children. Eaten in the hand as they walk home, juice dripping down their chins.

This is the sixth, no seventh, year she has been running her restaurant. Well, not exactly a restaurant. The four coarse wooden tables with equally rough chairs do not make a restaurant. An *ouzeri*, perhaps.

She certainly sells enough ouzo, along with the charcoal-grilled sausages and chickens, to farmers who sit for half an hour and want more than the hand-held *giro* or souvlaki.

Stella smiles. Seven years. She loves it. She loves being at the hub of the community. She loves the laughs and the banter. She loves serving food to the single men who all look a little crumpled and need some care. She loves putting extra sauce on for the children and extra chips when they buy a parcel of chicken to take home for their mothers. She loves Friday and Saturday night when she puts on the radio and the customers stay longer, drink more, enjoy themselves, the cool of the evening air adding energy to her limbs, and a bounce in her step as she serves and dances between tables.

The farmers who come are a rough but jovial bunch.

'Hey, Stella,' they call. 'Your potatoes are the finest in Greece,' and the place dissolves into uproar, no harm intended. They fling compliments at her, these, who once threw stones. She gives as good as she gets, not offended by their rough ways and serves free shots of ouzo to the authors of the funniest comments, revelling in their flattery. Once Stavros had joined in. Lately he is more likely to clatter the spatula against grill, demanding her help.

'Hey, Stella, don't put any more fuel on that fire!' the farmers hiss in a stage whisper, or 'don't blow on those coals, they will burst into flame,' they warn as she scuttles to see what he wants, casting them a silencing look as she goes, giggles and whispers following her through to the grill room.

Stavros' piercing blue eyes rarely turn to her as she enters these days. He will just throw the spatula onto the counter and go to sit outside. One time recently he had just spat the words, 'The sausages need turning,' and had taken the bucket out to get more charcoal.

It isn't that what he says is cruel or unkind or untrue. The words themselves are harmless. It is the way he says them, his tone a window into his mind. What does he think of her if he feels free to speak to her that way? If she were the butcher the tone would be different; if she were one of the farmers even, then he would not be so dismissive. But the edge in his voice shows the absence of respect. It leaves her on the brink of tears. At these times a quiet desperation lodges in her, creating an urgency, compelling her to do something, anything to make the situation different, the feeling go away, to make things better.

She sighs and scuffs circles in the dust on the tarmac with the toe of her shoe. He was the life of the place once. More farmers' wives had come then. He charmed them and made them feel special. He used to make Stella feel special once.

Stella stops grinding the dirt and looks over to the new sandwich shop across the road, just opened, and doing rather well it seems.

These days, when Stavros offers more than a grunt all he has to say is that they need more business, tourists. He has even talked about employing a foreigner to help bring in these tourists, as if this foreigner will have an unlimited line of hungry friends trailing behind them. Why would the tourist come here, to this village, the same as thousands of others scattered across the backwaters of rural Greece? A moth flies to the light. But these thoughts remain unsaid; these days it's better that way.

Stella peers across at the tourist. White shorts is still standing by the telegraph pole, rummaging in her bag. It is big for a handbag but not a rucksack. She takes out a phone.

Stella wants a mobile phone. She is not sure who she would call on it, but it would be fun. There would be no point in calling Vasso, she is right there in the kiosk during the day and next door when they go home. The butcher, next door? But the order is the same every week. The bakery is just across the road. There would be no point in calling Juliet, the lesson with her is at the same time every week.

The lessons are a silver lining to the cloud of Stavros' growing obsession with the need for tourist trade. It didn't take much to persuade him that learning English would be a good idea. She arranged a direct swap, a chicken dinner for an hour of Juliet's time. The lessons are going well and Stella studies when she can and becomes excited towards the day of her lesson. Last week they practised shopping conversations. Recalling the lesson, she forms her lips.

'I would like a dozen teacakes and a jar of marmalade.' Stella says out loud. She isn't entirely sure what a teacake is but she loves Juliet's marmalade.

The thought focuses her senses. A batch of bread must have just come out of the bakery oven, the warm mouth-watering smell thickening the air. They will come across with her daily order soon. Stella will pick out the end of a warm loaf for her breakfast.

She sucks on her straw considering how, overall, despite Stavros, she loves so much of her life. Hopefully Stavros will pull out of this mood and they will plod on until they are old and grey, serving hungry kids, adding extra sauce and dancing with the farmers.

The girl at the telegraph pole puts her phone away and takes out a purse. She doesn't look very happy.

Stella wonders if she should put extra sausages on, the kafenio is very full. They will sit there all morning and wander across when they get peckish for a *giro* or sausage and chips. She might even put a chicken on early. Someone may want to eat their main meal before mid-afternoon.

The girl in the shorts walks across to Vasso's kiosk and flicks through a little book before looking into the window. Stella is side-on to the open window of the kiosk and she cannot see or hear Vasso until she laughs. Stella knows this laugh. She uses it when she has made a joke; it is slightly withheld as if she is embarrassed. Vasso's head appears, pushed through the kiosk window, followed by an arm. She points in Stella's direction.

Perhaps the girl is hungry. Stella gets up to check the grill. It is almost hot enough but even the sausages will be fifteen minutes and the potatoes aren't peeled yet. The girl will either have to wait or go across to the sandwich shop. She can imagine Stavros' face if he found out …

She looks over to the new shop, and the Romanian girl who opens up and serves there waves at her. She seems alright but Stella has not really got to know her yet: she is new to the village. Stella nods in return and looks back to the square to find the tourist nearly upon her.

'English?' the girl asks. Stella wonders why she would think she is English. She has dark skin and dark, shoulder length hair, frizzy from the heat of daily cooking, and even darker eyes. But she seizes the chance to bring her English lessons alive. This is what all the work has been for.

'No, I'm Greek.' Stella smiles, feeling very pleased with herself.

The girl talks too fast and Stella struggles to keep up. The story begins to unfold. It seems there is some sort of a mix-up. The poor girl has got on the wrong boat and is miles away from where she was heading. Stella feels for her, she is only young. She goes into the shop and pulls out a second chair. But the girl is all but curled up on the kerb, her knees to her chest.

'No problem.' Stella tries to sound cheerful. 'I will drive you back to port and you can go to the Saros.'

The girl does not move.

'No problem, I will drive you.' Stella finishes her coffee with a lot of dry sucks, getting the last of the froth. But still the girl does not move. Stella takes a step towards her, hesitates, and then takes one back before committing herself and crouching down beside her.

'What is the problem?' Stella asks. She peers under the girl's hair which hangs lankly over her face.

The girl sniffs. Stella jumps up and skips into the shop, grabs a handful of paper napkins and hands them to the tourist as she crouches beside her again. The girl looks up from her knees, her eyes wide and wet with tears. She looks so young. Stella can feel her heart reaching out to her. She puts her arm around the girl's shoulders.

'Tell me.'

'I've been stupid,' the girl says. 'I only had enough money to get to the job on Saros.'

Stella sucks in her breath. This is tough. Stella has no money in the till. Again. She is not sure when Stavros empties it but it is becoming a more and more regular event. How does he expect the place to keep running if there is no money to even pay the butcher? He keeps saying they need to earn more, but for what?

A crowd of thoughts presses to the forefront of Stella's mind. Her eyes widen, her pulse begins to race. Stavros' obsession with tourists; he will want to take this girl in as a worker. He will think she is the answer to all his business dreams. This is not good. Things are unsteady enough between them and this would be a terrible burden to place on the girl, who is so young. Besides, he would also take advantage of her position and pay her next to nothing.

Under these thoughts is an angular, acid

emotion. She recognises it, she cannot fool herself. It would only be a matter of time before he would want to prove his manhood in one way or another with this poor unsuspecting girl if she were to work for them.

'How old are you?' Stella asks as gently as she can.

'Sixteen.' The girl still sniffs and studies her sandals, wiping the dust from them around her toes. Her nails are bright pink.

The girl is just a teenager. When Stella was first married there were rumours. Rumours about Stavros, about him before they were a couple. Rumours that he had been pushing his affections onto some girl who was too young. It wasn't the old, old days when people were married as young teenagers: these were the days of George Michael and Michael Jackson. She can remember the posters on her wall. It had come as a shock to Stella, the dirty looks he received when they moved to his village after they were married. The gossip behind his back, the sudden silences when she walked into the village shop. The sympathetic looks she received, with her being so small and childlike herself. None of it matched the image she had of her hero. He had made her laugh and changed the subject when she asked him to reassure her. The gossip subsided when she was introduced as his wife in church that first Sunday. After that he had been so attentive in public no one could doubt his love for her.

It silenced them all. She had touched on the subject a few years later, but he was not so jovial then and it was clear the matter was closed.

No, he must not meet this girl even if these rumours were never true. There is enough tension between them without adding a new dimension.

For the girl's sake and her own sake Stavros must not know she has been here.

'What is your name?'

'Abby.' The girl lifts her head and looks at Stella. 'You?'

Despite her worries Stella is also excited to be living out one of her English lessons. 'Stella. I am very pleased to meet you.' She grins. This was lesson one.

The girl smiles back. 'I am pleased to meet you too.'

Stella cannot think what to do next. She cannot abandon the poor child. For one thing the girl is sitting on the kerb outside her shop, and another, more compelling reason is if she and Stavros had been able to have children, their child would be – she pauses her thoughts to do the maths – twenty-four. She looks back at the girl, realising just how young she is.

'Where are your mother and father?'

'Never had a mum. She died after giving birth to me, haemorrhaged to death.'

'Hem are itch?' Stella curls her tongue around the word.

'Bled to death. Dad's back in England.' Her tone is flat.

'Ah!' says Stella, *"Aemmoragia"*. Are you here alone?'

'Yes.' Abby's eyes brim with tears again and Stella looks around for the napkins. The girl has them in her hand and she dabs at her eyes.

'So if we call your Baba, I mean Dad, he will send you money?' Stella smiles at her insight and this simple solution.

'No, he probably hasn't even realised I am gone yet.'

Stella sees the problem getting bigger. She turns her head but cannot see the clock inside. Stavros could come down any time. Stella has much she must do before he does. The farmers will be hungry …

'Ahh the sausages!' Stella exclaims in Greek and runs inside to put the sausages on. She also lays on a split chicken.

Without really thinking she picks up a bowl of potatoes and sits to begin her peeling in the sun. The girl looks up and Stella nods to the second chair which the girl, after raising herself like a boneless puppy from the pavement, relaxes her growing frame into, tucking her feet under her.

'So you are away-run?' Stella returns inside for a piece of newspaper to drop the peel on.

'You mean a runaway. I suppose I am, but not really. I have a friend who has her own flat, so I am no more a runaway than her.'

'You have your own flat?'

'No, I mean ...' But she doesn't really have the enthusiasm to explain properly.

'So what will you do?'

'The only thing I can think to do is to go back into town and try and find work there. I saw a couple of bars.'

'Ah yes, a good idea. I give you a lift into town.' Stella puts the bowl down on the pavement, wipes her hands and goes inside to turn the sausages. She looks at the clock. The girl must leave soon. There is Stavros and the chips must be cut.

Coming back to the pavement, she reflects, 'No. I

cannot drive you now. I must cut the potatoes. He will get very cross if the potatoes are not done. I give you money for the taxi.' She feels in her apron pocket.

'No, I wouldn't dream of it. I have a little money left which I was going to use for my breakfast. I will use that,' Abby says.

Stella's pocket is empty anyway. She balances the bowl on her knee and peels the potatoes swiftly and carelessly, dropping the peel on the newspaper between her feet.

Stella puts the knife and the potatoes down and greets a man coming across the road carrying a wooden box. He nods at Abby and calls a cheerful hello to Stella, putting the box on the floor inside the shop before marching back to the bakery. The shop fills with the smell of fresh bread. The aroma drifts out to the pavement and Abby's stomach growls.

Stella hacks a loaf in two on the counter with a heavy bread knife. 'Then I will give you breakfast,' she says, and hands the half-loaf to Abby and picks out the soft centre of the other half for herself.

'I will call a taxi now,' Stella says, chewing with her mouth open. She checks the clock. Time is moving quickly. The sun streaming through the shop's open door highlights a smear of grease across the clock's face. She can remember wiping it for the New Year, half a year of grease and dust layered on the splitting plastic face, but it works, so who cares.

'I guess so, thank you.' Abby picks up a potato from the pile of those to peel and looks at it without interest.

'The knife is in the bowl,' Stella says as she picks up the phone. She turns her back on the world as she speaks into the receiver. The village taxi driver, Nikos, is always fun on the phone, and Stella chats and the minutes pass. A large black beetle, a *chrisomiga*, flies into the shop. Stella thinks they are funny: they fly into things as if they are blind. Close up, they are beautiful greeny-gold colour. The beetle hits the grill hood, drawing her attention back to the cooking. With the receiver tucked under her chin, she moves the sausages to the side of the grill to keep warm and turns over the chicken, which is spitting above the hot coals. Nikos is telling her a story of a lady who booked his taxi to take her goat to her brother's, and insisted it sit in the back with her. She wipes tears of laughter from her eyes with the back of her hand and flicks the chip fryer on. The beetle flies past Stella and hits the clock.

Stavros may not be much longer.

'Sorry, Nikos I have to go, *yia sou, yia sou*.' She takes the phone from her shoulder and before pressing the disconnect button she remembers why she has rung. 'Nikos, are you still there? I nearly forgot, can you come to take someone to town? You are drinking coffee? Yes, it is urgent, she needs to go now. No, I understand your coffee will go cold, but she really needs to hurry.'

Nikos agrees to come as soon as he has finished his coffee. Stella knows this is the best she will manage. She puts the phone back in its cradle and pokes the embers in the grill before putting more sausages on.

'He is on his way.' Stella turns back to Abby. 'Five minutes, I should ...'

But her sentence trails off. Stavros is at the kiosk buying cigarettes.

'Perhaps you should wait for him a little way out of the village.' Stella tries to appear calm as she takes the girl by the elbow and lifts her out of her chair. The girl's eyes are like saucers, her mouth slightly open, not understanding Stella's manoeuvring. Stella picks up the bag to give to the girl who still has a potato in one hand and the knife in the other.

'What have we here?' Stavros calls in Greek as he swaggers across the square towards them.

Chapter 3

'So what's happening?' The shadows inside the kiosk render Vasso almost invisible in contrast to the sunshine. The wooden kiosk is dappled by the shade under the palm tree.

'Why did you send her over to me?' Stella sighs, leaning on the shelf that runs around the outside of the kiosk, which is burdened with bags of sweets, packets of chewing gum, a vase of ballpoint pens, and a box of individual flavoured condoms. It is all part of life.

'Didn't you say Stavros wanted a tourist to work in the shop?' Vasso is stacking cigarette packets in columns on the shelves inside the kiosk. Stella wonders why all old kiosks are painted mustard brown inside and out.

'Yes, but he would never have found one.' She sighs again and swirls her finger around a plastic box half full of individually wrapped chocolates. They are slightly soft and should to be in the fridge. She picks one out and unwraps it, licking the melted mess from the paper.

'No, probably not. And now?' Vasso puts her hand out to take the wrapper and pops her head out of the window and they both look down the square toward the *ouzeri*.

'Now he is sitting at a table with her eating chicken and chips.' Stella looks back at Vasso. 'Can I have a packet of pain killers?' She feels her forehead and closes her eyes.

Vasso reaches without looking and puts the packet of headache pills on the coin dish in the middle of the counter, a glass platter between her and the world. 'You know if she is to stay she will need somewhere to sleep?' Stella nods, opens her eyes and takes her hand off her forehead to chew at a finger nail. 'With Thanasis now in Athens I was thinking of renting his room. I will not be gathering the olives this year so the income will be useful. That's if she is staying.' Vasso picks up a newspaper and fans herself as the day's heat is growing.

'You're not going to gather your olives?' Stella searches Vasso's careworn face for an explanation. Her hair, as always, looks as if she has recently come from the hairdresser's but the lines between her eyebrows speak of the stresses she has endured over time.

'No. When we gathered them ourselves it made us a little money, but on my own I couldn't manage, and to hire people will take all my profit.' Vasso takes a bottle from under the counter. Rubbing lotion on her hands she qualifies, 'It was Thanasis' idea for me to rent his room. Two euros.' She nods at the painkillers.

Stella smiles, pays, pats Vasso's hand to reassure her that there are no hard feelings and returns, slowly, under the clear blue sky and warm sun, to music and laughter in the *ouzeri*. Stella's heart lifts a little at the sound of the revelry, it's like old times. When they first started there was often music, the radio was always on, smiling faces were the norm, there was dancing and laughter, and happy disorder. Her heart sinks again. Today's party has nothing to do with her; it is all Stavros, Stavros showing off to Abby.

Their weathered olive skins crinkled in smiles, trousers held up with knotted belts, shirt sleeves rolled up, missing teeth showing, the farmers are enjoying themselves. They have put the radio on their table. Earlier Stella had turned it on to drown out Stavros as he tried to get Abby to understand his Greek. Usually the radio is behind the grill, by the sink, unseen. Stella feels a little embarrassed with it being out in public. It has grime in all the recesses and the handle has kitchen paper wrapped around it which looks like it has been there for weeks, compressed, tattered and no longer white. She swallows two pain killers with a shot of ouzo.

The man on the radio sings with such intensity he might be declaring undying love. But he is not, he is singing about what he wants to eat. Mostly he wants fish, particularly red mullet, *barbounia*. The farmers are caterwauling along at the tops of their voices waiting for their chicken and chips to be cooked.

In the corner sits the girl. Her bag is on the floor beside her, and she clearly does not know what to make of the situation. She is sitting at Stavros' table and he is pouring ouzo. The sun is struggling through the dusty window, spotlighting the scene. The farmers stand to perform. They interlace arms, hands on shoulders, and dance in the tiny space. Stella moves chairs and tables out of the way, her eyes on Stavros who is grinning and flirting with the teenager in a tongue the poor girl doesn't understand. She looks slightly afraid. Stella is not sure if she feels more hurt by Stavros' actions in front of her or afraid for the girl's situation. Stavros is nearly thirty years older than … what was her name? Abby.

One of the farmers is full of life; the lunchtime impromptu singing has brought energy to his limbs. He is feeling good; he has '_kefi_', an appetite for life, joy. His hair is greying at the temples and his hands speak of years of toil, the skin thick and hard. But at this moment he is alive, his heart is full, he wants to dance, dance like there is no tomorrow, no field to dig, no olives to tend. To dance as if his life depends on it. He climbs on a chair and then jumps onto the table. It wobbles and threatens to collapse. The other farmers and Stavros cheer. The table holds his weight and he dances with his head brushing the ceiling, his friends kneel, as if about to propose, clapping in rhythm to encourage him.

Abby claps self-consciously, hands making such little contact with each other, no sound, but she is smiling. Stavros shouts '*Opa!*' and raises his glass above his head towards the man. Abby giggles.

The man on the table pauses on its edge. He is a youth again, he crouches low and then springs from the table, completing a somersault to the floor with a wobbly landing and everyone cheers. No one looks more surprised than he does at his success. They all laugh and applaud.

Through the window Stella spots her friend Mitsos across the square, steadily making his way towards the shop. He concentrates, each step a tentative shifting of his weight, the slightest of pauses for correction, and then the next step. Some days he is so unsteady he uses a shepherd's crook as a walking stick but today is obviously a good day. It's early for him.

His trousers bag at the knee and crumple around his ankles, making his walk look comical. His balance disrupted by his accident, twenty or so years ago, a long time before Stella opened the *ouzeri*. She had been still living in Stavros' town then, with his parents. She crosses herself and mutters 'God rest their souls', they were kind to her. A glance over to Stavros. He is locking Abby's gaze with his piercing blue eyes, he is encouraging her to drink ouzo.

The clock on the wall by the grill tells Stella how short the time has been since Abby arrived. She grabs some kitchen roll and smears the grease more evenly over its face. Reaching under the counter for the anti-bacterial spray bottle she viciously sprays the clock and wipes it again. The dirty paper thrown on the grill brings a sudden roar; the stubble of a feather on the bare chicken laid there ignites and extinguishes itself just as fast as it blazed. The clock only looks marginally better. A collection of dead flies obscures the number six behind the plastic face. Stella looks past the insect cemetery to her husband and the tourist. Stavros looks back, scowling; she averts her gaze out of the window.

This is very early for Mitsos. He normally arrives for a late lunch after sitting at the kafenio for a while. He comes nearly every day but is thoughtful enough to come at times when she is not very busy. She can then take her time to cut up his food for him. Life is difficult for him, with only one arm. At first he was embarrassed when she offered her assistance but now it has become a routine, a moment when they sit together without words. He doesn't talk about how difficult it is and Stella doesn't ask. He is a nice man, kind, sympathetic, quiet.

Today, as soon as he steps over the threshold he glares at Stavros and backs out again. He clearly is not in the mood for noise and high spirits. Stella nips across the room to him. She looks him in the eye, for understanding, support.

He has a kind of old-fashioned honourability about him and has indicated that the way Stavros speaks to her is not really acceptable. Stella knows he is her ally, nothing specific has ever been said, nor is likely to be, he has an old school manner about him but she feels sure she has read the signs correctly - he sides with her against Stavros.

She can't remember the first time she got this feeling about him but it was probably once when she had been cutting up his food, their faces close. There was no judgement, just an understanding. Stella had felt her cheeks grow hot, shame that Stavros talked to her the way he did, ashamed of her weaknesses, embarrassed that she did not stand up for herself. There is no shepherd's crook that can support her affliction. But Mitsos' looks had been so kind that she was gentle with herself and gained some strength from his presence. A good man.

'What is it?' He looks upset about something. She indicates the chairs outside, they can sit there. The dancing and singing continue but the open air dilutes the intensity. The air is fragrant with the scent of flowers, drifting from the next-door garden, the sun a caress on their skin. A cat is sauntering in the shadow of a wall down the lane to avoid the heat. Somewhere on the hill a cockerel tells the time, incorrectly.

'So?' Stella leans back in her chair, stretches her legs out in front of her and crosses them. She crosses her arms across her floral dress. She distracts her thoughts from Stavros by wondering if she should paint her toenails pink.

'I just talked to Marina.' Mitsos lowers himself into the empty chair. Stella is the only person who knows of Mitsos' secret love. The many cut-up lunches and dinners he has eaten at her shop have, slowly, over the years, cultivated a trusting friendship. She knows the story right from when Mitsos first saw Marina, through her subsequent unhappy arranged marriage to someone else who, on his death, left her with nothing. Poor Mitsos, out of the goodness of his heart, has a wish to improve the quality of Marina's life, to make her happy and secure even if she feels nothing for him. 'What do you think Marina needs most in the world?' he asks as he concludes his narration of their recent, and very brief, exchange.

Stella can relate to Marina and her harsh life. Although that is a bit unfair: Stavros works beside her every day, they are still a team. Marina, from what she has heard, was a single parent even though her husband lived in the same house. He was never there, and provided very little. She raised two girls by herself and after her husband died she started the corner shop with all the junk he left behind. Now the village wouldn't function without the shop. Stella admires her.

No. Stavros is not like Marina's husband. Stavros may have his hand in the till and the payments may be late for the butcher but they always get by. Not so for poor Marina, for her it was proved that husbands can be absent even when they are there. In this culture, where many women do not work, not being provided for is the same as not being considered.

Look at Vasso, she had the best husband in the world, he considered her with his every breath, loved and cared for her till death parted them and then left her a little something tucked away. Vasso holds her head high every day, always has her hair done, looks smart.

Being ignored has to be the worst feeling in the world. When Stavros ignores her she can feel her self-belief draining away, her joy in the world evaporates. It is only the fun she generates with the customers that keeps her from sinking. That and a nip of ouzo. She knows exactly what Marina needs.

After considering Stella says, 'In all honesty, she needs what no one can give her.'

'What's that?' Mitsos asks.

'She needs a memory of a husband who was good to her, who thought about her and who provided for her. With a memory like that she would feel like a different person. She would feel valued and loved and lovable. As it is she sees herself as unlovable, worthy of neglect and unworthy of being put first. You can see it with her children. She sees them as having so much value and herself as having none, she does everything for them she can, breaks her back for them and just considers it the "right" thing to do. Over the years she has neglected herself more and more and that has all come from him.' Stella pauses; Mitsos stays quiet, looking at her. 'Sorry. Did you want such a full answer?' She smiles but she is turning her head to look inside her shop. Stavros is still at the girl's table and the dancing has stopped. He is pointing to the dirty dishes and saying *'plenis ta piata'*, in Greek very loudly over and over.

Mitsos leans over and pats Stella's hand kindly.

'And you would know, Stella,' he says.

Stella lets a tear fall.

Mitsos stands slowly. Stella wills him to go away. She could easily imagine her head on his chest, his arm around her and releasing all her sorrow, hiding from the world, him making everything safe. It is a long time since her father died but still, sometimes, she feels like a child, with childlike needs. Mitsos is up, he pats her on the shoulder before he sets off again back across the square. The pat releases another tear. Stella looks over the road to see if the Romanian in the sandwich shop is looking at her but she is busy putting bottles of water into her fridge. Stella wipes the tears from her face and braces herself to stand.

'What are you doing sitting out here when I am in there busting a gut for the two of us?' On silent feet Stavros is beside her. Still seated, his belly is at her eye-level. His T-shirt is rucked over his stomach and she notices that he has black fluff in his navel. In the seven years they have had the ouzeri he has become so fat, and, with each kilo gained, less fun. He could be carrying twins he is so round. 'We have an opportunity and you just sit here!' he grumbles.

Stella's chest sinks and she exhales with his callous view of Abby. She is not an opportunity; she is a person, a child.

'I thought you were quite happy in there by yourself.' Stella stands, Stavros steps back but does not let her past into the shop.

'If you showed a bit of friendliness she might decide to stay. God knows we need some tourists to bring this place to life, put some money in the till. Get in there and be civil.' He puts his hand behind her arm and gives a push. Stella staggers forwards, finds her balance and, shocked, turns on him, but his face holds such malevolence she backs away and goes into the shop.

44

The farmers are quiet. Stavros must have served them as they are all busy eating and as a consequence they say little. The radio has been turned down.

Stella checks the sausages and spreads another split chicken on the bars over the embers, takes the cooked chips from the fryer and puts more in. The grill has been set up behind the counter with just enough room for one person to cook and serve. Behind the free-standing grill with a hood over it there is a narrow mirror-tiled corridor of space with glass shelves for glasses, misty from the grease in the air. Here she finds Abby, at the far end, peeling potatoes in the old marble sink which is already full of dirty pots. There is a line of filth where the sink meets the wall, darker than the greying white of the marble. Perched by the tap are a bottle of ouzo, and a bottle of gin with no cap. The whole area is in semi-gloom. With Stella's appearance Abby drops a potato on the floor. She bends to pick it up but hesitates. The floor is grimy around the edges, the central foot-width where Stella has walked it smooth is lighter, her path en-route from grill to sink, grill to ouzo, grill to gin, grill to sink.

Stella picks up the potato and tosses it past Abby into the sink. It hits a glass but nothing breaks.

'What does "*plenis ta piata*" mean?' Abby asks.

She looks so young.

Chapter 4

After a while the farmers begin to leave. Abby shifts in her seat. There is a toilet in the corner of the room divided off by a thin hardboard wall. During the course of the afternoon the farmers have demonstrated that it is not soundproofed. Will there be toilet paper? She crosses her legs.

She studies the picture of a donkey in a straw hat hanging on the pale green shiny wall. It must be gloss paint. The glass in front of the picture is greasy and smeared. There is a thin shelf around the room, high up, on which there are several ceramic swans and various other pottery objects. The room is hard and stark. Can she take a picture on her phone without offending the man? Back home friends will not believe this place. She will share it on Facebook. Fumbling in her bag she remembers the phone's battery is dead. While her hand is still inside she quickly feels for the fur of the tiny teddy on her key-ring, just for a second.

Stavros, his knees almost touching hers, shifts towards her. Abby makes a show of picking her bag up from the floor, pushes her chair away from him and hangs the bag on the back of it without actually leaving her seat. He keeps babbling at her in Greek, with the occasional ill-pronounced word in English. She cannot guess what the Greek words mean, like she could, sometimes, guess the meaning of words in Spanish or French class at school.

Seeing these Greek men dancing, being part of it all, a private impromptu affair, not for tourists, is thrilling. Real Greek life. She will keep a diary. What an experience! She mops her forehead with a paper napkin. She cannot imagine anyone back at home getting onto a table in the pub and doing a back flip, certainly none of the grey-haired men anyway. One of the boys high on something might, but he would probably break his neck. Besides, someone would start bleating about health and safety if anyone even tried to stand on a chair. No wonder there is no life, no spontaneity left around where she lives. No wonder everyone over thirty has no joy; they are all beaten with the stick of conforming to health and safety legislation. She decides she will write in her notebook until she can afford a diary. She decides she is not on holiday, she is 'on life'. She takes her pen from her bag and writes that line on a napkin. It can be the title of the diary. Stavros leans over but when he sees it is in English he loses interest.

She wonders if there is a minimum wage.

'How much will you pay me?' she asks in clear English. If she had ended up in the wrong place with no money in England there is no way she would have found work this easily. It feels unreal, but natural to this country somehow. The job offered will do for now anyway, no matter what they are paying. She is confident she will be able to get to her real job tomorrow, or the day after that at the latest.

'Ti?' the man answers, but there is no understanding each other. He stands. He gestures for her to stand too and she follows him to a space behind the grill with mirror-lined glass shelves stacked with glasses and plates, a sink full of pots at the end. It is filthy. The man points at a sack of potatoes and hands her the knife. Abby wants to show she is a good worker and looks around for the bin, wondering where to put the peelings. There is none to be seen, and without the language she feels stuck. He points at the sink.

After peeling two potatoes Abby hopes a day or two working here will earn enough. Her real job is in a bar with a crew of young waiters, neon lights, a dance floor, leather chairs, glass doors that open onto the street, all new. She sort of knows Jackie who is already there, it is her second summer at the bar, but then she is older than Abby, she has her own flat back home.

Abby pictures the bar lit up at night. She will learn how to make Margaritas and B52s, serve shots to lines of bronzed university students. It will be great. She will be on the beach all day and work all evening. She is sure they will still take her on if she is a day or two late. She might try to call again once she has a wage in her pocket and can offer to pay for the call. There is a phone on the counter. Or maybe she can find a charger for her mobile.

The peelings drop in the sink. Stavros has been lingering behind her but now he turns to leave.

'Money? How much?' She surprises herself at her forthrightness but rubs the pad of her thumb against the pad of her index finger to illustrate her words. Being in a foreign country is giving her confidence, it seems.

'*Perimene,*' he pats the air flat before he begins to turn away. 'Ah, *diavatirio,*' he mimes, opening a book. Abby just stares. He tucks his elbows in and puts his hands out to the side and whistles through his teeth, swaying as he turns away left and right. Abby reaches in her bag and thumbs through the phrase book in the travel 'at the airport' section.

'*Diavatirio,*' he says again.

'Passport!' Abby momentarily feels she has conquered the language, or at least a very small part of it, before frowning. 'Why?' she asks.

'Work,' he says in English, rolling the 'r'. Abby fishes deep into her bag and pulls out her maroon booklet and hands it to him. He looks her in the eyes. Abby turns to continue with the peeling. It is getting hot. It feels amazing to be so warm in just a T-shirt and shorts. If the pay is good she will stay and make enough to get to Saros. If not, she will stay today and use what money she has to take a taxi first thing in the morning to the town and see if she can find work there. She will probably do that anyway. This place is amazing, but it is a pit. She will probably only need two or three days' work in town to raise the money to get to Soros.

Abby stops peeling. Where will she sleep? She cannot afford a hotel, and doubts the village has one anyway.

Perhaps she can ask to sleep on the floor of the restaurant. She looks at the floor and decides, actually, it is not an option.

'Don't be so soft,' Dad said when they were cleaning out the garage together and she hadn't wanted to touch things with cobwebs on. Jumbled thoughts of home close in on her. Her bed, cosy, the smell of clean sheets. The hot water in the shower, her lavender soap. Dad's arguments for her not to go into the sixth form. Of course it would be worth it. She has already started the journey, to work her way through Uni.

Determined to prove him wrong, she considers her options. The floor will be fine if she buys a newspaper to put down first. No, the print will come off on her clothes. She could put the chairs together, but that would be too lumpy. She puts down the potato and goes into the room with the tables on the pretext of clearing up any discarded plates. There is a glass on one of the unoccupied tables.

Picking up the glass, she lifts the corner of the stiff, crackling, plastic tablecloth with its hunt scene running around the edge, of men in faded red jackets, hounds bleached by time and wear, but no sign of a fox. The table-top is a chipboard slab, on which there is a ring of green paint the same colour as the walls. She runs a finger across the chipboard, no dirt comes off. She puts a hand under the table-top and lifts. If it is not attached she could put two or three of them on the floor and sleep on them.

The farmers smile at her as they mop the juices from their plates with hunks of bread. She takes her hand from under the tablecloth and smooths out the creases and hurries back to the sink with the single glass. More likely Stella will find her a bed. The Greeks are meant to be hospitable and she seemed very kind. It does all feel almost too exciting.

Once hidden behind the grill she wipes her hands on the clean teacloth she has tucked into her shorts instead of the dirty apron Stavros had thrown at her. She reaches into her bag which she has slung in the only clean place, across her shoulders, and pulls out her key-ring with the limp teddy dangling from it. She palms the teddy and rubs him a few times against her cheek. The food and the early start and the heat from the back of the grill are making her feel sleepy.

The grill shakes as someone pokes the embers. Abby bundles her key-ring teddy away and picks up a potato but it is slippery. It skids out of her hands and onto the floor behind her.

Stella picks up the potato and tosses it past Abby into the sink. It hits a glass but nothing breaks.

'What does "per-i-menace" mean?' Abby asks.

'Wait.'

'Oh sorry, are you busy.'

Stella laughs. 'No, *"perimenis"* means "wait".'

'Oh, I thought he was saying I was a menace or something.' Her voice trails off.

'Why are you putting the potato coats in the sink?' Stella asks.

Abby looks into the sink where the peel has mixed with the dirty pots, knives and forks interlaced.

'I didn't know how to say, "Where is the bin?".' It's important to make a good first impression. Being sacked, that would be a disaster. The fragility of her situation seems to rush at her from nowhere.

Stella pulls a cardboard box from under the lowest glass shelf.

'Use this.'

She does not seem as friendly as she was earlier.

'Are you sure me working here is ok?' Abby asks, blinking away the beginnings of tears. She wishes she had slept more on the plane.

Stella seems to ignore her, her face is blank.

'Stella?'

'Yes, what?'

'Are you sure it is ok for me to work here?'

Stella looks her in the eye and her face softens; she pats Abby's arm. 'Of course, what else can you do?' But Abby senses Stella's reserve. She doesn't want to overreact. Dad is always saying she acts without thinking. Maybe she should take a taxi now and trust she can find work in town. Would that be an action or a reaction? Or an overreaction, perhaps. It can be hard to tell the difference. She wishes she had charged her phone battery. Maybe she could have got Jackie's number from someone.

The girl seems so young. Stella is sure she was

not so young at that age. She manoeuvres past her to get to the sink.

At seventeen she was still at home with her father and mother. She only suffered the occasional taunts in the village by then.

Stella piles the plates on the floor by her feet, picks out the peelings and throws them in the box Abby is peeling into, and runs the water until it comes hot enough to wash the cutlery. Everything is washed under a constant dribble of water.

The days at home with Mama and Baba had been sweet, although to some degree she had been angry at the world, angry that Baba married a gypsy, angry with Mama for being a gypsy.

Stella wonders what Abby's family life is like, what her home is like.

The forks done, she swills them and puts them, handles down, in a glass next to the gin bottle. She starts on the knives.

A home made of blankets, with sticks and branches holding the shape, children running in and out, their bare feet planting white footprints of dust on the colourful blanket floor. Typical. How she had hated those 'holidays', as Mama had called them. To Stella, visiting her relatives was torture. The women in long flowing skirts, breasts hanging loose under shapeless blouses, uncombed hair braided into plaits with ribbons floating round, cooking food. The darkness of their skin is the lasting memory.

Before she was six and school started there had never been any such 'holidays'. Then, with no warning, someone Mama had told her was her uncle picked them up on his moped and they drove away from home and Baba into the country for what seemed like miles, and then on a long straight stretch of road, he had stopped. Two women with hair down to their waists had come out of what looked to Stella like the enclosures that farmers made for goats, although this one looked less permanent. The women had been followed out by two teenagers, also wearing long skirts but instead of flowing tops they had tight T-shirts that didn't cover their tummies. Stella had thought this was a good way to keep cool so she pulled her top up too, and Mama had pulled it down again. Several children her age, and some younger, had come out after them, looking as if their hair had never been combed. The boys' hair was in knots and the girls' in rat tails, and they all had dirty faces, scruffy shorts and no shirts. Stella had wanted her Baba. Her Mama was hugging these people and that didn't seem right.

With the knives done and swilled Stella starts on the plates. She checks Abby from the corner of her eye. She is still peeling away but she is very slow.

One of the women had picked her up and Stella

had struggled. The woman smelt of cooking and wet washing. That was when a man in a suit came from inside the place. He had a baby in his arms, and when he saw Stella he passed the baby to the nearest person, made a joyous sound and took Stella from the woman. He smelt of tobacco and something else. His hair was long down the back of his collar and it looked wet. She didn't want to touch him. She remembered she had started to cry, louder and louder, until Mama had taken her into her arms.

Everyone seemed so happy. Someone played a guitar and after a while the younger children started to dance and then spin in circles. This looked fun so Stella had spun in circles too, until she fell into a dizzy heap with the other children. There had been spicy food which the children, sitting on the floor, ate with their fingers. A wind had come up and the plastic and blanket walls began to suck in and billow out as if the whole place was breathing. Stella had left her food to sit by her Mama, scared by the living tent. A dog came in and ate everything from the plate she had left on the floor. This also made her cry as she was still hungry.

On the way back Mama had explained that the people were gypsies, people who like to keep moving, without a home. As Stella was trying to make sense of this Mama had told her that the man on the moped and the one with the baby in his arms were her great uncles and everyone else she had met that day was a cousin, or second cousin. That made her, Stella, a gypsy too. It had taken some time to understand that Mama was a gypsy, but Baba wasn't, even though Mama had been born in the village. It was Stella's grandmother who had settled there before Mama was born. Mama had never lived the travelling life.

Stella puts the clean plates on their edges, leaning against the sink side; the racks above are full. There is no more room, so she puts some of the drier ones on the glass shelves behind her. The day is a warm one and they are drying quickly. At the height of summer they dry in seconds.

Then school had started for her, at six years old like everyone else, but not like everyone else. It had been clear later that Mama had taken her to meet her relatives so she would understand her classmates' reactions at school. If she hadn't known she was a gypsy or what a gypsy was it would have been a confusing as well as a painful time.

Stella rinses the last of the dishes, gives the sink a cursory wipe and turns to the glasses. They are piled on one of the glass shelves, stuck on ouzo rims. Stella hears the sound of one of the big black dozy bugs fly in but it doesn't venture past the grill. Far away a cockerel is crowing; a car going past drowns its cries. A glance at the potato bucket tells her Abby is far too slow. Stella shakes her hands of the washing-up water and wipes them down her dress. She takes the knife from Abby and uses it to point to the glasses and the sink. Abby begins on the glasses under the permanently trickling hot tap.

Stella deftly peels half a dozen potatoes. The skins that fall in the box are thicker than the skins that Abby had pared but with the amount of potatoes that they need speed is more important.

School had not been fun.

She digs an eye out of the spud with savagery. The potato splits in half.

She felt alone and was bullied. She did discover that she was quicker than the other children of her age. It was a mixed-age class so she often spent her time with older children. This did not help the separation she felt from her peers. Eight years of trying to belong, hating who she was by birth, desperate to fit in, pushed away. Her fourteenth birthday could not come fast enough. With her educational obligations fulfilled she and her peers left the classroom confines. Their energies directed elsewhere, they all went about their work in the villages, son following father so no one went very far, and neither did the prejudice, and to some extent the meanness continued. So Stella stayed at home, stayed indoors, except when she went on her walks.

Filling the bowl again, from the hessian sack

under the grill, reminds Stella she must order more potatoes. She shakes out the last dozen or so and sets about peeling them.

Then Stavros came into her life. She had been on a ramble up in the hills and he had just been there with his startling blue eyes, his broad shoulders, his flat stomach; he looked like an athlete. Stella remembers she gasped at the sight of him. He had been so polite and so considerate. They had talked and talked. Well, he had talked, Stella had listened. He knew so much, had seen so much. He was from a village all the way across the orange orchards on the other side of the plain. He had once visited Athens.

After their meeting he had come into the village to ask her Baba if he could take her out, and the entire village quickly heard. That had shut them up. The girls who used to look down on her now looked jealous. The boys who used to tease fell silent. Stavros was not only tall; he was broad across the shoulders. He delivered her from their prejudice, her heritage, and she loved him for it.

Stella lugs the bucket of spuds round to the front of the grill, next to which is a tiny deep-fat fryer and a square foot of counter surface on which to cut the yellowing misshapes into chips.

'Have you talked to her yet?' Stavros exhales smoke as he speaks. He stands half in and half out of the shop, his extended stomach a shelf for his hand as it rests between puffs, confident that Abby has no understanding of his Greek tongue.

'About what?' Stella says, her mind confusing the Stavros she used to know with this overweight, sweating, out-of-shape man talking to her. His irises are still an intense blue but the whites are mostly red. His face looks flushed and his eyes bulge as if they are about to pop out of his head.

'Make her stay. I think she wants to know how much we will pay her as she did this.' He rubs his thumbs and index finger pads together.

'Well, what are we going to pay her? We don't have any extra.'

'Tell her it is a trial.'

'Where will she sleep?' Stella asks as she finishes chopping. A child is walking with purpose towards the shop. She wipes her hand on some kitchen roll. She is not going to make this easy for Stavros. The boy comes in and orders two *giros* for himself and his granny, 'who is looking after me for the day,' he tells her. 'We are going to feed the goats later.'

Stella oils two circular pita breads and puts them on the grill for a moment, the oil sizzling, soaking into them. The meat on the spit turns automatically, all day, in front of a hot wire grid, cooking and turning, the

60

aroma drifting into the street luring young and old alike. Stella takes a hot pita and puts it flat on her hand, a piece of greaseproof paper protecting her from the heat. She slices some meat off the spit and it falls onto the pita bread. She mounds on top some pre-made chips that are a little cold now, yoghurt and garlic sauce, some tomato slices, and asks if he would like onions. He nods his head enthusiastically. Stella piles raw onions on the mound and then with supple twists of her wrists she rolls the whole thing up and tucks the greaseproof paper in at one end to stop any drips and hands it to the boy.

The second *giro* is without onions as his granny cannot digest them. His little hands can hardly hold the two bulky rolls, open ends uppermost. He walks away smiling, eating a chip he picks out of the top with his teeth.

'She cannot be paid nothing and sleep on the floor. What exactly are we going to do with her?' Stella asks.

'Why are you making this so difficult?' Stavros' face is going a livid red, and he throws his cigarette end into the street.

Stella knows that what he is really saying is, 'You sort out the details'. But this is not her idea. 'She is not sleeping on the sofa at our house, it wouldn't be right. And we do need to pay her.'

61

'Today can be a trial, but if we make more than normal tomorrow then we will decide what to pay her.' Stavros has no consideration for the girl. Stella is glad she stayed silent about Abby's desperate situation.

'And if we don't?' Stella starts to mix some more lemon sauce for the chicken. She pauses to jot down a list on a napkin before she forgets: more tinfoil trays for the take-away, two dozen mini-ouzo bottles and another sack of potatoes.

Stavros does not reply but goes out into the sunshine and across to the kiosk for a paper.

Stella had done the sums over and over. At one time she had not even thought how much money they made in the *ouzeri*. When she needed to pay the butcher she took money from the till. But as time passed there seemed to be less and less money in the till and more and more unpaid bills. Stella began to wonder where the money went. Slowly she began to take notice, then she started to do the maths.

After they were married and had settled down with his parents in his home town, Stavros and his Baba would often get together to play cards. The mood was jolly. Stavros' Mama rustled up plates of food. With the shutters closed they would settle into a night of joking and fun. The men would laugh and Stavros' mother would prepare coffees and chasers.

Sometimes they would stay up so late Stella would go to bed and wake in the morning to find Stavros' Mama asleep where she had sat the night before in one of the chairs.

Sometime Stavros would go out and play cards with his friends. Not often, but when he did he would not come home until very late and would be grumpy for several days, or elated, and his wallet would close or open correspondingly. His Baba laughed and slapped him on the back either way. His Mama was given a handful of drachmas when he won.

His card-playing away from home increased as time passed and Stella continued not to conceive. She had had tests done. It wasn't her. Stavros had refused to believe it was him; it was too big a knock to his self-image. He said less and played more. His mama said it was God's will and who are we to question what God decides? He would have his own reasons beyond our comprehension, He could see all.

Stella nips behind the grill to see how Abby is doing.

'Alright?' she asks. Abby starts. Stella wonders why she has her bag over her shoulders. It looks heavy and it cannot be easy to work like that. 'Do you want to hang your bag here?' She takes some coats that have been left for as long as she can remember off a peg on the wall at the grill end. Abby looks around for somewhere to dry her hands. Stella steps forwards and lifts the bag from over her head, being careful not to mess her hair or touch her wet hands.

'Thank you. Erm, can I ask what the pay is, please. I need to make plans to get to this job. I promised to be there …' Abby blushes.

Stella takes a breath. 'Today we try you. Tomorrow we pay you when we see how much more we make. OK?' It doesn't even sound ok to Stella. She feels her own cheeks grow hot.

'A trial?' Abby asks.

Chapter 5

The grill spits and hisses. Stella leaves Abby's question unanswered to attend to it. The tongs grip the chicken's legs and the splayed bird flips awkwardly onto its back.

'Why are you making this so hard?' Stavros hisses in Greek. He flicks his cigarette end into the gutter before entering the *ouzeri*.

Stella throws the spatula onto the counter and turns to face him.

'Now what have I made difficult?'

'Vasso, she tells me she has already said the girl can sleep at her house.'

'We do not have money to pay Vasso for somewhere for the girl to sleep and the girl cannot pay because we are not paying her.' Her hand on her hips.

'Well, it's done, it's agreed, tonight she sleeps at Vasso's on trial. If she stays, she pays.' He takes out another cigarette.

Stella sighs. It feels like they are dividing Abby up between them like a roasted goat. The poor girl should be on a boat to Saros, to a real job, a teenager's job, a bar, life, young people, not stuck in this village to serve old farmers.

Stavros sits inside on one of the wooden chairs and puts his feet up on one of the tables to read his newspaper.

'Abby.' Stella goes behind the grill. 'I must be true.' She is sure that she is not using the right word in English, perhaps honest would be a better word, but she goes on. 'We do not have the money to pay you to work. If tomorrow we make more money because the farmers like your pretty face then we can pay you. So it is a trial for us both. Vasso, that is the woman from the kiosk, she has a room for you. If you stay, after tonight, then you will agree a price to pay. This is all I can offer. I can offer no more. It is up to you.'

Abby finishes washing the glasses and wipes her hands dry on some kitchen roll.

'I have been thinking. You have been very kind trying to arrange a job here for me. I am happy to work today to pay for my meal but I think that perhaps tomorrow it is best if I go and get a job in the town.'

'*Yia.*' A gruff goodbye comes from Stavros as he leaves the shop.

'He is going for a sleep, it is his habit at this time of day. You need a sleep?'

'I did earlier but I am past it now.' Abby looks around the counter area. There is a picture of the old Greek King and Queen on the wall. 'How long have you had this place?'

'Seven years, since my Baba died.'

'Baba?'

'Dad.'

'Oh, I am sorry.' Abby looks at the ground. 'Um, can I use the loo I am bursting?'

'No need to ask!' Abby feels Stella watching as she takes the kitchen roll with her through to the presently empty café. When she returns Stella asks, 'You like Greece?' as she tidies the high counter.

'I have only been here, well, less than a day, but it's amazing. The people are so different.' Abby folds her arms and slouches to rest them on the counter top, still standing.

'Yes? Different how?'

'Oh, I don't know ...'

Abby cannot quite articulate the differences she is feeling. Sure, Greece looks different and it's hotter. A donkey brays and Abby declares, laughing, that this is just another difference, there are few donkeys in

England, and none in the towns. But it is more than that. The heat relaxes her, as it seems to relax everyone who lives here.

She lowers her head onto her arms and stares. The walls are green in the counter area too, but in here they are streaked where condensation has run down them. She recalls standing at a bus stop near to her house, the rain streaming down the glass sides. Two of the people in the queue for the bus were people she knew: one was her next-door neighbour and the other the lady who used to feed their cat when they went away on holiday. But they didn't speak to each other. It was not as if anyone was being rude, it was just that it was cold and wet. Abby remembers pulling up the collar of her coat and trying to dip her chin inside for warmth. The neighbour had put on a see-through plastic head covering that tied at her chin and everyone had pulled their shoulders up around their ears and tucked their arms into their sides to keep warm, hands deep in pockets. No one was going to expend energy or expose themselves to the chill wind just to have a conversation.

Here the sun has people lifting up their faces to feel the warmth, arms unstuck from their sides as they try to create the biggest surface area to cool themselves. There is no possibility of rushing in this temperature and, as things happen slowly, there is time to talk. She sees the people in the street demonstrating this all the time. The man who brought the bread this morning must have tarried for ten minutes or more talking to the lady from the kiosk. And the man who came out of the grim café at the top of the square to buy cigarettes from the kiosk seemed quite happy to wait, leaning on her counter, until she finished her chat and wandered with no hurry back to serve him. He had stayed and chatted with her a while as well. People are important here, more so than the jobs they do, it seems.

A restrictive weight is lifted from Abby with this thought. On reflection, she finds herself smiling despite her circumstances and she experiences a strange confidence that everything will be fine.

Stella, if nothing else, is being honest. Maybe they do need her help and really cannot afford it. Maybe they don't need her help and are being kind. Either way, she wants to stay for the 'trial' day to thank them for their kindness, and besides, she has got a tasty chicken dinner out of it.

Standing up straight she eases the strain on her full stomach.

Tomorrow she will go into town, but for now she has landed well and truly on her feet.

She must ring Dad though, and let him know she is safe. Stupid man.

Maybe she should take Modern Greek.

Languages are always useful. Even Stella, a Greek village woman, speaks English.

The other thing about Greece, Abby ponders, watching Stella adding some numbers in the columns of what looks like a home-made accounts book, is that it feels very safe, even as a single female. She has been into London with friends before and there were some areas where she was not sure she felt safe. Pickpockets, maybe even muggers worried her. But here she feels she can leave her bag unattended, hanging on the hook at the end of the grill with all her belongings and her phone, and no one will touch it, she is sure.

So much for England being the supposed civilised country. Half a laugh escapes her. Stella briefly looks up but her eyes are un-focused, she turns back to the ledger on the shelf behind the raised counter.

Abby leans against the door frame, the heat is making her feel sleepy. Her eyes close and she imagines what would have happened if she had turned up in some district of London miles away from where she was supposed to be. Abby doubts that anyone would care, let alone find her a job and a place to sleep. They would either just walk past her or, worse, someone might even try to take advantage of the situation. There is no way anyone would offer her somewhere to stay for the night. They would be fearful she was a psycho or, if they did offer a place to kip, they themselves might be the psycho. She would instantly be another homeless person, curled up in a shop doorway. But she cannot conjure up the feeling of cold, the sun is too strong, sweat runs down her temple. She opens her eyes and steps from the doorway into the shade.

'Greece is an amazing place,' Abby concludes walking round to see what Stella is studying. She points to a number on the page. 'Shouldn't that be a three?' Abby asks. Stella makes a sound of relief and quickly rubs out the eight, and pencils in a three.

'Are you missing your Baba?' Stella continues, looking at the book.

Abby had forgotten about Dad again. He will have read her note by now and no doubt has been trying to ring her. What were they, two hours behind in England? If everything had gone to plan she would have been at her job on Saros where someone would have a phone charger and she would have been able to tell him where she was and how successful she had been in getting the job and getting there. She swallows.

She wonders what he would have had to say about that, if it had all gone to plan. She had been really looking forward to the shock of doing that. 'Hi, Dad. I am in Greece working at a bar called the Malibu with Jackie. Earning money to put towards Uni.' Now she will have to wait, and so will he. Well, it serves him right.

She has done so well with her GCSEs, she knows it. Why did he think she would not put the studying into her A levels? Actually, she does understand. The whole "not working hard enough" thing was just a ploy. What he really meant to say was, 'What was the point in her taking her A levels as no one could afford to send her to university?' So she might just as well start working from sixteen and contribute to the household. Well, here she is, working at sixteen. But not for him. She will save enough to pay her own way through Uni. If she can make the tuition fees then a bar job while she is there will take care of the rest. Besides, there are always student loans.

'He has no faith in me.' she blurts.

'Faith, like you are God?' Stella looks up from the book with wide eyes.

'No, faith, like he does not believe I can do things.' Abby steps towards the door before turning to lean against the counter again.

'Oh. My Baba used to say: "How can you know what you can do until you try?' Stella shuts the book and puts it on the bottom shelf, out of sight.

'That's what I said, that I should try, and if I can't then I will give up.' Abby decides she likes Stella.

'It's the only way. You want a frappé?' She lifts her own empty glass.

'What's a frappé?'

'Coffee with ice.'

'Water's fine, thanks.'

'What you want to do that he doesn't believe and you haven't tried yet?' Stella spoons coffee granules and sugar into her glass.

'I want to go to university.'

'Ah, university. What a lovely idea. I would like to study something.' Stella uses a little electric whisk on her coffee and sugar with the smallest amount of water. The mix turns brown and then cream-coloured and shiny. She turns off the whisk and adds water and evaporated milk.

Abby says, 'Really! What would you study?'

'Business, I dream of owning an international business. Like the women in Hollywood films, who tell the men what to do and don't need them.' She laughs at her own joke and Abby joins in. She too would like to tell Dad what to do and not need him. Even without understanding the language she relates to Stella.

'Who is the man, is he your brother, your

husband, what?' Abby nods her head to the door, indicating the departed Stavros.

'Stavros, he is my husband. He saved me from a hard life, makes me belong.'

'Oh' is all Abby can find to say. From what she has seen of him and the way he treats Stella the price seems a bit high for whatever it is he has done.

Stavros stamps up the couple of steps into the kafenio. He grunts a hello to the men he knows and clicks his fingers at the owner for his 'usual'. Stella is just unbelievable. It is almost as if she wants things to get worse. His idea to get the tourist girl working there is just logical. Stella knows they need to pay things off, so they need to make more money. Something has to change. The first thing that should change is the way Stella behaves. The locals must be so heartily sick of her flirting ways; it's amazing anyone comes in at all. The same old stuff over and over.

He pictures Abby's face, glad for a new mental image to look on. And it is a face that doesn't show as many years as his wife's. Doesn't Stella realise how unseemly it is for someone of her age to carry on the way she does? She should take better care of herself. She should take better care of herself for him. She would be the first to complain if he wandered.

His coffee arrives and he grunts a thank you. Who is he trying to kid? His mind wandered after the first year of wedlock. He should never have married her, stuck the rumours out; they would have stopped eventually. The young girl would have grown soon enough and then some local boy would have plucked her and he would have been forgotten.

He takes a sip of his coffee. The kafenio will close soon; the owner, Theo, has a nap in the heat of the day. The floor-to-ceiling glass windows give Stavros a view of the whole square. There are very few people making their way anywhere at this time, which is a relief; he does not want to see any of the men he owes money to. He should have quit with the first debt. He can see now that trying to win enough to cover that debt somewhere else had been a mistake, as had the loan. But these things happen. It will sort itself out, just not today, and not any time soon unless Stella gets off her high horse and starts working with him, gets this foreign girl behind the counter. A young tourist in her little T-shirts and white shorts should bring plenty of locals in. For a while, anyway.

Why would the girl's father let her come to another country alone? The western ways make no sense. A girl of that age around here is seen in one of two places, on the school bus or at home, and with good reason.

The girl from his village returns to his mind. He

cannot even recall her name, but he remembers her big wide eyes and hair that shone and was so soft to the touch. Why had she been allowed to sit so long outside after church? No one came to take her indoors. What did they expect? She had spoken to him, not the other way around, asked him the time.

Stavros takes a sip of coffee, picks up the saucer and moves to a table nearer the back. Perhaps it's better not to be too visible, not when he owes money to so many people. He uses the teaspoon to scoop some undissolved grounds off the top of his coffee and curses Theo under his breath for not taking the time to make it well.

They will need to increase the takings by quite a lot. There's no cutting the outgoings. The butcher, the baker. Besides, he can't stop now, his bad run will have a season, it will end. It's not like he owes anybody a huge amount. It's just the number of people he owes now, it's getting awkward. Although if Stella would listen and stop piling extra chips on the portions, cut back a little here and there, count the cents. She thinks that grovelling to people with big portions impresses them. She was fairly pretty once, but that was years ago. Flirting with the farmers. It is demeaning, to her and to him.

He sighs and takes another sip. Theo makes the best, despite the grains.

He drinks the water that came with the coffee and lights another cigarette. He watches a woman and child walk across the square, the child reaching high to hold her hand, her little legs almost running to keep up. And all that nonsense about him not being able to have children. It was her, she didn't eat enough to keep a bird alive, let alone a child. Now, all day he has to listen to her nonsense. Spouting about how the business should be run, as if he doesn't pull his weight. She flits about the tables laughing and joking when he is sweating at the grill.

The problem is the village. Nothing but farmers and farmers' wives. Not much money. They will sit for an hour with one drink, taking up the table space. Tourists are the ones with the money, he has said it for years, but will she listen? She's learning to speak English, so why does she not put her efforts into finding tourists to come to the shop? They will pay double, and they do not sit all evening.

His coffee is nearly finished. He swirls the grounds in the bottom and waits for the liquid to settle on the top.

And this sitting all evening is Stella's fault too. She encourages them, tries to make it feel like a home from home. It is not a home from home, it is business. McDonald's does not flirt with you and give you extra chips. No! It encourages you to buy and move on. That is what they need, tourists who will buy and go, and make room for the next. Not locals who come in every night to chat with Stella and buy so little.

Perhaps this will change things with this foreign girl. He recalls her face. The child looks frightened, out of her depth. Stavros will take care of her, make her feel welcome, such a fresh young face ... He shuffles in his chair. She will be grateful for his consideration, and he will pay her a little something on busy days.

And she is all alone, with no family to consider. Yes, he will make her feel very welcome. No need for her to stay at Vasso's, when there is plenty of space in the house. She reminds him of the girl in his village before he married Stella. The talk was not good. Stella was a pass to respectability then, to silence the gossipers. Did he overreact? Too late now, he is saddled, and with this business, slaving away over a hot grill for unappreciative orange farmers.

He takes the final sip from the cup and puts it back in its saucer, and grinds out his cigarette.

The men he owes are likely asleep now in the afternoon, and those who don't live locally will not come to the village in the heat of the day. He should never have got mixed up with them. He chucks a couple of coins on the table.

He takes the back way home, just in case.

Chapter 6

The shop is all but empty as the heat of the day increases. There is not much to do so Abby asks if it would be ok to take a look around the village, walk up the hill. Stella says it is hot for walking, but as the girl insists on going she gives her a baseball cap someone has left behind to keep the heat off her head. It smells of goats.

As Abby leaves Stella sees Mitsos making his way across the square towards her. For a moment she is confused, she has seen him already today, but then recalls he left without eating, the noise of the farmers being more than he wanted. It is better he comes at this time, she can give him her full attention. A tractor obscures him from view as it rumbles to a stop. The farmer leaves the engine running as he jumps down and goes to Vasso's kiosk for cigarettes.

The tractor leaves, and as its noise diminishes it is replaced by the clonk and clang of goat bells. Mitsos looks up from his steady pace and Stella turns to see the mottled herd enter the village. The lead goat has some fine horns. There are one or two sheep mixed in with the brown and white ocean. If the shepherd is taking them in from the heat of the day, he's a little late.

Mitsos hurries his step as the goats come streaming across the square.

'Hello again,' Stella says over the unorchestrated bleating and bells.

'That lot gone now?' He nods to the shop to show he means the farmers, not the goats.

'Everyone has gone,' Stella says. She watches the dog bring up the rear of the herd, running this way and that across the tail end of them, in a very relaxed unhurried way, clearly in control and enjoying himself. The goat herder has stopped at the edge of the village to talk to someone and is completely unconcerned that this event is continuing without him.

'The girl?' Mitsos asks.

'Up the hill, having a look around.'

Mitsos steps inside the shop and shuffles to the table at the back.

'The usual?' Stella asks, but does not wait for an answer. There is half a chicken on the grill and two sausages. There are actually three but the third caught fire and has a charcoal coat on. Stella feels the chips with the back of her fingers. They are warm but not hot. She pours them into a stainless-steel dish and puts this over the grill. The cooking bars are black with the burnt juices and the undersides have small pieces of charcoal adhered to them. The coals are still hot but Stavros did not bank more on before he left. Another job she mustn't forget to do.

In the time it takes to arrange the meat on the plate the chips have started to stick to the steel pan but they feel hotter.

'Lemon sauce?' she calls and unscrews the bottle top.

'But of course!' he calls back.

The square table is so small their knees touch as she sits at right angles to him. He smells of fresh air and stored linen. She is glad he does not wear aftershave. Some of the farmers try to mask the smell of their animals with it and it gives her a headache. Mind you, she is not sure if Mitsos even herds his own goats these days; it can't be easy.

'How are you doing?' he asks. Stella knows there is not much she can say. Often the time spent companionably with Mitsos is in silence. The quiet says more than all the words she could think of.

'Managing.' Stella cuts the sausages up and starts on the chicken, which is trickier; it tends to slide on the plate in the sauce.

'Is she staying, do you want her to stay?' Mitsos watches her cutting the food, the sun through the window falling on one half of her face, her cheekbones defined.

Stella exhales loudly. 'I don't know. I suppose if the takings go up … She seems nice but …'

She pushes the plate across to him.

'I think I see trouble if she stays.'

They fall back into a comfortable silence.

'How are the chickens?' Stella asks after a pause. Mitsos had mentioned one of his hens has stopped laying in the hutch. A broody hen. She is laying elsewhere and trying to sit on the eggs. Stella cares about Mitsos' chickens because he cares, but what she would like to say is she wishes he was fifteen years younger, although she wouldn't really. She likes the creases in his face, particularly the ones around his eyes. But she has not ever dwelt on the subject more than that, pushing such thoughts away, forcing Mitsos into a father-figure role which he doesn't quite fit.

There is Stavros, and Mitsos has shown only kindness. She is just lonely and enjoys his attention.

Abby turns right, out of the square. There is a stone wall painted white snaking up the hill. The whitewash is so thick the wall appears iced, all edges rounded, gentle curves replacing sharp corners. Grass grows along the bottom but it is trimmed back, presumably by the passing of cars. Abby climbs the slope, the sun beating down on her white skin. She forgot to put sun cream on and already her shoulders are pink. There is a line of dust up the centre of the road. She has never seen a road like this in England: they always have puddles.

Maybe Stella has a phone charger; there are so many things to take pictures of. The whitewashed wall. The donkey in the field over the other side. The back yard of someone's house that has a line hung with huge white knickers side by side. The buckets and tins that have been painted and spotted blue and white and planted with geraniums, with shocking red blooms. Everywhere a postcard, but actually better than a postcard as none of it is staged, it is all real. Another back yard and a man is … Abby turns away. So revolting, how could he do that? Ok, so he has to eat, but to skin a goat in public, there should be laws.

Coming up from the square floats a clanking and clanging of bells. It must be a herd of goats. She turns to see but the lane has twisted and the view is blocked. Puffing up a track to the right she passes a gate with a home-made letter box, but it looks old and disused. It has a drawer front as a lid and there is a lizard sunbathing on the brass handle. But Abby is determined to see the herd of goats and jogs as fast as she can bear in the heat up the track until, before she reaches a tiny cottage, there is a break in the bushes and she can see the village laid out before her, including the goats in the square, so many of them, a heaving sea, ears flicking, white tails bobbing.

The lady from the kiosk is wafting a newspaper at them to stop them eating her wares and she is talking in a high-pitched voice to a man who does not look at all bothered. The animals begin to leave but the herder doesn't follow the goats or his dog. Abby waits until all the goats have turned out of sight and Vasso has finished wagging her finger at the goat herder, who is now buying a bottle of water from her. Abby turns from the scene to continue to climb the hill.

She decides to go past the cottage, which looks deserted, and along the outside of the wall that surrounds the grove of some sort of trees. The branches are black against the deep blue sky. There is not a cloud anywhere. Abby puts her hand up to shade her eyes. Her forehead is hot; so is her hair. She pulls the cap Stella gave her from her shorts pocket. It smells but somehow seems like a better option than the heat. She waves it about a bit to de-scent it and balances it on her head rather than pulling it on. She walks stiffly so it won't fall off.

Abby has been here less than a day and she is amazed by, well, just about everything she has seen. The people are so funny. One minute they shout and it seems like they will kill each other. In England, if two people in the street argued with the same vehemence, then it would definitely conclude in a physical fight, or worse, a knife being drawn. But actually no one would dare to shout like that unless they were really drunk, or married. But here they shout like it is life and death, other people join in, and then they act like nothing has happened. Abby finds it unsettling. How can she know when anyone is really angry? She quite likes the idea of being able to shout at the top of her voice without it really meaning anything more than her letting off steam. She would love to have shouted at the top of her voice at Dad when he said she couldn't go back to school to do her A levels. A levels are the gateway to University, University the gateway to a career, how can he not realise how important that is? It will define her life.

She supposes she should really let him know she is ok. The idea of being here isn't to worry him. When she gets paid tomorrow she will ask Stella if she can use the phone. Maybe they have call-boxes in town. She doesn't feel she can ask to use the *ouzeri* phone yet as she has no money to pay for the call, and it's not clear what her position there is. She certainly wouldn't ask the man, and Stella seems nice, but reserved. Like she hasn't quite made up her mind.

She passes what must be a chicken hut with little ramps up to a small entrance. She looks around her and sees one or two chickens crouched in the shade of bushes and the back wall of the orchard. A cockerel crows but none of the chickens takes any notice.

Abby makes her way towards a clump of pines that crowns the top of the hill. As she steps under them the relief from the sun surprises her. The ground feels springy and there is a hushed silence. It is a place Rockie would love, digging in the soft ground, finding sticks.

She turns, and her mouth falls open before forming into a wide grin. The village and the whole plain are laid out before her. Little whitewashed houses with tiny yards and regimented kitchen gardens huddle at her feet, squadrons of orange groves range across the flat plain, in the distance are dotted villages and even the nearby town hugging the coast of the bay to her left. The sea itself glistens in the sunlight, a living jewel.

The view looks, to Abby, computer-generated, unreal, as if a child has included all the elements that give joy: a white church atop a hill in the foreground, another further away in the mid distance, the sides of the hills they are mounted on chiselled to make terraces for more olive trees. The mountains in the far distance fade to purple and the wide open sky is an endless dark blue. Abby wants to say it is awesome, but it doesn't feel to be a big enough word. But she is in awe, she feels sure, in the real sense of the word.

'And I am here,' she whispers into the breeze, and the tops of the pines sigh in answer.

Although Stella has finished cutting Mitsos' food she remains sitting there as he eats. She looks idly out of the dusty window in the paint-sealed door to the restaurant part. If she unjammed the door and got nicer tablecloths they would probably get more families; they could even get some more tables and put them on the pavement. She knows that when there are one or two farmers being raucous inside it frightens the women and children away; the outside tables could be for them. But Stavros will not unjam the door, or agree to the buying of more tables. In fact the money they make does not seem to go very far unless ...

'Can you cut this bit, please?' Mitsos asks.

'Oh, sorry.' Stella beaks from her daydreams.

'I am asking you to cut my food because I was a fool twenty-odd years ago and got my arm blown off and you are saying sorry to me?' His eyes smile before the laughter that follows.

Stella smiles back and watches him eat for a moment. What would happen if there was no one to cut his food for him? What would happen if there was no one to cook for him? Life seems very cruel to elderly people, not that he is very elderly, he is only sixty-something, but people that are really elderly have afflictions that mean they cannot use their arms or, even worse, their legs. It seems wrong that people put in effort all their life and then when they get old, as if life has not thrown enough at them, they suffer afflictions.

Stella recalls Vasso had gone to see an old aunt in Athens once who had been put into a state-run old people's home. She had said it was an old building but more like a warehouse, the room was so big. People in pyjamas or in a state of half-dress were wandering around not really knowing what they were doing, and she said no fewer than three people claimed that she had come to see them as they were desperate that she should go into their cubicles so they would have someone to talk to.

She said that rooms had been built in the huge space with flimsy walls, enough to give each person something of a sense of their own space, each room with a bed and a chair. But none of the rooms had ceilings.

Her aunt's was better than most because she had taken with her a small chest of drawers and her own bed linen. She had framed pictures of her family on the chest and on the chair and a little rug by the bed. But she did not seem happy or well. People had wandered in and out of the room while she was there as if they were lost. She didn't venture to even ask about the bathrooms.

But that was in Athens. What happens here? What would happen to Mitsos if he fell up at his cottage on the side of the hill? Who would know? Well she would, because she would go and check if he hadn't been seen for a day or two.

And what will happen to her?

'What? What is it?' Mitsos ask.

'What?' Stella replies.

'You just made the most weird sound and then you ask me 'What?' He chuckles and continues eating.

When Stella had asked herself what would happen when she got old she very clearly saw herself without Stavros, and the thought frightened her, made her gasp out loud. But not only was there fear. She also felt – she tried to pin the word down – 'spacious', which she thought was a silly word, even though it fitted somehow.

'And now you are smiling.' Mitsos chuckles.

Abby finds it almost unbelievable that she is alone in Greece. Dad had never even been abroad until he met Sonia. But lots of her friends have been all over the place. She is probably the least travelled among them.

A dog barks down in the village and Abby tries to spot which yard it is in. It is answered by another dog and a little flurry of barking spreads across the village before dying down again.

Her friend Jackie, who is probably working at this very moment at the Malibu, took a gap year before university. She said there were only two problems in life, deciding what you want to do and finding the money to do it. Abby had thought at the time that deciding what you want to do was the easy bit but now, just a year later, it seems so much harder.

If Dad does not let her carry on in school then there is a whole world of choice. Travelling is obviously not so hard, maybe she could travel the world for a bit. Getting a job seems easy enough. There is lots of charity work abroad. In fact there seems little point in staying in England when there is a whole world to choose from. But there is the snag! The whole world to choose from. That's a lot of choice.

But the one choice she wants, to stay at school, go to University, seems to be denied her.

Stella stops smiling at the thought of being old without Stavros. She has no right. Stavros saved her from a very unpleasant situation which was destined to last a lifetime if he hadn't stepped in.

School memories rush at her and she pulls her skirt over her knees and folds her arms across her chest.

'Are you ok?' asks the ever attentive Mitsos.

'Fine.' Stella jumps up and goes through and behind the grill to get the ouzo, the good stuff, and two glasses.

She sits down again and pours and quickly takes a gulp.

'Come on, what is it?' Mitsos sits back, his belly extended, ready to talk.

'I just had a memory, I have it quite often.' She glances at him. His eyes are kind, as always. She is brave and says, 'Once, on my way back from school some kids followed me. Called me 'Gypsy', told me I was dirty. We were all about seven, I think. Well, they had stones in their pockets and they began to throw them.' Stella can remember the fear she had experienced, her little bare legs running up the road and the children chasing her. The first stone hit her thigh and she ran faster; the second hit her head. The taunts of 'gypsy' and 'dirty' bringing tears to her eyes, the rejection, the isolation, the being different. Even now, just remembering, she can feel tears trying to build, but her eyes stay dry, the emotion stuck somewhere below her throat. It was the premeditated act that hurt more than anything. The children already had the stones in their pockets, it was not on impulse. They had planned it.

Mitsos leans forward and takes a toothpick from the holder in front of the napkins.

'People can be very cruel.' He pauses with the toothpick. 'Children even more so.' He bites on the toothpick and, as discretely as he can, cleans his teeth. Stella looks out of the window in the door until he finishes. He says, 'I too have been considering my life recently, for what it is worth, and I have reached the conclusion that the only way to be content is to have absolute integrity. To fulfil all you believe to be true no matter what the cost.' He sips some ouzo and sucks his teeth. 'Then when people give you looks, say false or unkind things, you know that the fault lies with them. You have been all you can be and no one can ask for more.' He looks at her and she at him. 'Decide what you believe in, Stella, and the rest will follow. I just wish I had thought this when I was younger.'

'It won't change that I am a gypsy,' Stella says.

'Gypsy is the last thing I see. Focus on your other qualities.' He waits, but Stella does not respond. 'If you have a belief that making other people comfortable is a good thing then put your heart into that. You cannot at the same time think about your place in society as a gypsy. You will be so lost in acting out your belief, so involved in other thoughts, that being a gypsy will not come to mind. You cannot think two thoughts at the same time. You cannot both fill a glass and empty it at the same time.'

'But these thoughts just come. I wish I had never been to school. Some of those children are still here in the village, all grown up. They don't even seem to remember, but I know how they think.' Stella absent-mindedly arranges the salt and pepper pots and the serviette holder in the centre of the table.

'Don't give them power,' Mitsos says. 'It's like the stream up behind my house in the winter. It starts as a small trickle seeping out across the land; soon it wears a little groove, and then as the water collects it takes the easiest route. Soon the groove widens until it becomes a stream. If I leave it the water will always take this easy route. If it is a route that suits me I leave it but if it is a route that goes past my back door turning all the earth to mud it is a problem. So I take my spade out before the trickle becomes a stream and I dig the route I want the water to take. Your mind is the same, it will always take the easiest route, and that will be the route you think most often. It's easy, it has done it before. New ways are harder, but not if you start them early.'

'Yes, easy for you to say, but I already have a

river flowing through my mind.' Stella snorts an unhappy laugh.

'Then it just needs a little more constant work of letting your river flow into the channels you feel are good, your hospitality, your business sense, your compassion, your kindness. Focus on those and the river will be diverted.'

'What I would have given not to have gone to school.'

'And that right there is one of your worn replayed grooves. Either don't think it and think something else, or think, "Thank goodness I went to school and experienced that, now I know how important it is to make people feel welcome, make them feel at home."' Mitsos takes another sip of ouzo. 'I for one know, Stella, that without you making people feel welcome and comfortable this business would not be as thriving as it is today. It is the kindness you show.' He pats his empty sleeve, his own need to receive kindness.

At that moment a farmer, with a cheerful 'hello', comes in and flops into a chair as if it is his own home, timed as if to prove Mitsos' point.

Chapter 7

The *giro* drips oil down the farmer's hand as he banters with Stella for a minute. Mitsos raises his eyebrows, tightens his lips and nods at Stella. Stella succeeds in not looking at Mitsos but she gets the message. The farmer sees Mitsos and joins him at his table.

'One of my goats got stuck in my child's tricycle this morning, pulled the bell right off.' He laughs heartily.

Stella cleans up the counter area where she made the wrap and goes through to retrieve the ouzo bottle. The farmer eyes her up and down, and makes no secret of it.

'I am forty-six,' she scolds him.

'My older dog knows how to herd sheep better than my younger one.' He grins back at her. Mitsos is drinking the last of his ouzo. The farmer's retort makes him laugh. The ouzo sprays back into the glass, and he puts it down to mop his chin.

Stella wipes the table, smiling and tutting at the farmer before she returns the ouzo back beside the sink. The smile slides as she takes in the grubbiness behind the grill. She wishes she could raise the enthusiasm to clean but it all feels too much. Too many shelves to wipe, too much dirt to clean, too many years of neither her nor Stavros caring. She always puts the customers before that sort of thing. He puts his free time first. She will get some Ajax, glass cleaner. Vasso sells it.

'Do you know that this will be the first year I have had to do the accounts on my own?' Vasso says. There is a fan mounted on one of the shelves, blowing the warm air around inside her kiosk. Stella has the sun on her back, it is hot. 'My son has always done them, before him his dad did them, now it's me. I haven't a clue.' Vasso is up to her elbows in receipts and bills.

'I have to get ours done soon. I hate it too. It's a shame there's no one in the village who can do that sort of thing. I am not going to pay a town accountant to add some numbers.' She laughs at the thought. 'Do you have any Ajax?'

'No, but Marina does over in her corner shop.'

Marina, Mitsos' unrequited love. Stella knows she sells just about everything, but Vasso is closer and she knows her better. She doesn't really know Marina, never really got to know her for some reason. Of course she knows *of* her, everyone knows about everyone in the village. Marina's husband, she knows from experience, had not been such a nice man. Stella crosses herself anyway. He had once shocked her with how very unkind he could be, implied she was 'available' just because she was a gypsy. She had been twenty at the time, before she married Stavros, but he was married to Marina, in fact it was just a couple of years before he died.

'Hang on.' Vasso searches under her counter at knee level. 'I have two of my own, give me a couple of euros and you can have one.' Vasso pulls out a very old-fashioned-looking plastic bottle. 'Do you need kitchen roll?'

Stella shakes her head and puts two euros on the counter. Turning to go back to the shop, she sees the farmer she has just served in her *ouzeri* and Mitsos, making their way towards her, or rather to the kafenio.

'Thanks,' Mitsos says as he passes her.

The shop has hit its afternoon lull; it is too late for lunch, too early for dinner. This would be a good time to start on the shelves. She puts the bottle on the counter and goes through to clear Mitsos' dirty plates. She is washing them when there is the noise of someone at the counter. She shakes her hands dry and goes around the grill.

'Oh, hi.' Stella is surprised at how flat her voice is.

'Any customers?' Stavros asks.

'Mitsos and that Achilleas who lives over the other side of the hill with the three donkeys. Did you have a sleep?'

'Not much business then.'

'About the same as always at this time of day. Did you bring more charcoal?'

'It's not enough.' Stavros seems particularly grumpy. 'I suppose you sat and cut up Mitsos' lunch and chatted like you have all the time in the world.'

'Of course I cut up his lunch. He only has one arm, how else would he manage? That's the reason he comes here. What's wrong with you? You seem so grumpy, did you have a sleep or not?'

'This place, this hand-to-mouth living, frying and sweating all day, it's not enough.'

Stella decides not to say anything.

'Where's the girl?' he demands.

'The girl is called Abby and she has gone to look around the village.' Stella counts how many foil takeaway trays they have left.

'In this heat? What's wrong with her?'

'She's English.' Stella tries to stifle the giggle she can feel in the back of her throat.

'Why are there no chickens cooking, not even a sausage on the grill, what the ...' He stomps around to the grill. 'Stella! You have not even banked up the coals for tonight. *Panayia!*' He calls on his God. 'No wonder we are not making enough to get by on.'

'We are making the same as we did last year at this time, and our outgoings have not increased. Even the butcher has kept his prices the same, so how come we need more money this year?' She considers the structure of the next sentence before she says, 'Is there something else the money is going on that I don't know about?'

'Out of my way.' He pushes her backwards to get past her from behind the counter. He pushes her hard and she staggers. She hits the wall and her head hits against the peg that Abby's bag is hanging on. For a moment she is blank. There is only the pain. She blinks and rubs the back of her head to ease the intensity. She expects Stavros to say something, to ask her if she is ok, maybe even put a hand on her arm, help her to sit down. But there is no sound. She blinks again and focus returns, and she looks up. He is gone.

Stella is more shocked by his lack of remorse for

what he has just done than by the action itself. It is almost as if the shove was deliberately that hard. She holds the wall as she goes through to the four tables and pulls at a chair to sit on.

With her elbows on the table she waits until the world stops swimming and the throbbing subsides a little. Surely it was an accident. Presumably he went to get charcoal and didn't see her hit her head.

She hears a snuffling and a snorting as Stavros lugs in the coals.

She sits and watches him. Any minute, he will ask her why she is sitting down and then she will tell him, and he will be sorry for his strength and everything will be fine.

He looks over to her.

He says nothing.

He unties the top of the coal sack and builds up the fire.

He knows what he just did.

It was intended.

'You hurt my head.' Stella decides she must speak out. He had pushed her by the elbow earlier to get her to go inside and now he has pushed her again, but much harder. It is unfair. She stands up, the backs of her knees against the chair.

'You're not dying.' He says it quietly, his mouth hardly opening, dismissive in the lack of effort he makes to annunciate the words.

'You hurt me!' Stella's voice is high pitched.

'Forget your head, if you used it to increase business I would care far more but you flit and flirt, pile on too many chips, then they have no need to buy more. It's a joke.' His brow is wet with sweat. He tears off some kitchen roll and mops his forehead and the back of his neck, scrunches it into a ball, dries between his fingers and throws it in the fire.

'Perhaps if our outgoings were less it wouldn't be such a problem, and there is only one reason that they could be more than last year.' Her knees feel slightly weak and she can feel the blood rushing to her face. The muscles in her forearm tremble, her fists clench. She looks to see her position relative to the door. Adrenaline gives her courage. 'If you have a gambling problem you cannot take it out on me. I already suffer with the drain it puts on our money, and now your tempers as well.'

He steps towards her. 'So this is my fault?' He sneers as he spreads his hand, palm-upwards, to encompass the whole shop.

'No, the shop came from my dad. You haven't earned, you've just spent.'

No sooner are the words spat out of her lips than she wishes to suck them back in. But the saliva has not even dried on her lips when the grip he takes on her arms demands all her attention, his thumbs digging in, her muscles screaming at the compression, his fingers on her triceps, his short nails cutting into the skin as he grips hard. She opens her mouth to release the pain. The first noise is silence. Her head whips back and then forwards. He shakes, hard and strong. The snapping back and forward of her head leaves no room for thought. Her eyes spin. She loses sense of direction and with it her balance. Then she can actually sense her brain hitting the inside of her skull, which, in some quiet, calm part of her thoughts she considers is interesting as she did not know that could happen. The thought is obliterated by a tidal wave of fear that some permanent damage may be occurring in her neck, her head. The room distorts, her eyelids a dark red and then it stops.

He sits her in a chair like a doll.

'Did you have a good walk?' Stavros' charming tone drifts to her as if nothing has happened, his honeymoon voice, which he used on her when they were first married, and on the farmers' wives when they had first opened the *ouzeri*. She hasn't heard it in years. But she cannot look up or open her eyes; she cradles her head in her hands and just sits, listening to her own pulse in her temples.

Stavros receives no answer. But Stella can hear someone else in the shop and the sound of pages being turned. Her neck hurts, there is a throbbing inside her ears.

'I do not understand. "Then ka-ta-la-ve-no".' It is Abby's voice.

'Ok, ok.'

Stavros' English is so strongly accented it does not sound like English at all. Stella opens her eyes and looks up carefully. Her neck feels loose and fragile. He is dragging the coal back outside to put it around the side. It is all crashingly too real. Her perception of Stavros pivots on its axis and her knight turns into her oppressor. She is amazed at the speed with which it happens, and the completeness of the transformation. The man who saved her becomes the man who is harming her. The man whom she was proud of becomes the man she is ashamed off, the man she worked with now the man she will work against. In among all that emotion, the most startling find is that there is no love left. Not even a sentimental love; just sadness.

As this realisation settles Stella is aware that none of it is new. It has been going this way for years. This is just the defining moment that demands honesty, and she can no longer pretend to herself.

She hears the sack scraping around the corner. She counts down the seconds it will take him to walk back. He doesn't come in, he walks straight past.

'Oh, hi! I didn't see you there. What did he say?' Abby spots her.

'He hopes that you had a good walk.' Stella tries to hold her head up straight.

'Oh, how kind, what a nice thing to say. I think people are very lucky when they are married to nice people.'

'Me too,' Stella replies.

'You OK?" Abby asks. Stella looks as if she isn't focusing too well.

'I'm fine, I just need to sit, too much ouzo over lunch,' Stella says, looking away. Abby wonders if the problem is that Stella doesn't really want her to work here. She wonders if Stella would be happier if she wasn't around. Or maybe she needs to work harder.

Abby's shoulders are burning from being out in the sun. She puts opposite hands on each one to cool them but her hands feel hot too.

'What shall I do?' Abby asks. If she is as useful as she can be, it might cheer Stella up. Or maybe this is just the way she is, warm one minute, cold the next. That might explain why Stavros is the way he is, poor man. Still, he is a bit of a letch; there is no excuse for that.

It's late afternoon and she should really call Dad. He will be worrying about her.

'I was wondering, my phone has run out of charge, you don't have a charger, do you?' Abby asks. Stella looks at her as if she is speaking Swahili, so she tries again. 'Phone charger?' But still Stella does not reply, and she has gone very white. 'Can I get you something, some water perhaps?' Abby asks. Stella looks ill.

'Yes, water, please.' Stella's voice sounds shaky. Abby takes one of the glasses that she washed up earlier and goes to the fridge for the bottled water. She feels just slightly smug that she remembers not to get it from the tap but, actually, looking at the tap, it is probably a health risk anyway, even if the water was good. There seem to be no health and hygiene laws here. They should make a reality programme on restaurants abroad. It would be great.

'Here you go.' She watches Stella drink and then tries again, speaking slowly. 'I need to charge my phone so I can let my dad know I am okay.'

Stella cuts her off. 'There is the phone.'

'Is that okay? For England?' Abby asks.

Stella seems weary but Abby is drawn to the phone. 'Do you know the code for England?'

'There's a book underneath, bring it over ... There, 0044.' Her voice is soft, gentle; she doesn't seem cross.

'Are you ill, Stella? You don't seem right?' Abby dials, it begins to ring. 'Hang on, it's ringing. Hello! Oh. It's the answering machine. Hello, Dad, it's me. Just wanted you to know I am fine. In a place called ...' She looks over to Stella, but Stella's head is in her hands, eyes down. 'I don't know what it's called but I am fine. I'll call again when I get some charge. Bye.'

Stella looks up. 'You are lucky to have a dad.'

'Oh, don't you have a dad?' One of Abby's friends is always going on about how fantastic her mum is because she has no dad; they are more like mates than mother and daughter. Her mum is only sixteen years older than her so they go out clubbing together. Abby would rather have had a mum than a mate.

'Yes, but now he is dead.'

'Oh. I am sorry.' Abby puts the phone book away

and neatens some knives and forks on the counter top.

'He was a good man. My mother she came to this village on her own. She was working at the place they make cheese, the two green doors next the kafenio.'

'Oh, that building with no windows?'

'Yes, she worked there with the family. It is not so big, even smaller then. Now they have two people. When my mama worked it was because she was cheap and they gave her a small *apothiki* to live in.'

'What's an *apothiki*?'

'A room for things, things you don't use every day. But it had bathroom, not like new but with toilet and shower head from the sink, you close the toilet, it is a chair and you have a shower room.' Abby is a little confused by Stella's sudden talkativeness, but in the mood Stella is in maybe she needs just to talk. Sonia's like that. Suddenly talking non-stop. Stella continues. 'She had a little gas stove, one that you can carry. She told me all about it, she like it, she was proud. The room had a bed and a table, but you had to sit on the bed to use the table. There was no room for a chair she said.' Stella stops talking and rubs her neck. 'Abby, please give me the headache pills on the shelf there, no, down, next shelf, yes, thank you.' She takes two and drinks the rest of her water before she starts again.

'My dad he sees her and he gets to know her and

he is brave enough to marry her.'

'Er, sorry, why did he need to be brave?'

'She was gypsy.'

'So?'

'So, so? Gypsies are not the same as not gypsy. The people, they do not like gypsies. They think they are dirty and they steal. Some are dirty and some do steal, but not all. Gypsy have a heart like anyone else and they hurt like anyone else. I know.'

'So by marrying your mum, what happened?'

'Nothing. They have me and they are happy. We are all happy till I have to go to school.'

'I love school,' Abby butts in.

'You do not love school if you were gypsy, they throw stones at me.'

'No!'

'Yes! But then along came Stavros, who, can you believe, was good-looking then and he say he will marry me and then the people my age stop talking because I am married to a Greek and they respect him, just because he is Greek.'

'My dad has just married Sonia, she's Russian.

Everyone is saying it was not a good idea. Now he doesn't want me to go to school so I can help with the new baby when it comes. But why should I? It is their baby, not mine.'

'Better than school,' Stella says.

'Not for me. I want to stay on and do my A levels and then university. But Dad says "what's the point".' Abby draws out the chair next to Stella and sits down.

'Even I know the point of education and I did not like school. But if I could go to a school with no peoples I would have loved it, I love to learn things. I learn English.' She laughs and her head rolls back. She uses a supporting hand to aid it back to upright.

'I love learning too. Mostly maths, but I quite like computers, and geography. Besides, babies don't do anything, I would be bored,' Abby responds

'I wanted baby once,' Stella breathes.

'Haven't you got no children then?' Abby says, then reruns the question in her head to sort out the grammar but decides it doesn't matter, Stella's English is far from perfect anyway.

Stella shakes her head slowly. 'He cannot have them, he says it is me, but I think it is for the best.'

'I'm not sure I want kids,' Abby muses.

'Someone to look after you when you are old,' Stella says.

'I'll find a nice old people's home, better than being dependent on someone else. Where was your dad when he died?'

'At home, here, well just up there.' Stella lifts her hand and indicates a general direction. 'When he died was not so bad. No, it was bad. But after he dead then it worse. My mother was alone. Her gypsy family come. Some stayed, some took things. *Siga siga*, slowly slowly, as we say in Greece, they took everything. First the small things, my Mama's picture frames and her aprons. Then some men who said they were uncles come, two stayed in the house. They have her cooking for them and they just put their feets up.' She says 'put-their-feets-up', as if this is a new phrase to her that she has just learnt.

'That must have been hard on you.' Abby knows what it is like to have interlopers in her house taking her mother's role, the mother she never knew.

'I was not there, I was married with Stavros, living in his village. Every time I come the house was a little more empty, my mother was a little more tired and the men are little more bossy.'

'Is your mum still there?'

'No, she died also, after they have taken from the

house everything and left. I went back once and the kitchen table and chairs are gone. My mama was sitting on an olive oil tin. One of the men was sitting on a, how you call it, big square thing to makes houses, you know, grey, put them in a line then another line …'

'Brick, breeze-block?' Abby enjoys the challenge of trying to think what it is.

'Maybe, I do not know. Anyway that time I go to the toilet and the toilet seat is gone. This was in the house of my Baba, not the *apothiki* of the cheese factory. And the shower snake is gone. I go to ask her where I will find paper for the toilet, and through the half-open door I see the man who said he was uncle smack her on the face and walk out.'

'Oh my …' Abby does not finish her sentence, she cannot imagine how scary that must have been. She'd like to think she would have defended her mum but then the man could turn, and then what? 'What did you do?'

'I ran to her, she had tears on her cheeks, she held my hand so I could not run out after him. I ask if he has done it before and she says no but I did not believe her. So I stayed.'

'What, like the weekend?' Abby thinks she would have defended her mum, whatever the cost.

'No, I just stayed until Stavros came to find me and then he stayed. We had oranges and olives and I had Mama's job in the cheese factory because we needed money and they said she was a good worker. And then she died.'

'That's sad. My mum died before I met her,' Abby says.

'Yes, that is very hard.' Stella rubs her neck as she talks.

'I don't know. I never knew her.' Abby feels a pricking in her eyes and her breathing rate increases. 'More water?' She gets up to distract herself from what she is feeling.

'Yes, please, and push the fire a little and turn the chicken.' Stella stops rubbing her neck. She rubs her arms instead, as if she is cold.

'These sausages look like they're done. Shall I take them off?' But Abby doesn't wait for a reply. She moves them to the side of the grill to keep warm and turns the chicken.

'Why your dad say you must not have these Alpha levels?'

'A levels. Because I want to take them to go to university, but now you have to pay to go to university and Dad cannot afford it, so he thinks it will be a waste of time and that it would build my hopes up for no reason.'

'But education is not a waste, never.' Stella looks at Abby very seriously. Abby wants to give her a hug but instead puts the tongs down and fills their glasses. Stella still seems to be shaky.

Abby is about to go across to her when two boys walk in, not much younger than Abby.

'*Dyo giro, parakalo.*'

Abby stares at them blankly and wonders where her phrase book is.

'Say "*Yia*",' Stella prompts.

'Yia,' Abby recites.

'Yia,' one of the boys says. The other grins.

'They want two *giros*, I'm coming.' Stella takes hold of the table edge to stand.

'I've got it, tell me what to do.' Abby holds her hand up, palm facing Stella.

This idea seems to tickle Stella. She laughs gently. 'Two pita breads on the grill with some oil.' Abby follows the instructions. The pitas sizzle and she plucks them off and piles them high with meat and tomatoes, *tzatziki* and onions. She attempts to roll the first one,

113

and it is satisfactory. She is better with the second.

'*Dyo evro*,' Stella calls. Abby puts out her hand; 'dyo' she understands, two euros. She wonders if that is each or together but as each boy offers her two euros she presumes it is for each. They leave with happy smiles, one looking behind him for a last glimpse of Abby. She wonders how old he is, maybe her age.

Chapter 8

Stella sits alone in the remains of the heat. Loose limbed, looking up in the dusk to spot the first stars, she rubs the bruises. She wonders if she will go home tonight.

The last of the farmers have just left. As usual hers is one of the last shops to close. She takes a sip of ouzo and puts the glass on the floor by the leg of her chair.

The orange glow of light flicks off in the pharmacy leaving a pause of dark. A harsh bare bulb switches on, visible in the window above the shop. The noise of the television bounces off unadorned walls. The curtains are drawn, eclipsing the strip of light, muffling the sound. Stella continues to sit, listening. Shutters close, echoing around the village. A dog's bark is answered by another.

Vasso emerges from the kiosk and stretches. She took Abby to her home to settle in a couple of hours ago; the poor girl was exhausted.

Vasso's yawn is interrupted by a last-minute customer wanting cigarettes. His scrabble for change is waved away. The till is cashed up, he can pay tomorrow. She chains the metal shutters to the front of the free-standing drinks fridges, slots home the wooden panels over the windows of her kiosk and calls goodbye to Stella. She turns off her central lights, darkening the whole square. The moon bright in the clear sky, the stars sharp dots in the inky blanket enveloping the village. Her silhouette hurries towards her home, and sleep. She will leave the porch light on when she goes to bed to illuminate Stella's path to her own house, next door.

Stella levels her hands in front of her, fingers splayed, and stretches with her own, loud, yawn. As her eyes open she rotates her limbs inwards to show the matching bruises on the backs of her arms, angry, shocking. A knot forms in her throat and she blinks tears from her eyes.

The lights go off one by one before the metal-framed glass doors clang shut at Theo's kafenio. There is a sound of farmers talking, sharing last thoughts before wishing each other goodnight. Theo stacks the chairs that remain in the square, scraping them across to the lamp-post as he chats.

The same scene is played again and again, night after night.

With her thumbs under her jaw bone, Stella rubs the tears from her eyes with the pads of her fingers and sniffs. Over the past seven years, sitting outside her *souvlaki* shop, she has witnessed this curtain call, the finale to the sequence of events of village life at the close of the day, the continuity of events implying security.

But ... She doesn't feel safe any more. It only took thirty seconds. The smell of jasmine grows momentarily as a gentle breeze stirs the air and lifts the heat from her limbs. She picks at her dress to unstick it from her legs. She wants to lie down, become lost in sleep, but she cannot face her own bed. The process of getting into it will involve too much talk, or worse, heavy silence.

The voices outside the kafenio grow fainter. Theo, an outline, whose bushy hair bobs as he goes round the side of his café and opens a door which leads to his bachelor rooms above the shop, looks around before he steps out of view and, seeing Stella, waves good night. How different life would have been had her brief dates with Theo, all those years ago, become more. The age difference then had seemed unsurpassable. Theo, the same age as Mitsos. How time changes things.

She lifts her hand in acknowledgement, but he is gone and she lets it drop. Everything's the same as the evening before but all now unreachable, untouchable. Stella's focus is on a more compelling, immediate, reality.

She feels a tightening in her chest as questions collide, contending for precedence until one dominates. The foremost question: what if it happens again?

She looks around the square. With both Theo and Vasso gone she is totally alone.

There are no lights left in the centre of the village apart from those behind her in her own takeaway and only one of these remains on, a low-watt glow.

Stavros' shouting she is used to. Fists thumped on tables, even punches through door panels have been known, chairs flung across rooms, crockery broken, all common-place. The menace is there daily. But now it has overflowed onto her. Even if he never touches her again the trust is gone, the perceived safety shattered. He is no longer the Stavros she loved, although, even after the event, when she caught his eyes twinkling (for Abby), a smile on his lips (again for Abby), she was reminded of the Stavros she had married. The surge of loneliness and overwhelming sadness that rose from her stomach to her chest had taken her by surprise. She had nearly been sick.

Even in her sickness she could not lie to herself. The moment his grip tightened to pain he had granted her permission to let her suppressed feelings flow. But it was neither fear nor hate that gushed with her adrenaline. It was undiluted disdain that contorted her thoughts. A sad little man. A little man with the power to hurt her.

She takes another sip of ouzo.

A distant dog barks. It is answered by one behind the houses on the opposite side of the street. This starts another howling and for a short time the village is blanketed by the dogs' choir until one by one they quieten down and nothing can be heard but the cicadas rasping their loneliness in the heat of the night.

A light comes on over the bakery and goes out again. They will be up in a few hours. Stella finishes her drink and stands. She stretches, sways slightly, steadies herself, and turns to lock up. The glass is left on the pavement by her chair.

Inside the shop the grill is reduced to ashes. She checks (again) that the chip cooker is off and screws the top back on the litre bottle of lemon sauce. Someone has left a tip of a euro on the counter. She leaves it and extends her arm to turn out the light.

The bruise does not shock her so much as enrage her, drawing to her attention the empty, gnawing, panic feeling at the bottom of her stomach from which the ouzo has only just taken the edge. It reminds her of why she was sitting out in the dark drinking in the first place. How dare he take away her safety?

The mark is turning yellow in the centre.

She lifts her other arm into the light, displaying a twin bruise, in the same position, the same colour. Twisting her chin over her shoulder to see down her back, she can just make out the edge of discolouration on her shoulder blade, where she hit the corner of the wall earlier but hadn't noticed for the pain of her head on the coat hook. The twist hurts her neck. She switches off the light; the dark feels better. The moon her only illuminator, she steps back into the street and locks the door.

Tears are forming before she is even aware she has felt the emotion: delayed fear. Her throat constricts and her body spasms in the first sob. Emotion overcomes her. Her lungs feel tight and she gasps for air, sending further spasms across her chest, her shoulders twitching in response.

The night absorbs the scene, the darkness a cloak, allowing her privacy. Silently she shudders and heaves until her energy is drained. The feelings subside.

But the thoughts remain. There is the hint of a belief that she deserves this. Worse things happen to ordinary people. Why should she be spared? She has no status to say she deserves better treatment. Her gypsy legacy tells her that perhaps this is just her lot in life, as it was her mother's. Accept, don't fight the tide, was her mother's motto. Be insignificant and they leave you alone, she had said. Thinking like that makes this incident an unremarkable event. Her life, which until this incident she thought she had moulded as well as she could, suddenly seems pointless. Her future, whatever future she has, is distorted by fear until it is so twisted it feels impossible that it exists at all. She can see no way forward, no way out. Another wave of sobs rises unbidden but this time she sucks in air, lifts her chest and denies herself the comfort of succumbing.

She stands for a moment, preparing to go home. Across the square the cold light of the moon contrasts with the warmth of the breeze. The heat wave Greece is experiencing feels like August has come early, when shops will close and people will not move in the heat of the day as the temperature saps all energy and lays low even the most energetic person. But that is not yet.

With the thought of the future her head rises and her lips form a thin line. Determination invigorates her and she begins the unsteady walk home.

Alcohol-fuelled feet take her, haphazardly, to the crossroads at the far corner of the square. She turns left by the corner shop and up to the paved area by the church. No children play there at this hour but a ball rolls silently, blown by the soft breeze. For a moment there are two balls. She presses her eyelids together. Focus returns. The lane will take her towards the edge of town but she turns left again between the houses covered with bougainvillea. The path narrows and wriggles between whitewashed stone homes glowing in the moonlight, plots of spring onions and lettuce, plastic tables on porches with chairs leaned up against them at angles, so cats cannot sit.

She passes Vasso's house where Abby and Vasso will be safely asleep by now. She puts her hand out to steady herself against her wall and gains some stability. She pats the wall as if the stones themselves are her friends. On to the final lane before the village opens onto the orange groves. She and Stavros rent the last house. Vasso's outside light helps her to see the way. Stella murmurs a 'thank you' for her friendship.

Stavros, too, has left the lights on outside. The narrow porch is cosy in the warmth of the electric light, creating its own frame as its illuminating fingers stretch out to reach the leaves of the bushes on one side and the wall across the lane at the other.

A stark bulb is also on inside. Stella swallows. He may still be awake. She would like another shot of ouzo before she goes in. A shadow passes the window on the inside. She cannot face him.

She turns on the spot, trying to hold her determination intact, and walks quickly back down the lane to the church. She has no idea where she is going, just away. She staggers across the open area in front of the church, her legs wobbling, wishing her limbs more nimble, her mind more clouded. She tries the doors of the church but they are locked so she sits on a wide stone-slab seat to one side and rests her head on a carved stone pillar. She is warm now but she knows an hour before dawn the temperature will drop and her thin sleeveless dress will offer her no protection. She looks at her thin legs and despises how small she is, her tell-tale tan, her dark hair, which she shortened to her shoulders years ago to cut ties with her culture.

The moonlight does not enter the church doorway, and with the dark, and the length of the day, her eyelids close and allow her mind to escape for an hour or two in sleep.

The cold comes like a thief, sucking the warmth through the ground from the stones she is lying on before leeching the air and replacing the void with a nip of northern temperatures. The cicadas fall silent.

Stella's eyes are the last part of her to awake and she finds she is shivering. The cold has sunk into her bones, and despite her lack of rest her body needs to move, to chase away the shivers. She stands, her eyes closing again, and walks half asleep along the lane out of the village. It is too early for work, and she would rather go anywhere but home.

The temperature drops even more when the houses that line the lane give way to orange trees. Stella walks briskly and finds herself heading towards the olive hills. She turns up a track that climbs a gully and heads towards the nearest summit. Now she knows where she is going.

The track steepens and she puffs as she tries to maintain her pace, the exertion giving her the illusion of power and with it a feeling of hope. She is warmer now. Her breathing eases as the way levels slightly and she turns with the path, from the gully, up the spine of the hill, the summit teasing as each horizon offers another, dim in the half light, until finally she is at the top.

The panorama lifts her from her worldly troubles. The whole of the plain is laid out in one big expanse, the village a small cluster of red roofs at her feet, the fruit trees sprawling out, quilt-like, to the towns dotted around the coast, the bay itself heralding the dawn as the first rays of the sun sparkle orange across its tranquil turquoise surface. The mountains beyond look so bright, so joyous, Stella forgets herself and is lost in the wonder of the new day. Anticipation of the heat to come is reflected in the colours. The sun rises rapidly and Stella looks behind her. One tall mountain is between her and her own dawn, and the sun is already peeking over the top, the first rays causing her eyes to narrow.

Her father would walk with her up here and tell her, with a smile on his face, that anything was possible. Looking over the vista she would believe him, that the world is a magical place. That was long ago.

Her bruises throb with the rush of blood the climb has flooded through her veins. The contusions have developed a purple edge. She hopes they will fade quickly and the episode can be forgotten; she cannot contemplate the prospect of a re-occurrence. She feels that there must be a mistake as to how it came about. If there was an error, she knows, surely, it must be hers. She wishes she wasn't so physically small. Perhaps, for someone bigger, the event would have felt like nothing.

Images of her mother, and school, are banished from the processing. She will not be like her mother. She concentrates on the view, refusing to give the incident any more power. She has lost a night's sleep, that is enough. What did Mitsos say? Don't give it power, think of things you believe in.

The sun is over the hill and the rays warm her, her tanned brown skin turning to a rich honey in the light.

Her Baba would walk with her and, her legs going twice as fast as his, she would reach up and they would go hand in hand, somewhere beyond this point, down the dip and behind the next summit, but all she can see are bushes and scrubland, the memory faded, the promise of something wonderful just beyond reach: tatters of childhood dreams, fantasies of wishes. She turns from both dreams and panoramic view to head back down the hill. In the distance she can hear the sound of gunfire as dawn hunters shoot rabbits, their dogs barking in excitement.

Gravity adds speed to her pace, and the beauty of the sunny day a skip and a bounce to her tired tread. She feels free up here and wishes she could stay forever.

All too quickly she is back on the outskirts of the village. She waves to Vasso, who is imprisoned again. Vasso calls that Abby is still asleep and that she thinks it best to leave her, after so much travelling. She will come when she wakes, it was arranged last night. Stella goes straight to the shop and opens up to make herself a frappé.

She puts a teaspoon of instant coffee in a cup with a teaspoon of sugar and a small amount of water. The hand-held blender is noisy for the time of day but the mix quickly froths. The early morning discordant ring of church bells drowns out the electrical buzz, and rouses the village. She adds water and ice cubes, and the thick sweet foam rises to the top. She looks in the fridge for evaporated milk, which she pours in liberally.

Plonking a straw in her beaker, she flops onto the chair outside that she left only a few hours before. She slides down the chair, without the energy to sit up. She is grateful for the warmth, knowing that all too quickly it will give way to stifling heat.

The tiny sandwich shop across the road is open for breakfast, offering spinach and cheese pies, cream pasties and frappés.

The guttural sound of a tractor is heard before it is seen. It turns the corner into the village. Two dogs struggle to maintain balance on the flat back trailer it is pulling. The tractor's rusting orange paint is a contrast to the whitewash and blue shutters of the village houses. The dust kicks up from its wide, deeply grooved tyres.

Stella catches a movement in the sandwich shop. The girl serving smiles and waves to her before the tractor pulls up, blocking her view. The driver climbs down, his wife sitting half on his open seat, half on the metal wheel arch. Her black headscarf obscures her face. She wears the uniform of a farmer's wife, a straight skirt to the knees, ankle socks, comfy black shoes and a stained and out-of-shape T-shirt. She waits passively. The dogs curl up together behind.

The farmer returns, and the dogs spring to attention. He hands two paper packets to his wife and slides into his seat to drive across the road to the kiosk on the square. He descends again for cigarettes before approaching a group of illegal immigrants waiting, hopefully, for work, on the bench by the palm tree. They stand eagerly, in unison, to show their willingness. He selects two of the tallest and, with a twist of his wrist, points to the trailer with his thumb.

The dogs growl a warning as they jump on. The farmer drives out of the square at the top end, with the immigrants sitting on the back, legs hung over the number plate.

Stella watches them depart. There are more immigrants than there were last week. She wonders where they sleep.

A familiar thin profile shuffles into the square and heads towards her. She puts up her arm to shield her eyes from the sun and pushes herself back in her seat, sitting up.

'Hi, Mitsos. You're up and about early. Are you hungry?' she asks. The early morning light stretches out his shadow in front of him, his own path. 'There's no food on yet but I can make you a coffee.' Stella pauses, sliding her hand under her thighs, palms on the chair, ready to launch herself into action 'You could always get a sandwich from across the road and just come and sit.'

Mitsos raises his head from his concentrated effort and looks past her into her shop.

'He's not here.' She releases her hands from under her legs and slumps back into the curve of the white plastic chair. She smiles at him.

Mitsos, with a nod and the hint of a smile, changes directions and shuffles his way across the road to the sandwich shop. His belt has missed a loop of his grey serge trousers at the back and his shirt is bagging out as a result. He would be embarrassed if he knew that, but even more embarrassed if she told him.

The kafenio has opened its doors and the two men who were waiting are now sitting inside, cigarette smoke rising from their dangling hands. The corner shop is also open and some school children come out to slouch, resignedly, at the unmarked bus stop.

Mitsos makes his way back across to Stella, a paper packet containing his breakfast in hand. Stella stands and brings a second chair from inside out onto the pavement and returns indoors to light the single camping-gas ring for coffee.

The bus comes. The children march on board to the silent beat of unheard music, wires hanging from their ears, eyes glazed. The cluster of immigrants hoping for work dwindles until there is only one left, who dozes on the bench by the palm tree.

'Do you want to tell me?' Mitsos asks.

Stella shakes her head.

They drink their coffees and watch the world without speaking, the sun's heat intensifying with the passing of time, until Stella stands quite suddenly. Mitsos, startled, looks at her but she is gazing across the square to where she can see the back of Stavros as he lumbers into the corner shop.

'Best get things going before he's here,' she says to Mitsos, who smiles sadly at her. She goes inside the shop and puts on a cardigan she finds on the hook. It covers her bruises.

The sink plug is clogged with chicken skin and a ring of grease circles the stainless steel sink. Stella stacks the pots as best she can on the floor.

She hears Stavros cough as he comes in, a wheezing, hacking smoker's cough. He spits; she hopes it is into the bin, or outside.

With careful movements she wipes out the sink and scrubs along the line of mildew where it joins the wall. She does not want to draw attention to herself with careless noise.

She turns on the tap and wipes away the dirt.

'You were late last night,' Stavros says from the other side of the grill.

'Got talking to Vasso.' Stella decides not to soak the mildew with bleach. She cannot raise the enthusiasm, and lifts the dirty pots back into the sink and runs hot water over them.

'And this morning?' Stavros is raking out the ashes on the grill. This is normally one of the jobs Stella does before he arrives. He usually doesn't make an appearance until lunchtime service is well under way. It is not in his nature to be doing this to be kind.

'You hear me?' His tone is rough.

Stella squeezes more liquid on her sponge; it smells of lemons. She tries to think of what to reply but can almost not be bothered.

'Where were you?' He doesn't soften his voice.

'Went for a walk.' She puts a dozen rinsed plates up onto the racks above the sink, where they drip warm rain.

She works her way through the cutlery and wonders what Stavros is doing now. There is no more sound of ashes being cleared.

'You and your walks.' He sounds displeased; she hears a glass break and he curses.

Her 'walks' make all the difference, and always have, right back when she was very little: 'walks' with Dad when she was tiny and then 'walks' on her own when she grew. It was on one of her walks that she met Stavros. He'd seemed so worldly; now he seems pathetic.

Having finished the pots she opens a new sack of potatoes and pours half of them into the sink and begins to peel.

Why? She has seen so many films where the women run businesses, are assassins, beat corporations that are doing dodgy dealings, even women who box. So why is she peeling potatoes when Stavros usually lies in bed snoring? It isn't as if he sits and works through what they need to order, or does the accounts. If he did, and she couldn't, then maybe her doing the potatoes would be a fair division of their efforts. But as it is she who orders the potatoes, chickens, ouzo, tomatoes and charcoal, and she who does the accounts, the result is that they do not get equal leisure time. Imagine how well it would run if he peeled the potatoes and she managed the place …

She throws a naked potato into the large pan on the floor ready to be cut into chips.

But what if she hadn't married? She picks up the next potato, fumbles and drops it back towards the sink, where it bounces off the rim, hits Stella's apron and slides to the floor, rolling underneath the grill. She sighs and takes a ladle off a hook and, bending down, begins to fish under the grill. She retrieves an empty mini ouzo bottle, a fork, a torn lottery ticket and three cigarette ends, but no potato. She gives up, leaves the ladle where it has been firmly wedged by the grill's leg and continues her monotonous peeling.

Look at Madonna, Nana Mouskouri and Princess Diana. Stella crosses herself several times with the hand that holds the knife.

'God rest her soul,' she mutters.

'What?' Stavros pokes his head into the narrow gap next to the sink by the grill above the chip fryer. There is just enough room to see his bulging eyes and his sweating forehead. 'Have you finished those potatoes yet? The grill needs lighting.'

Stella drops the potato and the knife into the sink, wipes her hands down her apron and comes out from behind the grill. Stavros has cleared too much ash from the long grill pan; it is going to take longer to heat up now.

'Why are you sighing?' Stavros cuts each word. Stella backs away from his menace. She puts her right hand over the bruise on her left arm before turning away.

'I'll just get some more charcoal.'

'There's plenty here.' Stavros comes out from the space between the grill and the counter to let Stella in. She can smell ouzo. He picks up his glass and takes it outside. The postman passes on his moped and Stavros waves and lights a cigarette.

The charcoal bag is lighter than the potato bag.

She pours plenty in, until it empties, then she scrunches up the wrapping and puts it in with the charcoal. She turns to see if he is looking. He isn't. She takes out a small bottle of lighter fluid she keeps under the counter and squirts it over the charcoal: her secret. Stavros fails to light the charcoal every time and Stella gets an - admittedly, childish –satisfaction from lighting it with the first match. It makes Stavros cross, and it pleases Stella no end to see his face after he has been trying for a quarter of an hour to get it to catch, and her kindly relieving him and having it blazing within a minute. He doesn't think to use lighter fluid.

'Ha!' She exclaims as one match kicks up flames to the grill hood. She looks round to Stavros, who is motionless in the white plastic chair in the sun, his back towards her. Stella watches the flame curling and splitting, the orange against the grey of the steel. It might be hot enough in half an hour even without the ashes, she concedes.

She doesn't suppose Grace Kelly ever had to light a grill pan, or split a chicken come to that. She washes her hands in the sink. With the half-peeled potatoes, a bag of plucked chickens and the butcher's knife from the hook on the end of the grill, she goes into the area with the tables. On the window sill is balanced a cutting board which she lays on one of the tables.

'Oh, hi.' Abby announces her arrival. 'Hope I'm

not too late.' She walks past Stella and into the toilet cubicle.

Stella cracks open the first chicken and puts it on the next table, ready to lay it on the grill bars.

'That looks so satisfactory,' Abby says as she comes out wiping her hands on a piece of toilet paper.

Stella brings the knife down with such force that the table wobbles.

'Did you sleep well?' Stella asks, breaking chicken bones, thinking how barbaric her job is. She doesn't like chicken. She lives mostly on chips and salad from her garden.

'Yes, thanks. I was so tired. It was an effort even to get out of bed this morning.'

Abby had every intention of getting up as early as possible and going into town to try her luck at getting a job there, with the vague plan that if she didn't find anything she could get back to the village before lunch.

But when Vasso had come in the night before, Abby had woken and got up for a glass of water and they had talked, or mostly mimed. Vasso had been so funny. Abby had laughed until her sides hurt when

Vasso asked if she wanted milk in her tea and mimed milking a cow whilst sort of mooing. At least she thinks it was a cow, maybe a goat. The thought makes her start to giggle all over again and she tells Stella the tale.

'She is very funny lady,' Stella agrees, laughing herself.

'Anyway, what shall I do?' Abby looks around.

'Potatoes, in the sink.' Stella crashes the meat cleaver through the bones of another chicken.

'Ok, but can I ask, why don't you buy ready-cut chips? It would save you so much time.'

'Yes, but not money, potatoes are cheap.'

'Yes, but your time is valuable. Imagine how much you would have to pay someone to make chips and see if ready-made aren't cheaper. I bet they are.'

Stella looks at her, brow lifted. 'I had never thought it that way around.' She brings the cleaver down again with a loud crack.

Chapter 9

The insecurity of her position urges Stella to continue with her routine as if nothing has happened. She knows things must change, that they will change but while she is unsure of what action to take her normal routine is very comforting. As usual there are no customers before eleven. Abby and Stella talk about costing up someone's time to see which day-to-day tasks are viable. Chip-making clearly is not. Stella is amazed at how much she doesn't know about running her own business and asks Abby where she has learnt so much. It keeps her from brooding over Stavros

'School. I did business studies at GCSE. I wasn't really interested then as it was all theory. This is much better, sort of on-the-spot training.'

'Yes, but who is training who?' Stella laughs.

Stavros barks Greek at them from the chair outside.

Stella jumps at the suddenness and the loudness. She looks at Abby.

'What did he say?' Abby whispers.

'Why you whisper, he no understand.' Stella

glares at the back of Stavros' head. 'He says we not to talk English, you need to learn Greek, but really he does not like that he doesn't understand. How you say in English "Fork him!"?'

'It's not pronounced exactly like that.' Abby giggles, but Stella is not listening. She stabs a sausage on a long two-pronged fork and jerks it upwards in a rude fashion in Stavros' direction. He is facing the road, watching the world, unaware, calmly smoking. What is the point, Stella asks herself? She looks at the sausage on the fork, why continue as if nothing has happened, it cannot stay the same, everything must change, is there any point carrying on these day to day chores when tomorrow who knows where they will be. She returns the sausage to the grill muttering Greek swear words under her breath until she grows calm.

Abby is working well today.

'Hey Abby, what would you do with the *ouzeri* so it makes more money?' she asks. Abby's eyes shine and she becomes quite animated.

'First thing I would do is I would wrap fairy lights around the tree outside, show something is happening.' She goes on to say that she would open the door to the restaurant part and put more tables and chairs outside. Stella laughs at this and says that she has been saying it for years to Stavros but he doesn't want to unstick the door.

'Why don't you just do it?' Abby asks

'It is not like that, I can't just do things. I watch my Mama make my Baba happy but she had to ask for everything. Then I watch her make the 'uncles' happy and the only way she got anything was to ask. Then I watch Stavros' Mama make Stavros and Stavros' Baba happy but she no ask for things, but then she didn't have anything either. It feels wrong just to do something without asking.'

'Yeah, but we are not children!' Abby seems to find it rather amusing that Stella, and the Greek women Stella knows, need permission to do things.

'Maybe I am just not strong enough to unstick the door,' Stella says, but she doesn't open her mouth very widely as she says it and the words are muffled.

'Have you tried?' Abby looks at the door.

Stella is brushing the floor around the tables and Abby is cleaning the glass of the picture of the donkey with the hat on. Stella chooses not to answer. There is a commotion in the takeaway and they both look round to see the two boys from yesterday, along with four more.

'Yia,' Stella greets. 'Go on, you serve them,' she whispers loudly in English to Abby. Abby blushes and puts down the window cleaner and goes to wash her hands. The one who spoke the day before asks for six *giros* in Greek, but Abby doesn't move. Her eyes wide, she appears rooted to the spot.

'What's wrong with her?' Stavros barks. He has raised his weight from the chair outside and stands leaning against the door frame. The boys turn around and stare at him.

'She does not understand and it is making her scared. You understand being scared, Stavros,' Stella snaps. Two of the boys snigger and Stavros' face tenses, his eyes popping out and his face going extremely red. 'Abby, they want a *giro* each, one *horis kremidi* – er, without onions,' Stella tells Abby.

Abby jumps into action and makes a great job of the *giros*. She hands them out to the boys who randomly take them. As she passes over the last one she says, 'Horace cream midi.' The boy who had looked at her the longest yesterday makes a point of touching her fingers as he takes this one and thanks her in English, prolonging the eye contact.

'*Dodeka evro*. Twelve euros,' Stella calls, and each boy hands over two euros to Abby. But when she counts it all together there is an extra two euros. The boys leave smiling and Stella tells her it is a tip. Stavros steps in and takes the twelve euros before it even makes it into the till. It is the first time he has done this openly. Stella feels a strange relief that at least there is no more pretence. He walks off towards the kafenio.

Stella hopes he will pay off some of his debts rather than just drink it away.

'Shall I write a note to say what he has taken and put it in the till for when you cash up?' Abby asks.

'What is this "cash up"?' Stella flops onto a chair, and exhales. It all seems such a waste of effort.

'You know, at the end of the day, see how much you have made, so you can calculate your profit.' Stella loves what Abby is teaching her but just at the moment it feels too much. The change in her position with Stavros lurks in her mind. His actions convincing her that he has debts. It weighs heavily. How big are the debts?

An hour later two more boys come in for *giros* and then towards lunchtime a mix of regulars and new faces sit down for chicken and chips and salad. They each leave a tip and Stella watches as Abby smiles, her stack of euro coins growing in the dish Stella has put out for her.

'It won't be many days before you can go to Saros with these tips,' Stella says kindly, but with a sad edge. She is enjoying Abby's company and she loves that she is speaking and improving her English every day.

'Yeah,' Abby says. She looks at the clock. 'And I have been in Greece just over thirty hours.' She gives a brief laugh before her smile fades. She looks at Stella, her eyebrows rising slightly. 'It will be strange starting again somewhere new, getting to know people and things, again.'

'And exciting,' Stella announces. The girl needs her freedom. What Stella wants is just from selfishness, replacing what she lacks with Stavros for good companionship. It would be easy to pull Abby into her life for her own needs, but it wouldn't be right.

Abby takes a bowl, the potato sack and a knife to a table, the light shining through the window making the drops of water on the bowl's edge glisten. She runs her finger around the edge before beginning to peel and watches the remaining traces of water evaporate in the heat. Stella crouches behind the counter. The thin bottom shelf is only used for one thing. She blows the dust off as she gets out the accounts books again. If she does a little every day she might get up to date. Taking them to the table next to Abby, she looks through. So much is missing, days and days of takings not written down. Now they have to give receipts by law, the roll on the till will have to be added up for each day and the amounts entered in the book. It is a mammoth task. Stavros has never even opened the book. He probably doesn't even know of its existence.

Stella looks at the pages again and the job seems almost too big to even begin. She looks over at Abby; her potato-peeling is getting quicker. One column:

Stella will do one column and then the job has begun. She is a little amazed at her decision and, application.

The day is getting hotter; the sound of motorbikes and tractors passing decreases. Dogs stop barking, the cicadas increase their decibels. Stavros rolls down the awnings outside using a long metal pole with a hand-turned crank at the bottom. It squeaks as it turns. He has a cigarette in his mouth and Stella can see the ash getting longer and longer with each turn of the winching handle until it finally falls onto the crease of his T-shirt above his stomach. Half the profits are right there in that round belly of his, the other half spent on his debts. Stella has not had a new dress since the one Vasso gave her last year, and that was a cast-off from one of Vasso's nieces. She turns back to the books.

The early afternoon passes quickly. Stavros announces he is going for a sleep. As he walks away four hungry farmers arrive, order chicken and chips and wait, impatiently, to be served.

After eating, the farmers seem to string out their meal. Every time Abby stops busying herself in the safe recess at the back of the grill, she goes through and asks, with her freshly learned phrase, if they are all right, 'Ola endaxi?' She smiles as she speaks, a tell-tale red flush beginning on her neck. They take it in turn to ask her for a variety of things, gently teasing her lack of Greek, enjoying her smile, her freshness.

Eventually, very full and happy, leaving much of the extra ordered food on their plates, they say they will return tomorrow and that it has been the best meal they have had in a long time. They meander out, eyes lingering on Abby. Stella has a sinking feeling that Stavros might have been right. Abby is creating more business. It should make her happy but she cannot see this ending well.

The farmers all leave a tip. One leaves two euros.

Abby seems happy and takes the pots to be washed.

'Abby,' Stella calls to her behind the grill. Abby has put the radio on. 'Usually it is very quiet now for a couple of hours. I go to my English lesson with Juliet. Usually I close if Stavros is not here. Today I leave you in charge?'

'Oh! Er, OK. What if it all goes badly wrong?' Abbey twists the tea towel she is holding.

'Don't worry, I will tell Vasso to come in if she sees anyone coming this way and you can go to her if you have any problem.' Stella feels no qualms in leaving her. Abby is picking up the basic words quickly. Besides, she needs to believe she is fine to be left. Stella must talk to Juliet alone. Without another word she marches out into the heat of the sun.

She lets Vasso know to keep an eye on Abby as

she crosses the square. Vasso tells her that the cardigan she is wearing is hers; she has been wondering since last autumn where it had gone. Stella smiles, keeps it on and walks off. The sun feels very hot today, the cicadas' grating hum so constant it becomes unnoticeable. They normally don't start till later in the year but the heat is bringing the seasons forward.

Mitsos is just leaving the kafenio to go home. He calls out to let Stella know that his nephew will be baptised soon and the whole village will be invited: will she come? Stella calls back that of course she will, she wouldn't miss it for the world, and as she walks on she knows Stavros won't go and this could be an afternoon for just her and kind old Mitsos. It makes her feel quite excited. She turns down Juliet's lane and relishes the peace and quiet. It is so central and yet feels almost as if no one lives in the lane, it is so private. She couldn't live there, she would be afraid to be so isolated, but she loves to visit.

The cardigan is very hot and she would like to take it off.

Full of flowers and blossom, the garden is introduced by wild roses trailing on the metal arch over the gate. Juliet's car stands in the gravel courtyard which is bordered by huge spiky plants in ceramic pots along the wall and across the front of the house. Down the right-hand garden wall are pomegranate trees, twisted and split, laden with last season's dried and cracked fruit hanging close to the ground. The raised patio in front of the house has a table with chairs around it, to one side a big sofa with a white throw.

'Hi. How are you?' Juliet greets. She gets up from the sofa, putting her books down.

'I am fine, how are you?' Stella responds parrot-fashion, wondering how Juliet can wear jeans in this heat.

'Very formal. I think we are past that stage. A little bird told me you have a visitor.' Juliet smiles.

'What is this "a little bird", like in the trees?' Stella is amused.

'You say that when you want to say you have heard something from someone and don't want to say who it is or when you can't really remember who you heard it from.' Juliet clarifies. She takes her red-blonde hair out of its pony tail and smooths it across her crown before restraining it again.

'Ah, I see, so a little bird means someone in the village told you I have a visitor.' Stella smiles. 'I like this "little bird" talk. Yes, she is called Abby and she is from England and now I speak English all day and she says that I am improving.'

'You have improved. It is flowing more. Well done.' Juliet seems a little taken aback by Stella's sentence.

Juliet sits down on the sofa and a cat jumps onto her knee.

Stella strokes the cat and sits next to Juliet, perched on the edge of the sofa as if she might slip off. Juliet lays one arm over the back of the seat, relaxed, assured. Stella's toes have turned in. Her shoulders rounded, she looks like a child beside Juliet. The cat jumps from Juliet's knee to hers.

'Do you want some tea, or some iced water?' The pergola over the porch is dense with a passion-flower vine. The sunlight pinpricks between its foliage but the shadow does not diminish the heat.

'Yes please, either, either.' Stella pronounces the word in both of its possible forms. In one of her lessons with Juliet they watched a black-and-white video of a song by a couple who could not get on because they pronounced things differently. She had enjoyed the song but it did make learning English difficult if there were different ways to pronounce everything.

Juliet, goes in for the drinks, giving Stella a moment to think. She strokes the cat, who settles on her knee. Juliet knows so much; she has lived in England all her life. How long has she been here? Only a couple of years. She is worldly, she is divorced and probably, and most importantly, she does not gossip.

The tray is laden with iced tea, biscuits and napkins. Stella dreams of being this civilised. But with Stavros, what is the point?

'Stavros,' she says out loud. Juliet is with her in an instant.

'What has he done?' She looks at Stella and settles back into the sofa as if she has all the time in the world.

Stella takes off the cardigan. Juliet sits upright, and her eyes widen as her hand goes out to touch the bruises, but stops before it reaches them.

'Oh my God, are you ok? What happened?'

Stella can hear Juliet's breath has quickened as she asks.

Stella relates the incidents. She hears her voice tell the tale and in the telling it seems unreal, something out of the newspaper. It feels so unfitting that she begins to doubt that it really happened, at least not to her. She strokes the cat quite rapidly. Over the wall, across the hills, there is a movement, and in the turning of her head to see the goats scramble up the hill she is given proof that it was all real. The pain shoots down her neck into her shoulder.

She winces and turns back to Juliet to finish her tale.

Juliet has tears in her eyes, her face drawn down with sadness. Stella is shocked. She had expected her to immediately jump into the: 'I am so sorry this has happened to you' spiel. This is not what she thought would happen. She feels guilty for bringing Juliet into her sordid life. The horror of the event becomes more real; her own tears well and silently fall.

Juliet sits quite still, looking straight at her, until she finally says, 'What do you want to do?' This completely takes Stella off her guard. She wasn't aware that she could 'do' anything about what has happened.

'How do you mean?' she almost stutters.

'If he has done it once it is unlikely that he will not do it again, which leaves the question, "What do you want to do?"' Juliet is firm but kind.

Stella has no idea if she wants to do anything. She wants life to be as it always was, running the *ouzeri*, maybe even improving it, living next to Vasso, waving goodnight to Theo, cutting up Mitsos' food. She suddenly misses Mitsos quite violently and sucks air in, a reflex to the surprise of her attachment to him. No, she does not want to change a thing. Except Stavros: she wishes he just didn't exist.

'I want Stavros to not exist.' Stella laughs before tears blur her vision and she shivers into sobs. Juliet is by her side with an arm around her shoulder. Stella turns her face against Juliet's T-shirt. Juliet rocks her gently.

'I have done "bad marriage", Stella,' Juliet says. 'It dragged me down and kept me under. I did the classic, I worked harder at it. He didn't. But you know, you know deep down in your gut, whether something is worth working for or not.'

Stella emerges from Juliet's T-shirt and Juliet uses the shift to nip inside and bring tissues. Stella blows her nose noisily. The tears on her cheeks have dried in the sun to salty war paint, white against her dark skin.

'Sometimes the event, like catching someone kissing another woman, can mean nothing, the woman he is kissing just a tool, an invention to bring a crisis to a point, so that deeper issues, that are too scary to broach, can be talked about. It is possible, in talking, that you can come together again, even better than before. The event, the woman, is just meaningless. Then, if you love him, it is not about moving apart, it is about moving closer together. Both of you work through the pain, not of him kissing another woman, but the problems you have together, that were the catalyst for that kiss.' Juliet takes a breath.

'Other times the event is for and because of itself. He wants that event to happen. Then you know there is no point in working, trying. It's time to part.

Sometimes, I know, you can confuse the one for the other and stay working and trying hard with something that is dead and buried.' Juliet looks at Stella. Stella looks puzzled. She has not understood all that Juliet has said. The ideas are too complex for her comprehension of English, the speech too fast.

'You know, Stella, deep inside, if it is worth working for,' Juliet concludes. Stella understands this but it brings her no joy.

'The feelings say "no", there is nothing to work for, but then I remember how he saved me.'

'Saved you?'

'Yes, from the bullies and the bad words about me being a dirty gypsy. He gave me, er, I do not know the English word for it, er, *axiopistia*, how you say?'

'Credibility,' Juliet mutters before going on. 'But Stella, he did not marry you to give you credibility. That was not his reason for marrying you?'

'Well, no.' Stella wipes her eyes. Another cat appears and sits at her feet, staring up at her.

'So his reason for marrying you was some other reason, love, whatever. It is you who sees that he gave you credibility, it is not he who gave you it. It was a fortuitous consequence.'

'Fort tu tus co ...' Stella begins to spell out.

'Luck,' Juliet condenses.

'Yes, but being married to him did give me this, without that I could never have opened the *ouzeri*, I would not have dared, and no one would have come to the "dirty gypsy".'

Juliet shakes her head at Stella's last two words.

'Yes, but like I said, these were consequences, results,' Juliet states. 'He did not marry you to give you all that, without benefits for him. He loved you and wanted you and all the other things that were his reasons. The bottom line is you do not owe him.'

'But without him ...'

'Without him who knows what you might have done? Maybe you would have set up the shop, maybe you wouldn't. Maybe you would have found a business partner in the town and set up a taverna there and been even more successful. Maybe you wouldn't.'

'But ...'

Juliet takes Stella's hand. The cat decides he has had enough of all the commotion and jumps onto the floor to be with his friend.

'I'll tell you an old Chinese tale.' Juliet settles

herself, inviting Stella to do the same.

'There was an old farmer who worked his crops for many years. One day his horse ran away. Upon hearing the news, his neighbour came to visit. "Such bad luck" he said. "Maybe", the farmer replied. The next morning the horse returned, bringing with it three other wild horses. "How wonderful", the neighbour exclaimed. "Maybe," replied the old man. The following day, his son tried to ride one of the untamed horses, was thrown, and broke his leg. The neighbour again came to visit saying, "what bad luck". "Maybe," answered the farmer. The day after, the army came to the village to enlist the young men. Seeing that the son's leg was broken, he was no use to them and they left him. The neighbour congratulated the farmer on how well things had turned out. "Maybe", said the farmer.' Stella smiles at the tale. Juliet continues.

'For years I stuck by Mick. First I worked at it thinking that it was me, then I worked at it for the boys, then because I felt I was being harsh, then because I felt I owed him. I thought of all the good things that had happened since we had been together and then I got real.

'The day-to-day reality was sucking out all my joy of life, reducing me to believing I could do no better, that I deserved nothing more than I got.

'It's a trap. I got stuck in it, but I eventually

figured it out and left. But do you know what?' Juliet waits for a reply.

'What?' Stella's voice is small.

'I didn't even have one bruise to tell me who he was.'

Stella sits wide-eyed, waiting for more. But Juliet closes her mouth and Stella is left to think over Juliet's last sentence.

Chapter 10

'What shall I do?' Stella asks. She strokes the cat curled in her lap.

'I have learnt that everything we do in life, even the little things, depends on what we want. Our actions decide how we live,' Juliet says. 'The difference between me now and me when I was married to Mick is that when we were together I would do whatever felt good or was easiest in the moment to make my life nice and then kept wondering why the result was always the same.' She sniffs, a brief controlled sound. 'But I think I wanted that same result, it fitted what I thought I deserved.' She squirms and settles herself with one leg tucked under her. 'During the divorce and after the divorce and, most importantly, coming here, I have experienced so much in Greece.' She looks out past the wall of her garden to the hills, 'I have watched myself and changed my view of myself. Now - and this is the big difference - I think what I want the outcome to be first and take the action second to make sure it happens. Even if the action needed is hard. The result is I get what I think I deserve.' Juliet encourages the second cat onto her knee. It jumps up and immediately curls in a ball to sleep.

'Then I must to become magician. I want him to

disappear. Then I go on, only he is not there,' Stella retorts.

'If you want to carry on as if nothing has happened, see if you can.'

'What do you mean?' Stella asks.

'Well, is the shop in his name or both your names, or your name?'

'The shop is rented, so is the house.'

'I thought you had a family house here?'

'Yes, but when Mama she died we sold the house and the land to pay off Stavros' debts.'

'Ouch! So whose name is the shop rented in?'

'No one, we just rent it from Mavros. The same with the house, but this is rented from someone else.'

'So if he left then you could just carry on?'

'Why would he leave?'

'Oh, I don't know. I am just seeing how the land lies.'

'What is "the land lies"?'

'It means seeing how things are.'

'So if someone else had told you how things are and you forgot who it was you could say "A little bird told me how the land lies"?' Stella is smiling.

'Yes.' Juliet laughs, lifts off the cat from her knee and gets up to go indoors, returning with a bottle of water. 'Do you want to go inside and I'll put the air-conditioning on? It's so hot.'

Stella gets up and the two settle in Juliet's white front room. Stella sits on the slightly shabby white sofa and Juliet pulls up a very comfortable-looking chair. She has a remote in her hand, and with a single press of a button the room begins to fill with new air. At first it is not noticeable, just the noise, then the moving air only accentuates the heat, but after a few minutes it begins to cool them both. It's delicious.

The room looks very western to Stella, but she likes it, everything white, except a huge deep red eastern-looking rug over the tiled floor. There is a small wooden table on which is Juliet's laptop, its colourful screen in contrast with its surroundings.

'Why does your computer have your name in big letters?' Juliet has often used her computer as a tool for teaching. Stella now knows about Google and YouTube.

'Oh, I have not shown you that. That's my web page for my translation business.' She gets up and

157

takes the laptop from the table and gives it to Stella. 'Good, isn't it? A friend of mine wrote it. He is in Pakistan now but he might go to England. He's got a job offer there. Actually, did you meet him? Aaman, he helped me with my garden.' Juliet touches the screen; she seems far away.

Stella says nothing.

Juliet comes back to the moment.

'But we are not getting much English done. Do you want to do a lesson today?' she asks.

'I have learnt about birds and land.' Stella smiles, but it does not reach her eyes.

'Yes, but it is not a proper lesson. I will not be charging you a chicken dinner,' Juliet says with a smile, but her voice has a caress in its tone as if she is aware of how raw Stella must feel. They sit companionably for a few minutes.

'You know I did not go to school much, but I learnt to read and write and I have the business. But do you know of what I always dream?' Stella does not wait for a reply. 'I dream of doing an international business.' She sits back at the grandeur of the words she has just spoken. But then suddenly sits upright. 'Do you get your work from England?'

'England and here. I am registered as a translator

with the British Council here, and now with my website I get translation jobs from all over the place. Last year I translated a whole book.' Juliet sounds so confident.

Stella's eyes are shining. 'So you have international business!'

Juliet laughs, 'Yes, I suppose I do.' The cat is scratching at the door and Juliet slides off her chair to let it in.

'I want international business.' Stella twists her tongue around each word to try to say it without an accent.

'I think your chips would get very cold if you posted them abroad.' Juliet laughs. Her laughter trails into silence. The cat is purring.

'I think he could make trouble with the girl.' Stella's voice is flat.

'How do you mean "trouble"? You mean like hit on her?'

'Like he hit me!' Stella's jaw drops open and she stands as if to leave, looking through the glass in the door as if she would have a view all the way to the *ouzeri*.

'No, no,' Juliet puts her hand on Stella's wrist

and gently pulls her back to sitting.

'To "hit on" someone means to flirt with them.'

Stella exhales and visibly relaxes.

'Yes, I think this will be next.'

Stella walks back slowly, soaking in the illusion of freedom the conversation with Juliet has created. She wants to live Juliet's life, be brave enough to be a single woman, with her own house, no fear.

Next door to Juliet's is an abandoned barn and next door to that a low small dwelling with a large yard. Georgia, who lives here, loves her flowers, each tended in a pot of its own, thriving as only she knows how to make flowers thrive. The space is an oasis of colour and textures, quivering petals and spiky succulents, the display of a nature lover. Stella would like to stop for a chat but in the jungle of Georgia's passion there is no sign of her. Stella walks on.

She kicks a stone in the lane. It skims before her and gently rolls to a stop. The dusty lane is a mix of compacted soil, embedded shiny-topped stones and determined weeds. Whitewashed backs of single-storey houses provide a wall on her left, the handmade ceramic tiles of their roofs flaking with age and algae.

The concept, the possibility of being alone, is both thrilling and scary. She has never been truly alone in her life. She shivers in the heat and twists her wedding ring, slipping it along her finger and pushing it back on as she walks, until she dares to pull the ring right to the end of her finger. She stops it coming right off with the tip of her opposite index finger, wiggling both to make the ring spin awkwardly.

It almost feels as if she has a choice. For now, she pushes her ring back on. Her spine straightens; the top of her head skims the blue sky as she continues down to the end of Juliet's track and onto the lane.

A man with a rounded stomach drives by on a slow motorbike, looking left and right, with nothing to do. He spots Stella and slows his motorbike down almost to a stall. He looks the length of her and smiles. Stella has no interest in looking back and he throttles forward.

What if Stavros uses his charm on Abby? A momentary jealousy squeezes her heart until the Stavros of yesteryear fades and reality is resumed. She does not wish this on Abby, but more than that she does not want to lose Abby's friendship. She is fun; the hours spin by running the *ouzeri* with two girls. This is only the second day Abby has been with them, and yet if she left now the space she would leave would gape painfully.

It seems strange to Stella that even though she wishes Stavros gone she admits to herself it would hurt, to some degree, if he were to want Abby and not her – 'twisting the knife', another of Juliet's sayings. But she is not sure if the hurt would come from losing him or losing Abby.

She turns the corner towards the square.

'A little bird told me the lay of the land and I am thinking you are twisting the knife.' Stella chuckles. English is full of nonsense. But then so is Greek. She often says 'listen so you can see' when she wants someone to listen to her to see her point of view. She also says 'slow the oil' when someone is exaggerating.

No, the twist of the knife, the wound, would be from the loss of Abby's friendship, not Stavros.

The square is bathed in the heat. It is reflecting off all the hard surfaces. With the sun directly overhead, the area of shade the central palm is casting is very small.

The lifting of the charcoal sacks and the potato bags when they are full. That is when she would notice Stavros gone. Sometimes when she is really tired and leaves him to close up, but that is not often. Stella runs through the daily chores but there is nothing she can think of that she does not or could not do herself. The clients would probably not even notice he wasn't there

162

any more. But nevertheless it would feel scary, it would feel lonely, but mostly it would feel as if there was little point in it all.

As she passes the kiosk Vasso looks up from some knitting and says 'Hello' in English, acknowledging where Stella has just been. Stella smiles and replies, 'I'll be back.' She knows this phrase makes Vasso giggle. As she reaches the *ouzeri* she can hear Vasso saying to herself over again 'L' beeback' and giggling.

Stavros has been her pivotal point for so many years. She wakes first and leaves the house without disturbing him, taking delight in her ability to give him the extra sleep. He turns up at the *ouzeri* later and she can see all the work she has achieved freshly through his eyes. The place fills with hungry farmers, she knows he can hear her taking the orders, suggesting an extra portion, another ouzo, making them happy, filling the till. She often cleans the place whilst he sleeps in the afternoon and takes pride in her achievement on his return.

He is her witness and without him her days will make less sense, in fact there is a strange void over both home and work when she imagines him absent.

The evening shift passes unremarkably. She chats to Abby, who is asking her about who lives in the village and what most of them do. She is entertaining company as she seems to know something about everything and she gets very excited if Stella can add to her knowledge of the world. The only indication of her youth is her relentless energy until she is quite spent, and then she is suddenly exhausted. Stavros keeps a low profile, he does not mention what has happened, he keeps all conversation to practical matters. Stella wants to say everything to him and nothing, the time has passed for talk. That time was probably years ago but neither of them noticed. The day seems false, suspended.

Stella lets Abby go a couple of hours before her and an hour before Stavros, who leaves saying he is tired and is going home to bed. Abby has earned a reasonable wage in tips and Stella has added enough to it that she will not lose any of her tips in paying for her bed. Vasso has been very modest with her price.

Stella potters around, serves the final *giros* when the bus from town drops off the last few returning villagers. She piles the remaining plates in the sink, checks the chip fryer is off, rakes the coals over and decides she has had enough. She too will go early.

She will persuade Vasso to do the same so they can have a nightcap together. That will cheer her up. Vasso loves a drink but gets tipsy after just a glass, and then, unintentionally, becomes a comedian either in everything she says or everything she does, sometimes both. Stella smiles at the thought as she approaches the kiosk.

'Long day for you today, Vasso?' Stella comments.

'Ach, I have this book that is meant to help me with my accounts and I have been trying to work it out. When we didn't have to give receipts nothing had to add up, you just told the tax man how much you earned, he doubled it because he thought everyone was lying and then he taxed us accordingly. It was a lot simpler.'

'Yes, but everyone did lie about how much they made. Come on, let's go and have a night cap,' Stella says.

'That's because they knew the tax man would double it!' Vasso chuckles and locks up.

They walk along together, past the church, chatting about nothing in particular. A screech owl sounds and sets a dog barking. The single dog turns into many. Someone shouts for his dog to 'shut up', another voice tells the man to stop his noise; genial, light-hearted. The dog's owner laughs and wishes the other person goodnight, and a shutter bangs closed.

As they reach Vasso's house Stella says, 'Er, shall we go to mine for the nightcap?'

'Oh.' Vasso hesitates and looks towards her own

home and yawns, her hand on her gate. 'OK then.' She takes her hand away and continues the leisurely walk on. The warm night air is a delicious relief from the day's heat. The stars are bright, no neon to dim their glow.

Stella feels relieved that they are going to her house. She cannot face Stavros alone. Vasso is a valuable friend, but Vasso has had her own set of worries. The decision not to tell her about Stavros is made from kindness. At the least she would worry, at the worst she would get involved. Besides, much as she is an irreplaceable friend, Stella knows Vasso does not understand why some things should not be broadcast.

The light is on outside Stella's house but the inside light is off. Vasso and Stella are quiet as they enter the house, to avoid waking Stavros. The house has three rooms: a bedroom, kitchen and bathroom. The bedroom door is on one side of the fridge, the bathroom on the other.

Stella unearths a bottle of gin from under the sink and takes the ouzo from the fridge and holds them up to Vasso, who points to the ouzo. Stella pokes about in the time-darkened wooden cupboards in the kitchen as Vasso perches on one of the dark wooden chairs. Ever the good hostess, Stella brings a plastic bowl of crisps and a metal takeaway tray of peanuts along with the ouzo.

'Do you want something more than that to eat? I have brought some sausages and I have some *kefalotyri*,' Stella asks, but Vasso dismisses the question with a shake of her head, a handful of peanuts crammed in her mouth.

'I'm fine with these. I couldn't eat cheese at this time of night.' Her half-gaze lands on the green-and-white 1970s kitchen tiles above the stained and pitted marble counter top. Stella pours them drinks. She takes her glass to the window, the aniseed nectar gently burning the back of her throat as she swallows it in one. She returns to the bottle and tries to unscrew the top noiselessly so as not to draw Vasso's attention to the speed with which she swallowed the first draught.

'Fill me up again,' Vasso laughs. She has begun on the crisps and the crumbs make their way onto the shelf of her ample bosom as she talks. She is stretched out as much as the hard wooden chair will allow, her legs crossed at her slim ankles, a long arm over the ladder back.

'Such a nice girl.' Vasso accepts her top-up.

'Who?' Stella says.

'Abby, a lovely girl. Helped me fold my washing. We had the funniest conversation using mime. She likes reading, computers, and maths, can you believe?'

'Doesn't surprise me. We had a conversation

about business, and I was amazed at what she knew for one so young.' Stella briefly thinks how her own child, if she had had one, would have been so much older. She wonders what he or she would have been like, but then feels glad she has no such child. The situation would be worse now if there were offspring to consider; she wouldn't have only herself to think about.

'With only having boys, it was interesting to spend some time with a girl. I kind of wished I had had a girl too. It's a different world.' Vasso sighs and takes another drink. 'Nice girl,' she repeats. 'The house gets a bit empty sometimes with Thanasis gone to Athens. You get into a routine of washing and ironing and cooking for someone else. *Stifado*. I made *stifado* before I left for the kiosk this morning so Abby would have something to eat when she got home. Did you cook?'

Stella stares at her and grins.

'Oh, sorry, yes, a hundred chickens and a million sausages.' Their chuckles settle and are followed by a comfortable silence.

'I like her being around, but I can't help but think, well, maybe ...' Stella stammers and looks towards the bedroom door.

'Ha! You mean Stavros.' Aware of how loudly

she has spoken, Vasso hushes herself to a whisper. 'I'm not blind, Stella. I see how he treats you and you pretend everything is fine. I cannot imagine what it is like for you. I was married to a saint, God rest his soul. No wonder the Lord took him.' She crosses herself three times. She takes another drink of ouzo and drains the glass. 'Fill me up, Stella, I'm going for a pee.' With this she crosses the room, fumbles and bungles the opening of the door to the bathroom, shoulders the door frame, laughs in response, tells the silent Stella to hush, enters and shuts herself in.

Stella drains her own glass and refills it to the top. She could just ask him to leave, just demand he go back to his own village. But he has no reason to go, there is no-one left for him there. If he refuses then her demands would become a declaration of separation and she could well imagine that she, the 'dirty gypsy', would be the one forced to leave. No, she cannot ask him to leave.

She refills the crisps bowl and cuts some sausages into pieces on a plate. She arranges the offerings with paper napkins on the table. She can hear Vasso in the bathroom singing to herself but there is no sound of Stavros' rhythmic snore.

She picks up her ouzo glass and sits.

A noise outside alerts her, not the usual sound of a dog on the scavenge or a cat being careless. Without moving, she looks out of the window but all is dark. Then there is a shape. It grows larger. It is approaching the house. Stella stands. It is a person, but who would be calling so late and why? Is it Abby? No, it is too large.

Stavros!

'Oh, are you home already?' He barely looks at her as he closes the door behind him.

'I thought you were in bed.' The ouzo spins her thoughts. Nothing is open at this time. Farmers are in bed. A familiar feeling of the inevitable fills her empty chest. To get a glass of water he walks past her to the sink. There is a smell of scent, perfume. In Stella's mind an image of Abby. The ouzo has loosened her enough to allow her to be brave. 'Where've you been?' she demands.

He finishes drinking. 'I got talking to Vasso,' he slurs nonchalantly.

'Vasso? At the kiosk?' Stella's heartbeat increases. A strong acid taste is in her mouth. She is about to contradict him, when he goes on to say, 'Yes, sat for a while at the kafenio and then went for cigarettes, got talking, you know how it is. Thought you were still at the *ouzeri*.'

'So you have just left her?' Stella asks, her eyes narrow.

'Is there anything to eat? Yes, just now.' Stavros opens the fridge as Vasso comes back in the room, the fridge door obscuring them from each other.

'There is also Marina. Now she didn't have a nice husband either, he was even worse than yours. When he died he left her nothing. Look what she did! It took guts to open that corner shop, but now' – she brings her hands up in front of her and waves circles to illustrate the enormity of what Marina has achieved – 'what would we do without her?' she concludes and tries to close the fridge door as she goes past.

On hearing Vasso's voice, Stavros jerks straight from his chilly search. He remains static, looking at Stella trapped like a rabbit in a headlight. The closing fridge door stops against his immoveable stomach. He breaks his stare, his bastion of attack brings words to his mouth.

'Watch it, woman.' His gruff attitude more of a warning than his chosen words, he pushes back against the closing fridge door.

'Oh!' But Vasso says no more. With raised brow she looks at Stella.

Stella's gaze is fixed on Stavros.

He looks from Vasso to Stella, shuts the fridge door with a slam which, after another strong stare, is followed by the slamming of the bedroom door.

Vasso drinks the remains of her drink and picks up her bag. 'Early morning,' she states.

'You don't need to leave.' Stella has not moved yet.

'I think I probably do.' Vasso puts her arm around Stella, who fits neatly, and gives her a hug. 'Goodnight.' Her voice is soft.

They kiss each other on both cheeks and Vasso gives Stella's hand a last squeeze.

After she is gone Stella takes a blanket from the cupboard in the bathroom and tucks it under her arm.

The night is still, the warmth gentle, the stars bright. But it brings Stella no joy.

The square is empty, no light in the village. She unlocks the shop but turns on no light. The green walls are eerie, the place hollow. She pulls tables together. It is a strange bed she has made.

Chapter 11

The sausages are browning quickly and Abby does not know how to ensure they are cooked on the inside with such a hot grill.

'Stella?' Abby says. Stella is sorting through cutlery, making sure it is all clean.

'What?' she snaps. Abby decides conversation can wait. She goes through to the eating area to find three tables pushed together, she drags them apart and swings chairs under them, four to each.

There was no 'good morning' when she arrived, just a tea towel thrown at her. It felt shocking and Abby wondered what she had done. She put the pots away and still Stella did not speak to her. But she did move the pots out from where Abby put them to shift them to a lower shelf, followed by a harsh glare.

Abby considers whether she can put up with the hot and cold behaviour much longer. She probably has the money to go to Saros now.

'That doesn't belong there.' Stella snaps when Abby puts her tea towel down on the counter top.

Abby says nothing but stares, wondering again

what has she done wrong.

Yesterday they had chatted on so many subjects. It had been fascinating and it had been a real buzz to explain to Stella some of the things she had learned about business at school. She had felt like she belonged. She hadn't even thought to ring Yiannis in Saros. She had almost made the decision to stay. She had even written a postcard, with a picture of a kitten in a sock hanging from a washing line, to her Dad to tell what had happened and to give him her address. Besides, moving again, getting to know new people, what was the point? She isn't at all sure that the Saros job is really what she wants.

'Sweep in there.' Stella points to the room with the tables and chairs.

Abby snatches the brush leaning against the wall and sweeps, digging into the corners the behind the tables.

'Here, spray it with water, for the dust.' Stella bangs a spray bottle on one of the tables. Her tone is still harsh.

'Stella, is there something wrong?' Abby asks quietly.

'What can be wrong? You tell me Abby.' Her eyes flash but she does not look Abby in the face.

Maybe she should go to Saros today.

Sure, she likes dancing and partying as much as the next person, but she isn't really a party animal like Jackie. In all honesty she enjoys a good book just as much as a night on the town. So the bar job might or might not suit her. But at this rate there will be no choice.

Given a choice she feels sure she would stay. The old-fashioned feel of the village is cool. There are lots of old farmers in the unfurnished café on the square and they stare a bit, but none of them means any harm. It is just, well, it seems they are a bit bored really. No, maybe she would be better off going to Saros. At least everyone would be her age there. At least that's what Jackie said.

Abby finishes sweeping. She checks the food, moves the sausages to a cooler part of the grill and goes behind to put on the radio, which is by the sink.

'Turn it down.' Stella barks but Abby's hand is on the knob to do so before her sentence is finished, it had been left with the volume turned right up.

Dancing is fun. But you can't talk to people in a bar, the music is always too loud. At least here she has got to know Stella a bit, when she is not in this weird mood, and Vasso who is hilarious. Also she has spoken to a man called Theo who owns the café where the old men sit, and he pointed out a house set back off the road a little just beyond the square that is a bar – a real bar with a pool table. She walked past, but felt too nervous to go in. There were two groups of boys sitting outside, one lot a bit older than her and the others in their teens. She recognised the boys who had come in for *giros* and given her the two euro tip.

The bar wasn't rocking; the music was quiet enough to talk. They had a huge screen so you could go and just watch TV as you drank. She would go if she had someone to go with.

There is a low rumble. Abby comes round from behind the grill and looks out of the door up to the sky. Clear blue. But the rumble comes again. She steps outside and looks about her. Out towards the sea is a bank of dark clouds rolling their way towards the village.

'Looks like rain,' she says cheerfully to Stella. The hot air needs freshening.

'Not in this village. Always passes us. The next village gets it,' Stella replies, clipped, as she writes in her order book.

'Really?' Abby looks at Stella but Stella does not answer. Abby takes the bag of potatoes outside with a knife and a bowl. Maybe if she is polite and waits Stella will tell her if she has done something wrong. She had

176

been willing to stay later last night but it was Stella who said to go. She had been almost insistent, and she had been happy and kind in the way she had said it.

"Actually Abby," Stella stops, lays her pen down, wipes her hands on a cloth and picks Abby's bag off the hook. 'Just go!'

Stella takes Abby's bag and marches passed her into the street.

'What? Hang on, I ...' Abby scrabbles to stand, drops the knife and potato to run after her bag. Stella disappears behind that bus which has paused to pick up the school children. Abby rounds the end to see Stella stepping from the bus back down onto the pavement.

'Where's my bag? What's going on?' Abby shouts.

'Your bag is on the bus. You are leaving.' Without another word Stella marches off.

With one step aboard the bus to retrieve her bag a hiss of compressed air closes the doors behind Abby, as she reaches her bag on the first seat the bus jolts forwards, throwing her against the seat.

Out of the window she can see Stella striding back across the road. There seems to be no reason for this sudden flare up.

Should she have insisted on staying last night when Stella made the suggestion she left early? She was cheerful and laughing then, so it must have been after that. Abby had left and walked back to Vasso's. The meat and onion stew Vasso had made and left on the stove was amazing, although Abby's stomach had been full of all the chips she had eaten during the day, she still had two bowls full. Had she eaten too many chips at lunchtime? Should she have offered to pay for them?

After that nothing. She had gone to bed early, written a second postcard to Dad, with a picture of a dolphins leaping out of the sea, read for a while, heard Vasso crashing in at some late hour and then slept well, and she hadn't been late arriving this morning. She had got up early enough to give the card to the postman. Apparently there is no post box in the village. But posting a card to her Dad didn't have anything to do with Stella.

The bus makes a turn and picks up some more children and then heads back through the village, the way it came, towards the town. Stella is inside the shadows of the *ouzeri*, leaning on the counter with her head in her hands. A drop of rain runs down the bus window.

Abby can feel a lump in throat. She swallows. They had talked so much yesterday, she felt she had known Stella forever, that she would know Stella for ever. At one point when they had been working Stella had held onto her waist as she squeezed passed behind the grill, another time Stella had swept her hair out of her eyes for her when she was turning the chickens. Really tender, caring. Abby's chest feels hollow and heavy at the same time, the lump in her throat bigger.

'Well stuff her!' she hisses to the window as the orange groves speed past. The village recedes behind her, she sniffs and wipes the back of her hand across her eyes.

If it is not something she has done then it's just how Stella is, hot and cold. A whole summer of Stella's moods and Stavros' creepy looks might be too much. She looks at the diminishing houses of the village through the back window. She will miss Vasso, and Stella when she is in a good mood. But the whole moody thing is boring. She wipes her eyes again. She will have to buy the books again that she has left beside her bed, and a new toothbrush.

Abby had shown no signs of guilt when she arrived this morning. Stella leans against the counter, her head in her hands, the noise of the bus leaving the village behind her.

She had almost not expected her to turn up this morning. She has a nerve. Although, to be fair, Stella isn't quite so sure now it was Abby's scent she had smelled on Stavros. Perhaps she shouldn't have been so hasty? Besides it isn't as if she wants Stavros any more. So why stop someone else having him?

No, that isn't it. She thought Abby was a nice girl and deserves better, but now, after this? But after what? Stavros lying and smelling of perfume isn't proof that Abby has done anything. What if she is wrong? Oh Abby.

Stella grabs some kitchen roll and wipes her face, blowing her nose noisily. Abby did nothing but help and be kind. Yesterday she had been like ... Stella stiffens, as the words come to mind 'like a daughter'. She fears she has just made a big mistake. She knows deep down that she has not behaved rationally. But after a night sleeping on the tables, is it any wonder? It's not Abby's fault though. Probably ...

Abby counts out her money for the boat to Saros. With her tips she has just enough.

'Next one, she leaves, you are lucky, fifteen minutes.' He points to the big ferry boat in the harbour and passes her a ticket.

There is a rumble. Abby looks up to the gathering grey clouds and feels a droplet of rain. Her bag is light without the books, she boards the ship and trips up the stairs to the first deck, from where she can see the town, the orange orchards and, so close, the village. The boat is rocking already with the wind that is picking up, her hair blows across her face and some strands stick with the occasional raindrops. It is still very warm.

Inside is calmer. Abby counts what's left of her money. If Yiannis is not true to his word about the job, if the job has gone or if she cannot find the place, she is in serious trouble. Whatever happens she will not ring home for help, she will find a way. She looks out over the sea which seems very large. Waves are starting to break over the concrete jetty, and in the distance the sea is a moody green, with occasional whitecaps. She takes her key ring teddy from her bag and holds him against her cheek.

The rocking of the boat increases and over the tannoy someone shouts in unintelligible Greek. Some people get up and leave the bar area she is in. The barman stops wiping the counter and slings his cloth to one side. He looks up at her briefly, picks up some glasses and disappears through a narrow door between the shelves of bottles.

She stares out of the window and watches the skies darkening. The voice shouts through the speakers again but it is meaningless to Abby. At least twenty minutes have passed. Abby looks around to see if anyone else is impatient, but the bar is empty, the bar tender is idly polishing glasses.

She waits, the boat is rocking quite hard now. Eventually she stands and wanders over to the bar, weaving a little, trying to keep her balance.

'Are we late going?' She asks.

'We don't go, you no hear? *Apagoreftico*.'

'A what?'

'*Apagoreftico*, too much wind, they order all boats to not leave.' He holds a glass up to the light.

Abby swallows and turns away. She doesn't want him to see the tears threatening to fall.

The descent to the harbour is as in a dream, unreal, the skies a deep grey. Her pockets empty of money, friendless and alone, she sits on a bollard as large droplets of rain fall, teasing the dusty ground, the flowers in the pots around the harbour releasing ozone. The light has a strange white quality.

'Hey lady, it is going to rain very hard very soon, you must go indoors,' says a man inspecting one of the ferry's mooring lines.

But where to go? It is ridiculous, one minute she has a job, a room, the next she is being bundled on a bus, not even given the opportunity to get her books, oh and her hairbrush, from Vasso's. Quite honestly, things could not get any worse.

Even in the avalanche of bleakness there is a nagging fear that there is something worse, something she has forgotten. It is remembered in a flash, sinking her to the floor, her legs twisted under her, the wind knocked out of her, all blood drained from her face. Stavros still has her passport. She loses all will to move, all power to fight.

'*Eisai kala*? Eh? Er.... You ok?' Abby looks up through filmy eyes, she recognises the man from the bakery, his warm bread every morning her breakfast.

'This not good for sit.' The rain begins to fall sparsely. 'Going village?' He lifts her from under her arms, helping her to stand. Her face is wet from the light rain. Abby surreptitiously wipes her eyes anyway. In a daze her thoughts contract to the present moment. At least if she goes with him she will be sitting somewhere dry. The village no longer matters, she is only interested in how she will survive the next minute - how stupid she has been. She should never have given her passport to Stavros. Stupid. She should have told the bus to stop and make Stella say whatever was bothering her, face her. Stupid.

She pulls herself to her senses and finds she is in a dry car heading back to the village.

There is another rumble and then the clouds disgorge their contents without reserve. Stella rubs her neck. It is still sore and she still has a headache. The rain is running down the street like a river within minutes. The heavy droplets ping off the parked cars like peas. The sandwich shop closes its doors to stop the rain blowing in. A man with a newspaper over his head runs from the kiosk to the kafenio. The rain brings a different heat. Ozone fills the air. The smell of wet dust comes up to her from the pavement as she stands watching the spectacle. The grey sky deepens and the growling comes more often. Lights come on around the village and shutters creak closed.

Then, a flashing strobe sheets across the sky, casting deep shadows on everything for a fraction of a second, leaving Stella blinking in the after-dark. She wonders if Abby is somewhere dry. To throw her out at the beginning of a storm, what kind of person is she?

She waits for the lightning to come again, and this time the thunder is fast upon it.

'No one will come to eat day,' Stella announces to herself. 'Sometimes these storms they last a couple of hours, but with this one, I think, the sky will go as black as night.' She realizes it would be nicer if Abby was here with her. 'Stupid woman.' she chastises herself. 'Stavros does wrong and you blame it on a child of sixteen. Stupid.'

Stella had just turned sixteen when she had gone down to the cheese factory to get her mother some feta. Wrapped in a cloth and paper she carried it under her arm when the bus from the town had stopped in her path. A group of boys she had known from school got off, amongst them one called Demosthenes who, on spotting her lurched and made a grab. The boys played catch with the cheese, Stella running widely from one to the other, the laughter growing, the throws more abandoned until Demosthenes himself threw the package into the bus. Stella had scuttled after it, the concertina doors closing after her.

She had not told the bus driver to stop. She was afraid to get off, to walk back to the village, the boys might still be there. But with each moment of her fear she was half a kilometre further from her home. She had walked half way back from town with the sweating cheese to her mother. The memory serves to remind her how young sixteen is, how dangerous the world could be. She crosses herself and prays for Abby's safety - and forgiveness.

She watches for a long time and then the rain begins to ease off. The water stops pouring from the gutter above the shop, and the sky lightens a little. Stella steps into the shop and, from a peg on the wall at the end of the grill, she lifts a folding umbrella. Even if she drove to town Abby could be on the boat by now, gone to Saros. 'Stella, you are a very stupid woman.'

Abby repeats Vasso's name and mimes the roof of a house. Eventually the baker's eyes shine and he grins. 'Ah, *spiti*, Vasso. House Vasso.'

'Yes.' Abby feels relief. Facing Stella can come later. Her passport and her stuff take priority. As they pass the *ouzeri* Abby slips further down the car seat. She is dropped on the corner just as Stavros strides down the lane, shoulders hunched against the rain, passing her by Vasso's gate. He says nothing and strides on. The rain becomes strong again. A gust drives the rain through her clothes. Abby shakes herself off on Vasso's porch. The skies are darkening even more. The usual village choir of dogs has stopped barking. No cockerels crow.

The front door is unlocked, as always. Abby flicks the kettle on. She patters down to her room at the side of the house. When she sits up in bed, the view from the window is down towards the village. If she stands straight on to look out she can see the rows of orange trees in lines telling the seasons. Goats taking shelter from the rains trim the pale underside leaves, cats slide through the undergrowth trying to keep out of the rain.

Coffee in hand, Abby makes herself comfortable,

propping her pillows up and listening to the sound of the water on the tiles, on the window and on the sloping metal roof of the tool shed in the garden. She has never seen a downpour so intense. It distracts her from reading. Even though she isn't cold she puts on her jumper; it feels comforting. It is as if someone is on the roof pouring bucket after bucket of water down past the window. She gets up to look at the ground outside. Where is it all going?

The pale dusty garden has become a deep, rich, reddy-brown, the rain soaking in as quickly as it is falling. No puddles and no streams: the ground is a sponge. She sighs and returns to her seat on the bed, her coffee and her book. No sooner is she settled than the lightning shoots a flash across the valley, lighting up the room in high relief. She opens her mouth to count out loud the interval before the thunder, but she is not quick enough. There is a dark and menacing roll.

She switches on the bedside light. The room appears dull by comparison with the spectacle.

She wonders what to do about her passport, she could try talking to Vasso but they can barely communicate, she might ask Stella directly but she would have to know what mood she was in. Confronting Stavros himself is not a good idea, there is just something about him, a bit scary, and creepy. Perhaps she could ask the English teacher to help, she must speak Greek, what did Stella say her name was?

She will ask Vasso, but she is not going out in this rain, she will wait until it stops or until Vasso comes home. Her little room is comforting, safe.

Part of her wants to watch the storm, witness the local weather, but the other part tells her a storm is a storm, and if she does find a way to stay on at school, all the reading she can fit in between now and September will be of benefit. Trying to forget about her passport she pushes on with the book on economics. It is a possible choice for one of her A levels. She got a grade A at GCSE.

The chapter on supply and demand is next. She can relate that to the *ouzeri*, maybe learn something she could have implemented. She skips the chapter she is on, bookmarking the page. The lightning sheets across the window and then cracks into jagged fingers down the darkened skies, lighting up twisted trees and angular buildings. The thunder rages again, louder than before, prolonged.

The light flickers. She watches it splutter once more and then die. She turns it off at the switch and wonders if she should check the rest of the house. The thunder crashes again in unison with the sheets and cracks of the light. Up in the heavens the blanket glow illuminates the clouds from above, showing layer after layer of heavy rain that will soon be falling, the forked lightning now being saved to spear the ground.

Stavros chucks the sodden newspaper onto the counter in the *ouzeri* and shakes off the rain from his legs and arms before pulling his tight T-shirt from his stomach and letting go, bouncing off the raindrops.

'Why are you here? There will be no people,' Stella says, not looking at him, still watching the rain, which is building again.

'No bloody food in the house. You feed the whole village but not me,' Stavros grumbles, mopping his bare arms with some kitchen roll.

Stella does not answer.

He takes a plate and loads it with half a chicken and five sausages, pouring lemon sauce liberally all over it. He takes it through to the restaurant area, pushes the blanket Stella slept under off the chair onto the floor and sits eating, using neither knife nor fork, just his bare hands and his teeth.

Stella cannot watch. She turns to look at the rain again. The gutter above the shop must be broken. The cascade is worse than before and the noise is loud and slightly frightening.

'What were you and that woman cooking up last night?' Stavros belches between mouthfuls, thick with saliva.

Stella turns to see if she has heard properly. Is he seriously asking her to defend her behaviour?

'Vasso came for a drink. She was not at the kiosk talking to you. Which leaves the question what were *you* cooking up last night?' Stella is alarmed by her bravery, and no sooner have the words reached his ears than she wishes them unsaid. Unsure of the possible reprisals, she takes a step backwards.

'That is no business of yours.' He rips some meat off a chicken leg with his teeth, grease on his lips, and pulls at the dangling tendons with his fingers.

'Isn't it?' Stella feels the strength of Juliet behind her. Juliet would speak up, and so should she. 'On paper you are my husband, which means if you are out with other women then it is my business.'

'Who said it was women?' Stavros laughs with his mouth open and Stella can see his half-masticated food.

'The stink of perfume on you,' Stella retorts.

'That was his wife!' Stavros sounds triumphant.

'Whose wife?' Stella asks, but she thinks she already knows the answer.

'The bastard that took my money.' Stavros throws his chicken bone onto the plate. It skids forwards across the ceramic surface and drops over the edge onto the table as he stands.

'Took it? Or you gave it to him attached to a deck of cards?' Stella says.

'If our life is such that I play cards to entertain myself then you should be grateful it isn't women, or drink for that matter.' He pours himself an ouzo.

'I am delighted, no ecstatic, that our money is "only" lost on cards, not drink and women. You must think I am an idiot, Stavros. I work here, slaving all day, every day, thinking I am making enough money to cover our outgoings, but the reality is I am covering your debts. So how much did you lose?'

'If I had won you would not be complaining.' Stavros lights a cigarette.

'Gambling is a fool's game. There is no winning. If you could win, casinos would never stay open. So how much?'

'If I had won there would be more than just you fawning over me.' He puffs on his cigarette at if it is a cigar.

'Meaning what?' Stella asks.

Stavros smiles to himself.

'If you mean Abby ...' Stella's voice does not sound like her own and she is surprised by the force of emotion behind it, her throat tightens and she cannot finish her sentence.

Stavros turns, a trail of smoke across his cheek with the speed. His blue eyes have a dark glow to them. His shoulder and hip follow his head until he is facing her.

'Abby?' he bellows.

At that moment the thunder crashes. Stella jumps. The rain is falling fast, in sheets. Behind Stavros the sky is so dark that lights are coming on all over the village, the road a swelling river. A car crawls past, its windscreen wipers on at full speed, making no impact on the rain sliding off the roof.

'She's just a kid!' Stavros exclaims.

'Exactly!' Stella retorts.

The slap is so hard that spikes of pain run up her nose and her eyes water.

It doesn't register as an action from him. It is just pain searing through Stella's cheek bone. His blue eyes stare into her, making contact in a way he has not done for years, searching for her surrender. Stella's eyes narrow: he isn't having it. She pushes to get past him out into the street, but as her hand touches his shoulder he shoves her back with such a force that she stumbles against a table. Shock pumps adrenaline, and energy surges to her muscles. She rights herself and lashes out at him, fear and anger mixing into a pool of uncontrolled aggression. She catches him by his hair and pulls, bringing his face down to meet her, his bulging eyes wary and wild, like a captured animal. He pulls his head back up but Stella clings on, their eyes level. She can see all the red veins in his eyes, smell the chicken on his breath, the individual greying hairs of his unshaven chin. She is repulsed.

The air exhales from her body with a gush and she doubles over, his fist buried in her stomach. Her hand releases its grip of his hair, both arms covering her stomach, defending and protecting.

'Sterile, dirty, gypsy, whore.' She hears the words spat at her as another blow hits her shoulder and she drops to the floor.

Her rage shrieks though her limbs, her legs scuttering. She is determined to stand, to face him. She fights for balance. Each attempt is met with a savage blow, to her shoulder, her thigh. With each blow her body grows weak but her mind is strong and she will not submit. Determinedly she finds her feet, every hit taken as another chance to defy, submission not an option. She blocks the pain, stubbornly facing him.

Denying defeat; she will not be crushed.

He reigns dominant over her. His body is alive with power, with the satisfaction of making good contact with each blow. The smack of fist against muscle, the pleasure of her cowering. The contortions of her limbs trying to protect her. He enjoys bruising, obliterating. Demanding acquiescence, he rages, unreachable.

She hits the floor again with force. With thoughts for survival paramount she tries to curl into a ball, but her limbs will not obey. In line with her face she sees the toe of his boot. She twists on the ground, her arm over her ear. The boot misses her face. The pain in her ribs refluxes her dinner and she coughs, but there is no mercy. The boot into her kidneys brings the message that she might lose her life. Does he know what he is doing? The blows land again and again, the impacts merging into one. Beyond pain, only reflex

Stella is no longer quite there. At last he falls, staggers back against the door frame in a squat and then, as if exhausted by all the effort, slides to the floor.

Stella lies still, wishes herself invisible. Between fingers she peeks at his face, his bulging blue eyes, shot red, staring at the floor. He looks spent.

Keeping noise and movement to a minimum, careful to not disturb his trance-like position, Stella uncurls. She rolls onto her knees and winces with the pain. Stavros does not move. Using a chair, she lifts herself to her knees, tries to focus. Her eyes are watering, thin strands of her hair stuck across her eyelids, over her lips. The table edge provides support as she tentatively stands. Finally on her feet she tips her chin up and looks down on Stavros, who remains motionless, panting, subdued.

With stiff limbs Stella walks past him. The lightning cracks and lights up the street. The rain has increased and the darkness is almost complete, the sun invisible. Stella steps into the street, the rain mixing with the tears of anger and pain, loneliness and loss, humiliation and degradation. The dirty gypsy.

She wants to run. The thunder grumbles before it cracks again and with a sheet of white lights up the molten, glistening village. Her legs will not respond. She feels as if she is moving through winter honey. She leans her weight forward to give some momentum, one foot scraping as she moves, the ankle not doing her bidding.

It seems to take hours to just reach the top of the square. She turns up her street past the shop. She glimpses Mitsos in the corner shop talking to Marina. She is glad he is not looking out, witnessing her humiliation. The lightning is on top of her and the thunder rages. Lights go out. The shop and the kafenio are in darkness.

Past the church into her lane, where Vasso's house is unlit, Stella pauses and draws in breath. She wants to lie down. She wants to close her eyes.

Her legs are going to collapse. There is a panic in her chest. All she wants is to get home, to close the door and climb into bed. She urges herself on, willing her legs not to give up.

The porch steps seem insurmountable. Dropping to her hands and knees, she crawls up. The door is open, no need to lock anything in the village - until now.

She climbs the door frame back to standing and locks herself in, bolting both top and bottom. With renewed energy she slowly and painfully checks all the windows, securing all she can. The final steps to the bedroom seem almost beyond her. Once inside she locks that door too and sits on the bed, pulling the covers around her, then sinks to the floor. She curls up as tight as the pain will allow. Pushing against the floor, she slides under the bed and pulls the covers she has dragged with her around her and over her head.

Dark and warm.

Chapter 12

Stella can hear the nylon cover she had pulled under the bed creating static with her hair: tiny noises, little clicks, only just audible until the thunder crashes. The shutters are closed, and under the bed with the cover over her there is no light, the lightning belonging to another world. Thoughts stay dormant. Warmth and dark and silence prevail.

Without the light visions come, memories that endorse her situation.

Walking home that day when the children threw stones at her: only now, the stones that landed are the bruises of Stavros' boots. The taunts in the school yard, the ring of girls and boys jeering 'dirty gypsy' until the teachers ushered them inside: the same words on Stavros' lips.

Walking up the dried stream bed she had presumed was safe: it was little-used except by the farmers who used the land along the sides or sheep and goat-herders who channelled their animals to pasture through its dusty course. The stream had not run for years and the passing of animals and men had flattened the path, the hedges on either side cut back by yellow teeth. Stella, swinging her arms as she ambled, picked spring flowers for her mother. The white flowers grew in abundance, the purple ones less common and worth searching for along the way. The bunch in her hand expressed the joy of the season.

As she rounded a corner a familiar sheep corral came in sight, a structure of plastic grain bags, wooden pallets, discarded bed-ends, and paint-peeling doors. The scruffy white dog left to guard the goats came running at her, barking as it always did when the animals were in their pen, ankle-deep in their own faeces. The dog, she knew, was all bark and no bite, so she paid it no attention.

As she reached the enclosure's makeshift gate a good-looking boy from school, Demosthenes, popped his head out.

'Hey,' he had chirruped. 'We're shearing sheep, you wanna see?'

Stella could hear other boys inside the covered enclosure.

'Who is it?' a voice from within demanded.

Demosthenes' head disappeared back inside.

'It's Stella.'

'What are you talking to her for? We don't want her in here.'

'Dirty gypsy probably thinks this pen is her home. One of these goats is probably her mother.'

Stella had begun to walk away. She heard the boys being shushed inside.

'Hey!' She didn't want to turn but Demosthenes had not seemed unkind. 'Don't leave, they are just mucking about. Come and see us shearing.' He lifted the metal shears, like a big pair of scissors, two long triangular blades sprung on a curve of metal. It was unusual for anyone to be friendly to her and his voice was very soft. To belong, to be one of them, to be accepted: his offer was tempting. She didn't walk towards him, but she didn't walk away either. 'There are some baby goats, you should see. So cute.'

'Why are you being nice to me?' she remembers asking.

'Why wouldn't I be nice to you?' He held his hand out to her to lead the way to the entrance of the pen.

Inside were three other boys, all of whom she knew from school. They were usually unkind to her. She pulled away from Demosthenes. His arm had swung around her shoulders.

'Come see the baby goats. Nektario, show her a baby goat.' The boy addressed looked about him until he spotted one and with a quick deft grab he had the goat's hind leg in his hand, the kid bleating for its mother and its release. The mother goat pushed past another boy, concerned for her offspring's safety.

Just as Stella was about to tell him he was hurting the goat he put an arm around its middle and lifted it from the floor and shuffled his way to Demosthenes. The ceiling of the pen being high enough for goats but not for people, he walked with knees bent, his feet sliding on the slurry of goat droppings and urine. Stella stayed were it was shallow but one of the boys stood ankle-deep.

Demosthenes took the beast and held it out to Stella. Stella remembers the shock she felt at Demosthenes' gentleness, his eyes locked on her eyes. She took the goat in a dream.

The animal stayed passive for a minute or two and no one said anything, Stella looking at the goat. When she raised her eyes she found all the boys looking at her. The animal gave a twist and Stella's grip could not hold him.

'He wants his mother,' Demosthenes announced, although the animal seemed happy enough just not to be restrained, finding its balance on wobbly legs. 'He wants his mother because he needs his milk.' The boys were looking at Demosthenes. The Pied Piper was calling and they knew it.

'He wants his mother to suckle milk - from her breasts.' Two of the boys sniggered, one wide-eyed at the situation. Stella remembers her uncertainty. He had been friendly until now but that sentence marked the edge of a precipice.

Demosthenes snipped his shears together.

'He needs to drink from his mother's' - there was a pause - 'breast.' All three boys sniggered this time. 'Or he will die.'

He snipped the shears again. Stella glanced to her side, gauging the distance to the entrance. She turned from him to leave the pen, wondering if she would make it worse by running. One of the boys stepped in her way; they had surrounded her.

'Animals die without breasts.' The giggles held menace. Stella looked about her for the best option to get out. One of the goats nudged one of the boys from behind and he stepped forward into a pile of goat droppings mixed into a green cream with urine. It made a squelching sound and one of the others looked down and laughed. With their attention drawn elsewhere, Stella turned and lurched for the gate. Demosthenes blocked her way. She stood motionless, the ambiguity of the situation now clear. The baby goat hobbled up behind Stella and began licking her hand. She had been skinning cooked beetroot before she came out and her hands were pink and no doubt tasted divine to the small beast.

Demosthenes raised the shears. The boys stood mesmerised. Stella's body was filled with adrenaline, her arms shaking, her legs unsteady. He took the shears and pointed one of the ends at her, between the eyes, inches from her skin. One boy gasped. The end of the shears trailed an invisible line through the air, down to her breast and then up to her shoulder. Fear held everyone still, their feet glued in the dirt.

The point of the shears moved closer. Stella looked frantically around her, her dangling hand feeling the goat. She stroked the kid's wiry fur, the act designed to reassure herself resulting in a small bleat.

The tip of the coarse metal shears rested on her shoulder and very gently traced over her collar bone and into the hollow at the base of her throat. Stella looked from one boy to another, pleading with her eyes. They did not see her; they were mesmerised by the tip of the shears on her skin.

The shears came to rest by the strap of her t-shirt. Demosthenes teased the sharp end under the strap. The boys all held their breath. Stella's eyes widened.

Snip.

Stella's hand shot up to stop her top falling. With the sudden movement, the baby goat by her side bleated in alarm.

Its mother made a dash to protect it, her belly pushing past the back of Demosthenes' knees. But Stella did not stop to see him overbalance. She wasn't sure her catch had been quick enough to preserve her modesty. In the commotion of goat and teetering balance her legs seemed to respond before her thoughts and she found herself outside, arms across her chest, running, the boys' laughter and Demosthenes' swearing fading with each step.

She felt dirty after that. When any of the boys were within sight the humiliation returned. In class, Demosthenes looked at her in a way that made her feel unclean. For a long time she showered before and after school and before bed as well. When her Baba asked her why, she disguised her obsession with hygiene as constipation, the toilet being in the same room as the shower.

Her 'constipation' had lasted for a long time.

The thunder cracks. Stella becomes aware of her situation. She peeks out from her hiding place. The room is relatively light, a layer of dust on the floor. She pulls the covers over her again. She is not ready.

The tiled floor is hard so she shifts, trying to make no sound. She wants neither sound, nor light, nor vision.

She can see no point in life.

Her existence seems to have no purpose.

Without purpose there is no point.

The dark almost engulfs her as she lies there unmoving.

But there is light, just a pinprick, coming from within.

Slowly she becomes conscious of herself.

Not the person people had told her she is. Not the dirty gypsy. Not the available slut. Not Stavros' wife. Not tiny Stella with frizzy shoulder-length hair. Not Stella when she closes her eyes and becomes Stella behind the eyelids with a beating heart. This is Stella with billions of capillaries and conscious thought, a miracle of life.

Her breathing deepens as her thoughts transcend.

She pushes the counterpane off her head and crawls slowly out from under the bed. The pains over her body are an offence to the value of her life. She stands in stages and switches on the lights. The mirror on the wall reflects someone she does not recognise, small, vulnerable, cowering. She raises her chin and stands tall. There is a large black bruise on her arm.

Using the mirror, she checks over her body; there are bruises everywhere. She can see her ribs are black from shoulder to hip on her right-hand side, and there are marks on her arms, and many on her legs. Her ankle, although it hurts, shows no sign of bruising. But it is her face that surprises her the most.

There is not one bruise, not a trace of the skirmish anywhere above the shoulders.

Stella is at first delighted, but then shocked. What if Stavros avoided her face on purpose, to hide his act. If that is the case, this was not an act of passion: this was a considered assault.

Stella, wrapped in her awareness of the miracle of existence, feels great pity for him. He too is a being struggling for life, for happiness. His way of trying to attain it has merely shown how small and scared he really is. It is sad, but for him, not for her.

She opens her wardrobe and takes out her only dress with long sleeves. She will not share these events with the whole village. There are lots more sad people out there who have also displayed how scared and small they are – not least Demosthenes, who regularly comes into the *ouzeri*, and these days leaves embarrassingly large tips.

What has happened is private, an uncomfortable crossroads to a new path in life. Stella knows she can cower with fear of the unknown future or rejoice with the start of something new. She has already chosen.

She must have lost more weight; the dress is baggy on her. She cannot remember if she has eaten today.

The rain is still drumming on the roof but has clearly eased. The thunder is loud; the storm is not over. The heat is still thick.

Stella unlocks the bedroom door and looks around the sitting room. Home. Just as it was when they moved in. Nothing changed. No personal touches. Not a single piece of furniture theirs. Nothing to fight over.

One of them needs to find somewhere else to sleep.

She doesn't care which one of them it is.

The kitchen reverberates with a loud cracking splitting sound but there is no pyrotechnic display to accompany it. The creaking splitting sound grows. Stella forgets her world and focuses outside, seeking the source of the disconcerting noise. She unlocks the front door and opens it. The rain, close by, is lit into silver chains by the porch light. The creaking sound continues. It is an unnatural sound, somewhere in the direction of the village.

An alarming crash follows and a dog begins barking frantically, somewhere near the square. Then nothing.

There is a silence between rolls of thunder, in which Stella can hear voices.

She steps outside and sees a figure hurrying along the bottom of her lane. Thoughts of her own life evaporate. She steps into the deluge. Her ankle hurts. Grabbing a stick as an aid, she hurries towards the square.

Abby throws her teddy key ring on the bed and runs to the front door. She grabs the umbrella on the porch table and is out into the dark. No street lights to show life, no cottages with orange eyes. All is dark. She marches towards the square: the sound came from there. In the distance she can hear voices. She breaks into a trot. She can see silhouettes of people and something large across the road, twisted, contorted, multi-limbs reaching the dark sky. She slows as she approaches the shape. She can smell the wet earth.

The tree's roots stretch up, unseen limbs bent, stringy toes hanging with earth. It lies immovable.

Movement draws Abby's attention beyond the mighty fallen tree. People are rushing, raised voices calling the alarm. She snaps out of her wonder at the hidden underside of the eucalyptus and skirts around and into the square. Still there are no lights but there is a lot of shouting. Many people stand in the rain or under umbrellas, looking into a darkened space.

With a cough and splutter the lights at the kafenio come back on. Abby blinks.

'*Panayia*! Marina!' Vasso stands beside her.

'What is it?' Abby follows her line of sight to a dark corner of the square where the people are gathered and the fallen tree has splayed its branches. The man from the kafenio, Theo, is running about in the dark space, pulling branches out of the way, calling something.

'Oh my goodness, the shop!' Abby exclaims. She looks to see if she can recognise any of the remains, and then, 'Oh my God! The people! Marina!' She steps forward but has no idea what to do and she stops. She looks at the other villagers also standing staring, shock on their faces, unmoving.

Theo shouts louder and then turns to the waiting group of people to call something. Some of the villagers go running in various directions, others head towards the remains of the shop. Discarded umbrellas flutter across the square in the breeze. Abby has no idea what is going on and she turns to Vasso to try to make some sense, but Vasso is gone, running to her kiosk. Only Abby remains stationary.

She is fixed, not stepping in any direction until she hears her name. Vasso is calling. The kiosk has many torches in stock. Abby quickly catches on and pulls a packet of batteries from the plastic display strip, three for the price of two. She loads them into the torches, clicking each one on and off to ensure that it works, a Morse code of semi-panic. Vasso stuffs them all into a plastic bag.

Abby finds a rhythm, batteries, click, batteries, click, but Vasso pulls her by the sleeve and they run to the darkened catastrophe and pull torches from the bag, flicking them on and handing them to everyone there.

'*Natos!*' someone shouts. Abby recognises the word from when she had made her fruitless phone call and got some old woman. 'There.'

There is a tangible change in the air. The people are animated, but the thunder rumbles its disagreement. The lightning briefly provides a view of the immense task before them. The branches and leaves of the tree cover the area, the thicker branches spiking the earth and denying access to the shop.

Those who had run off return with axes and saws, and in the torchlight a furious determination of work begins. Abby can do nothing but watch. She wraps her arms around herself, even though the air and the rain are warm. Vasso is back in the kiosk on the phone. The villagers work in unison. The thunder cracks with such a noise that Abby puts her hands to her ears. The clouds crash together to signal their disapproval.

The villagers chop and saw, and large branches shift their weight as they become detached. Abby at last can see a part she can play, and leaving her umbrella to spin in the square she grabs the nearest felled tentacle and pulls, heels slipping on the wet road, her weight arched backwards, across the road, to the still fountain. Other villagers are doing the same and the tree is quickly thinned to its trunk. The rain is lessening, and as it does so the voices of the men, inside what is left of the shop, became more audible.

Abby again finds herself without a role, her hair plastered to her face and neck, her clothes soaked.

The grumble of thunder – no, not thunder, the sound is too gentle, too earthly. A tractor rolls into the square with its lights full on. It drives straight for the shop's remains. Its headlights make the enormity of the event plain. The shop is crushed beneath the trunk of the eucalyptus, its tortured, de-limbed core straddling the spine of the shop's roof. Theo is shouting and gesticulating to the tractor driver. The driver manoeuvres his vehicle slightly. The sound of another diesel engine can be heard and a JCB appears out of the swirling rain.

Vasso is by her side again. She nudges Abby and points to the JCB driver, and then to herself. 'Cousin,' she says in English.

Chapter 13

Stella hobbles as quickly as her ankle will allow.

She stops abruptly in the road.

The black shape of the upturned tree strikes her as ungodly. She crosses herself and sidesteps its roots.

'*Ti egine*?' she calls to the people hurrying in front of her as she reaches the church. The wind and the rain whip the words into the sky unheard. She hurries on to find out what has happened. The possible enormity grows the more people she sees in front of her, rushing.

A tractor sits in the square, its lights blazing, lighting up the world in orange relief. A JCB grumbles into view.

She hears Vasso's voice say the word 'cousin' close by. She shuffles towards her and sees Abby is also there. Relief mixes in with her chaos around her. She wastes no time and wraps both her arms around her and hugs, losing herself in the balm of Abby's proximity.

Through Abby's hair she asks Vasso 'What happened?' but there is no need for an explanation of the tree to which Vasso points. Stella releases Abby enough to turn her head and looks the length of the trunk. '*Panayia!*' she exclaims, 'Marina!' as she realises where the trunk has fallen. Her own emotions over Abby are forgotten in the greater calamity.

Vasso mutters in Greek, which does nothing to calm Stella's wide-eyed shock.

'Is anybody in there with her?' She turns to Abby as she asks, her arms still around her. Abby shrugs. Stella repeats the question in Greek. Vasso shrugs. Abby and Stella turn fully to face the shop, letting go of each other, but standing close enough that their shoulders touch.

The men put a chain under the eucalyptus and it is attached to the teeth of the JCB's bucket. The digger's wipers are on full speed. As the bucket is lifted there are many shouts of '*Siga*' from the workers and watchers, and the tree is lifted very 'slowly' from the collapsed little shop. No sooner is the strain taken by the chain than Theo rushes under the trunk and within a couple of minutes he reverses back out again, pulling a man.

Abby gasps. Stella takes hold of her arm, using her for a support. Abby has never witnessed an accident like this before. She wills the man to move but he lies motionless.

'Mitsos,' she hears Stella gasp, and she feels the juddering of Stella's sobs through the arm that is bearing her weight.

Abby turns to her. Stella's eyes do not move from the prone man. She takes a step towards him but Vasso is by her side and puts a restraining arm on her.

'*Ohi* Stella,' Abby hears Vasso say gently. Abby puts an arm around Stella, who is crying openly now.

The village men converge around Mitsos, and he is lifted as if made of eggshells and carried right past Abby, Stella and Vasso. Stella reaches out an arm as if to touch him but Vasso gently pulls it back to her side. They take him up the road behind the shop and into a house. Theo is not with the carriers. He has gone back under the hovering trunk, emerging to point and shout instructions. The tractor judders forward and pushes the trunk to one side while the JCB still holds it clear of the shop's main roof beam.

Theo disappears again, accompanied by another man, under the trunk, and this time they come out carrying a woman.

'Marina,' Vasso shouts, and runs towards her. Stella stays in Abby's arms, crying. The village women converge and, holding hands beneath Marina, carry her in the same direction as Mitsos. As she passes Abby and Stella, she smiles. Vasso's face is grave as she bears her weight.

'*Ela*,' someone shouts back in the collapsed shop.

The skies are brightening by the minute and the lights of the tractor and JCB illuminate someone gathering armfuls of goods from amongst the debris of the shop.

'*Ela*,' he calls again, 'Come on,' and other people hurry into the mess and pick out goods, unconcerned about the contents, gathering like hungry ants. Abby is appalled at the looting. She remembers hearing on the news about looting in England where a millionaire's daughter had taken a pair of trainers. The idea disgusts her. She steps forward, unsure how to make her stance clear, enraged and ready to do battle. As she nears someone they hand her tins of dog food. Abby searches for a way to express herself but the man passes two more tins and pushes her by the elbow and points to Theo's kafenio. She at once realises her mistake.

Abby can feel her face growing hot, the heat prickling around her neck. She is glad of the still-dim light. The tables in the kafenio have growing piles of goods upon them. The villagers are hurriedly saving them from the rain for Marina.

Abby springs into action, gathering as much as she can, stretching her T-shirt in front of her to act as a pouch. She runs back and forth with flour, biscuits, bottles of bleach and plastic dolls.

Stella is doing the same but she is moving slowly. Abby wonders what is wrong, she seems to be limping a little. The tension in her throat has gone since she hugged her but she wonders how long before her next turn of emotions.

Stella ignores the burning in her legs and the pain in her ankle. The bag of sugar she is carrying splits in her hand. She drops it and wipes sticky fingers down her dress before picking up a plastic-wrapped mop head. She takes the couple of steps up the kafenio steps carefully. Her ankle feels weak.

'Are you OK?' Abby asks as she drops dozens of packets of tights from her T-shirt pouch. 'You're limping.'

Stella drags her thoughts away from Mitsos and reaches for a lie, and then wonders why she should save Stavros from the embarrassment he deserves. But the events of earlier seem small in comparison. She has ascertained from Theo that Mitsos is alive, but no one knows how badly he is hurt. Besides poor Abby cannot know if she is coming or going, literally, she certainly doesn't need added complications. She will explain everything at a more suitable time. She wipes her face on her sleeve and turns to collect more goods.

'Stella?'

'*Ti*? Oh, limping, yes, I fell.' She hurries back into the rain, washing away the tears. One minute she saw Abby as everything in her world. But then she felt life was over when she saw Mitsos pulled out of the rubble. Her chest had sunk inwards to her stomach and all life force had drained from her limbs. An overreaction , perhaps, after all that had happened, her upset with Abby and Stavros.

The crying was probably from the shock of earlier and the storm, she reasons. Marina has worked so hard to make that shop work and now, in the space of minutes, it is all gone. All that hard work, gone. All the chat and banter building up regulars, pointless. The years of refining her methods, wasted. All the fiddling with the grill to get the optimum heat.

Then she realises she is internalising about herself, and the tears stop.

A gaping hollow insides her chest heaves. She needs to see Mitsos. Calm, safe, caring.

She breaks from the line of people recovering all they can and goes to the house behind the shop, Marina's house.

She doesn't knock. She walks in, hears voices upstairs, people in the kitchen, a kettle boiling. She goes up the wooden stairs.

'She's fine, she's fine,' Kyria Katerina from opposite the church consoles her at the top of the stairs. 'The doctor is looking at her now.' Katerina was a nurse before her arthritis got so bad and her hands knotted up.

'Mitsos?' Stella asks. Her bruises seem to have come to life again, throbbing and aching.

'He's ok, he's in there.'

Stella goes into the next room. Kyria Katerina follows her. Stella looks at Mitsos, lying so still.

'He's unconscious, but his breathing is steady. The doctor says he is not worried. Nothing broken, it seems. Lucky man.'

'Yes.' Stella hardly moves her mouth to reply. She cannot believe the surge of feeling rushing through her. She wants to hold him, kiss his sunken cheek, smooth his thick grey hair. He is older, but not that much older. Some women in the village have married men more than fifteen years their senior.

Marina, for example. Her husband was thirty and she was fourteen, or perhaps fifteen, when they married.

Marina. The thought comes like a lead weight. Mitsos' lifelong love. Here he is, in her house, both of them having escaped disaster. And how is it that he was in the shop anyway? Mitsos hasn't spoken to Marina properly for years. Now they will have plenty of time to talk. This is bound to bring them together. How could it not? She sighs.

'He'll be fine, don't worry,' Kyria Katerina says with the positivity of someone happily employed, and she steps forward to smooth his bed and tuck in the edges.

'Yes, now he will be fine.' Stella closes her emotions back into the box she has only just learnt she has. It doesn't seem to want to shut.

She takes a last look at Mitsos' relaxed sleeping face and leaves.

Vasso is downstairs in Marina's kitchen. They return outside together and find Abby. They walk homewards together.

'Abby, so much is happening, my feelings are everywhere but I made a very big mistake this morning. I cannot ask you to understand but please stay, give me a chance to explain everything to you, Will you? Will you stay?'

Abby nods. Now is not the time to talk of passports or money, they are all exhausted, emotionally and physically. Despite Vasso's insistence that Stella comes into her house with them for something to chase out the effects of all that has happened, Stella returns home alone, squeezing Abby's hand before she leaves, promising they will talk.

The clouds have lifted, but it is evening so the sky is still dull. No lights are on in her home and Stella is sure Stavros is still out. She did not see him amid all the activity earlier.

She needs to sleep. There is no denying the pain in her ankle and, judging by the way her left arm hurts to lift, she thinks she may have at least one broken rib. The weight in her chest pulls her shoulders forward. She refuses to think of Mitsos, or Marina.

The house is all echoes and silence. Her bed is waiting for her.

When they first moved in, they complained to the landlord that the bed was not suitable. He promised a replacement, but it didn't happen and they got used to the gap. Stella splits the two beds apart with her knee. The two singles are cheap and light, the mattresses thin. Stavros' side has a dip moulded into it. Using her weight against her lower leg, she pushes it with disdain. Her right leg seems to be the only part of her that doesn't hurt.

She lifts the bed onto its side, the thin mattress falling off. She slides the base through to the kitchen. She pushes the mattress after it and throws some sheets on top. He can put it together himself. She grabs a kitchen chair and takes it into the bedroom.

Locking the door and wedging the chair under the handle, Stella carefully lies down on her right-hand side, pulls a sheet over her head and falls asleep, cutting Mitsos food for him, their knees touching under the table.

Chapter 14

The day's heat has already built. Shutters are open and the cicadas are singing. There is a smell of sheep in the air, and fresh bread.

Last night it seems Vasso had no idea she had even left yesterday. This morning she made her a coffee and gave her a time check as if she were going into the *ouzeri* as normal.

Abby is unsure what to do. Stella apologised and asked her to stay last night, but even so, she is not sure where she stands. She decides to wander casually to the *ouzeri* and see how Stella reacts. She puts her books in her bag and leaves nothing behind - just in case.

Outside with the sun on her face, even with the emotional roller-coaster ride she is on there is a bounce in her step. Life is very exciting in Greece, it beats being bored at home. She is glad Marina and Mitsos were not badly hurt. Theo was so brave.

A few immigrant workers wait in the square. Abby smiles in their general direction but they do not acknowledge her, almost as if they expect to be ignored.

Vasso, who left the house an hour before Abby

stopped reading and finally climbed out of bed, waves a cheerful hello as she walks up to the kiosk. The glass-fronted fridges sparkle in the sun. The shade under the awning is a sharp contrast to the whitewashed wall behind. She wants to ask how Marina and Mitsos are this morning but she does not know have the Greek. She points to the fallen tree trunk, on the crushed shop, which is rapidly being dissected into manageable lumps by a man wearing a checked shirt and wielding a chain saw.

'Marina?' She adds a thumbs up and a sceptical look. Vasso returns her own thumbs up and babbles two or three sentences in Greek, and then laughs. She points to Abby's leg and makes a snapping motion with both her hands and a wet harsh sound with her mouth.

Abby's stomach flips. She restores her calm and asks after Mitsos, who just gets a thumbs up, no snapping. Abby is relieved. She waves as she leaves, and Vasso calls in a low gruff voice 'You be back,' and cracks into laughter. Abby taught her 'I' and 'You' last night after they had showered off the tree debris and sweat and were sitting in dressing gowns. Abby is about to correct her grammar but decides it is funnier the way she has said it and just laughs as she walks on.

She does not quite get to the shop before Stavros steps out and locks the door behind him. He points to his car and then the direction of the town.

Abby frowns, now what? Is this him telling her to go now as well? He points again and then strides over and opens the passenger door. Abby is not ready to leave. Besides, she needs to talk to Stella first, and get her passport back. She looks into the shop but it is dark, Stella is not inside.

'Stella?' She asks.

'Shhh.' He puts his finger to his lips. 'No Stella.' He waves her into the car pointing to the deep-fat fryer in the back. Abby has no idea what Stavros' intentions are. None of his actions suggest that he wants her to get in the car to make her leave. He is insistent.

'Work.' he says, his one confident word in English. She climbs in. The plastic seat is split in many places and the gashes have opened like wounds, the edges peeling back, hot sharp corners cutting into her bare legs.

He has the chip fryer on the back seat and the inside of the car smells acrid even with the windows open.

The dashboard is covered with dust and bits of rubbish and the well of the passenger seat is filled with empty cans and plastic bags. A collection of charms and elastic bands hang from the mirror, which is cracked. Abby does not want to touch anything. She pulls her shorts down as far as they will go and wishes she had worn the grey ones.

Stavros heaves himself in, his door creaking on squeaky hinges. Air escapes from his seat as he sits. The car takes some revving to get it going and then with a judder they lurch away into the middle of the road.

He is a dangerous driver, heeding neither signs nor other road users. By the time they reach the town Abby would decides she'll return by taxi, whatever his plans are.

But it seems there are no plans. Once in town, they drive slowly from one shop to the next. Stavros has his window down and kerb-crawls, stopping frequently to talk or to call a greeting. Each acquaintance dips his head to look in at Abby, who pulls her shorts down even more and puts her bag on her knee. She resents this show, in which she is the main attraction, but with growing anger she tolerates the steady pace until finally he pulls up at a shabby-looking place, its windows filled with stickers that obscure a mess of articles stacked in the window. It is not a shop, it is a storage unit, stuffed with discarded junk. A microwave door balances on top of a radio with no front, a television with no case around it supports a video player balanced at an angle on top, countless articles, most of which Abby cannot identify, all sitting on a tangle of electrical wires, adaptors and fuses.

Stavros gets out and, ignoring her, carries the chip fryer into the shop.

Abby waits. And waits. And waits. Finally she gets out of the car to stretch her legs. She was right, the seat has left various grubby impressions on her behind. Just as she is trying to assess the worst of the damage, Stavros comes out of the shop and with a sneer, he too looks at her bottom. Abby defiantly faces him, her bag providing cover for her shorts.

Still grinning, he puts a different chip-fryer onto the back seat and gets into the car, leans over and pushes the passenger door open.

Abby gets in. He hasn't actually done anything she can say is wrong; it just doesn't feel nice.

He drives just as manically back to the village.

The shop is hot. Stella is not there and Stavros sets her to cleaning the mirrored shelves behind the grill. She hadn't realised how tight the muscles in her shoulders had become until they relax with this confirmation that she still has a job. She looks at the shelves that he wants her to clean - God knows they need it.

Stavros greets the butcher who arrives with the meat for the *giro* slung over one shoulder. The butcher takes off the sheet that is covering it and slots the three feet high skewered meat layers into its upright position in front of the grill. Stavros flicks a switch and the electric bars that surround the turning spit glow red hot in seconds. The butcher doesn't linger.

Stavros becomes aware of Abby watching the process. He rummages under the counter and gives her something called Azax. It is a bottle of window cleaner that looks as if it was designed fifty years ago. Abby likes the retro style but it is not a spray bottle: it just has a nozzle with a hole. She inverts it and squeezes, and it burps and emanates an uneven, blotchy spray. She wipes with a piece of kitchen roll and cuts through years of grease. The paper is black; the glass no longer misty, now smeared with a thick white-grey. Abby can feel the beginnings of a reflux action and she breathes deeply to overcome it. She wonders why Stella is not here.

Stavros has trouble lighting the grill and Abby delights in trying to memorise the words he uses, obviously swear words.

The bottom shelves come out so she leans them against the back of the grill and allows gravity to lure the Azax down the sticky surface. Once she has cleaned a couple of shelves and sees the sparkling difference, Abby feels rewarded. It is quite a Zen job, she decides. She takes her time. It is hot anyway and her limbs feel sleepy with the heat. She can hear a donkey bray behind the shop – somewhere near the pine tree top, she decides, maybe by that cottage that looks deserted next to the almond grove. The view from up there is breathtaking, it reminds her of Uncle Brian who has a huge model railway in his attic, with miniature trees and sheep in the fields, tiny houses, and, her favourite since she was so small Uncle Brian had to lift her up so she see, a shepherd with his dog under a bridge, the train going over the top, almost real. She would love to go up the hill again and look down on the rows of oranges. Maybe today when Stella turns up and Stavros goes for his sleep, she'll go for a walk, like she did the last time.

The memory of Uncle Brian triggers thoughts of Dad. She must either phone or write him another card. She called last night, after her shower, but got the answer machine again. Postcards are good, though. There are no arguments with them.

She breaks off a new handful of kitchen paper. She can hear Stavros pouring chips into the fryer, she wonders if he peeled and cut the potatoes himself. It doesn't seem likely; maybe they were already in the fridge.

Postcards. Day two was a kitten in a sock, day three dolphins. She wonders what she will send today. There is a good one of an old man in a traditional Greek white skirt thing and red shoes with pom-poms on.

She presumes Stella has not come in because of

her fall. She wonders how she is but does not have the Greek to ask Stavros. Mind you, Stavros looks like he has slept under a hedge. Literally. He has tiny twigs in his hair. When she saw him first thing she had tried not to stare.

With the bottom shelves spotlessly clean Abby moves on to the higher ones, taking a chair to stand on. Stavros keeps poking his head around the grill to see what she is doing. She decides he is definitely a bit of a letch. Stella, in one of her good moods, is so full of fun and life that Abby cannot work out why she is with this guy. He is creepy, sweaty. She considers. No, he has not one redeeming feature. She sniffs and moves on to the next shelf.

The chair is not tall enough and she cannot reach the top shelves. The ones above the sink look as if they have not been cleaned – ever. There is something black in the corner of the top one. Abby doesn't really want to find out what it is.

She continues with the shelves she can reach. The smell of the chickens cooking begins to sweeten the air.

Abby continues her work rhythmically, focussed on the task. When she does think, she is thinking of her school friends, and sometimes of Stella, whom she feels she really does seem to have some sort of connection with, even though Stella does blow warm and cold.

Is Jackie wondering where she is? She doubts it. All her money gone on that boat ticket. Since the boat was cancelled, could she get a refund? Mind you she earned it in no time. The bar might be more fun, it would certainly be less heavy, more steady. She could still go, it would probably be fun. Maybe she will go nearer the end of the summer, for a sort of fun time, rather than work. The money here is enough. The tips are great. She has some regulars.

Anyway, she is back now and she is working, she feels she is within her comfort zone. She likes her little room at Vasso's. It is the first room that is truly her own. Vasso is not about to barge in and demand she tidy it up like Dad does at home. But, then again, she doesn't have to, she keeps it tidy anyway. She likes it that way.

Vasso is hilarious and Stella is, well, like she imagines a mum to be, when she isn't being moody.

Abby has got to the back of the second shelf. It is disgusting. She pokes at the corners with a kebab stick to get out lines of mould growing between glass and wall.

It had been a big enough deal running away to Greece in the first place. That was way out of her comfort zone. But she had been so angry. He cannot tell her what to do with her life. She had to show him that she was independent.

It had been a bit rash, perhaps, a bit too spontaneous. An Internet booking at 4 p.m. and flying at 4:30 the next morning. She had been amazed at the bustle of life at the airport at that time of day, especially after the empty, silent, train she took to get there. And the silent house she left before that, Dad snoring, the dog not even stirring.

She blinks a couple of times. She had also wanted to show Dad what life would be like without her if he did insist she didn't go back to do her A levels. That hadn't been a nice thing to do. She will write on today's post card that she is sorry. Well, not straight out like that, she would never hear the end of it. She has apologised in an indirect sort of way, saying that she hoped he and Sonia and the baby were ok and not to worry about her. She will try to phone again, at some point.

The only way to reach the top shelves will be to stand on the sink. The big marble bowl looks like it will support a house, it is so solid. With the bottle of Azax in one hand and the kitchen roll in the other she climbs from chair to sink. The sink edge is narrow but balancing with one foot on either side she can just about reach.

She bends and takes a knife from the sink and uses it to reach the back corner, standing on tip-toes, she hooks the black object in the far corner and scoops it towards her. There is a layer of mould over it, which crumbles as she drags it.

Stavros pops his head around the grill again. He steps into the passage and takes a glass from one of the clean shelves. Abby continues edging the object to the front of the shelf, but it keeps slipping from the knife end. At first she thinks it is a potato that has been there since time began, but as it comes to the edge of the shelf and the mould falls away it takes on a form.

She hears a rushing noise and looks down. Her feet are still straddling the sink and Stavros has reached between her ankles and turned on the tap. He holds a glass under the tap and the water runs into it. He has not turned the tap on fully and the glass fills slowly. Abby feels vulnerable and wishes Stella would come.

She alters her position ready, with some embarrassment, to put both her legs onto one side of the sink. In doing so the angle of vision on the black object changes and she can see thin lines of white. It comes as a rush that it is the skeleton of a mouse.

Abby's throat constricts and she is about to squeal when she feels something rubbing her leg.

Stavros' glass is full and with a wet knuckle of the hand holding the glass he traces a line down the inside of her calf just below her knee.

Abby freezes, with her knife behind the dead

mouse, until, with no thought, she flicks the sack of bones and mould at Stavros' face. She doesn't mean to. It is a reaction. She opens her mouth to apologise when Stavros explodes with what can only be a string of expletives, brushing his face and hair as he backs out from behind the grill.

Abby is too horrified by his degree of anger to find his reaction funny. She jumps down from the sink, dithering about whether to leave or apologise.

Where is Stella?

She can see through the gap between the grill and the chip fryer that Stavros has gone outside, still brushing off his clothes, before pulling out and lighting a cigarette. She feels a little safer with the distance. Stavros bends over and shakes his head once more, running his fingers through his hair to ensure no dust remains.

She can imagine the scene when Stella comes.

'Hey Stella, I understand now, your husband is a creepy letch, no wonder you are so grumpy.'

Or maybe, 'Stella, I like working with you, but I have to say I cannot work alone with Stavros because he's a smarmy git.'

Abby sighs. She stays behind the grill, but she is pretty sure Stavros won't come back in. A customer comes in, a regular, and Abby peeps out from behind the grill before stepping boldly forward and deftly making him a *giro*, without onions she remembers, and with a smile that belies her mood she hands it to him.

He smiles back and says, 'Thank you, kind English lady,' as if he has been practising. He tips her two euros before he leaves.

'Damn!' Abby says out loud. She is happy here. Why does Stavros have to be here? Stupid bog-eyed toad. She slams the till shut.

Ok, she can handle this. This is just another test of her abilities. There will always be creepy guys, and this a good chance to learn to deal with one. Creepy guys should not win.

She goes to her bag and takes out her purse. With the tip she may just have enough.

She walks straight past Stavros, who is sitting outside smoking, and continues towards the bakery but turns down a side lane. The sun hits her like the opening of an oven door. The blast of warmth becomes bearable and her tension eases. She walks with purpose but not fast, the sun demanding that she take her time. She found this strange little shop when she explored the village on her first day.

There it is. The ancient cracked mannequin in the cluttered window has on a 1960s crocheted tank top and a pair of sailor's trousers, creased across the thigh and across the calf, with wide bell-bottom ends. Dust has settled into fading brown lines across the creases. Next to it is a wooden towel-rack with blue muslin laid over it. On the floor of the window is a pair of roller skates, a bucket and four tennis rackets.

Abby pushes the door open. The bell above the door rings. It is comparatively dark inside and Abby waits to be greeted or for her eyes to adjust, whichever happens first.

Her eyes adjust and she takes the blue muslin from the window. She suspects it isn't just a piece of material, and she is right. The muslin unfolds into a pair of 1970s wrap-around trousers.

'Cool,' Abby exclaims and turns to look for the shopkeeper. There is a little white-haired woman, her head on her chest, asleep in the corner, next to a free-standing full length mirror. Abby hasn't the heart to wake her, but she must. There is a price sticker on the trousers but it is in drachmas. She takes the opportunity to look around the shop. There is a diving suit with a big brass helmet and weighted boots. Beside this is a single tank with a harness to wear on your back, attached to a hose leading to a spray nozzle. Abby presumes this is for gardeners or farmers. A rack of clothes, a jumble of colour and another pile on the floor in front of it. There are some postcards that look as if they have been there since the first tourist stepped on Greek soil.

'*Ti thelis*?'

Abby jumps.

'Do you speak English?' What are the chances, Abby wonders. An old lady in a village in the outback of Greece, why would she? She wishes she had brought her phrase book.

'Of course.'

Abby is more surprised by the accent than the English. She sounds like the Queen.

'Oh, er, I wanted to know how much these are. Where did you learn your English?'

'They are clearly marked 5,000 drachmas.' The woman laughs, pulling the price sticker off. 'I was born on Corfu. Mother did domestic work for a very well-to-do British family and took me along for the fun. I played with the children of the house in the gardens. They taught me English and I taught them Greek. They're yours for two euros. You know they are faded down one side where they have been in the sun?' The woman tries to hold them up but, as she is sitting down she is too near the floor for them to fall evenly. She struggles to get up, shifting her weight this way and that.

'Let me.' Abby steps towards her and take the trousers. The woman is right, they have faded all down the left leg. 'Awesome,' Abby says. 'And this top?' She holds out a cheesecloth V-neck shirt with embroidered flowers on the front.

'That's a bit nicer, three euros.'

Abby picks out five euro coins . 'Do you have a changing room?'

The woman points to a red curtain folded over the arms of two mannequins who are touching fingers across a corner.

'I heard you are working at Stella's. Poor girl.'

'Who, me? I am not a poor girl! I love it.' Abby's voice is muffled as she pulls her strappy T-shirt off and replaces it with the long-sleeved cheesecloth shirt. It looks great in the pitted and musty mirror.

'No, Stella.' She enunciates perfectly.

'Stella? You mean her ankle?' Abby slips off her dirty white shorts and battles to work out how to put on the wrap-around trousers.

'No, I mean having him for a husband.'

Abby comes out, folding her shorts around her strappy T-shirt.

'Don't I know it!' She glances though the window as if he might be there, spying on her.

The woman stands and fusses, looking for a bag. Abby says she does not need a bag but the woman continues until she finds one. It is a thin blue plastic one that smells of fish.

Abby wants to know more about what she thinks of Stavros but it seems the moment has gone. It would be awkward to ask now. Besides, she cannot be away from the *ouzeri* too long. She thanks the lady and smiles as she catches her reflection in the mirror next to the woman. She looks like the hippies she saw that time Dad took her to Glastonbury. She smiles again at the memory and then remembers the postcards that look as if they have been in the shop since the dark ages. She chooses three; she likes writing them. It's fun, like writing a diary but someone gets to read it.

'How much?' she asks.

The woman jerks her head back, chin up. Abby has learnt that this strange nod means 'no'.

'But I must pay for them,' Abby insists, opening her purse.

'You hang on to your money, my dear. I have a feeling you may need it.'

Abby gives her a quizzical look and decides she

is just weird.

On the way back to the shop she passes by Vasso's for some stamps and gives her a twirl.

Vasso says, 'Twiggy.' Abby is surprised she knows who Twiggy is.

Fully covered up, she walks past Stavros, who looks her up and down and snorts and returns to concentrating on his cigarette.

Abby hopes the point has been made.

Chapter 15

The weeds by the whitewashed walls down the lane's edge are browning. There is the usual scuttle of unseen creatures as she passes each clump of struggling foliage. She aches everywhere. The hot shower has only taken the edge off the soreness. Stavros did not come home last night. Stella, instead of feeling relieved, felt strangely disappointed. The bed in the kitchen was her statement, to tell him 'the lie of the land'.

It is as if his not coming home had taken the choice away from her. As if he is still in charge.

She enters the square, the sun searing up at her from the paved surface.

Vasso has a queue of three farmers and a pair of tourists at the kiosk, big people in shorts and sandals. Presumably the large people-carrier parked incongruously on the kerb is theirs, so shiny compared to the usual tractors. The sight of the tourists brings the slightest bounce to Stella's step; her improving English is a joy to her. It feels more positive than thinking about Stavros. It proves she is more than a punch-bag.

'Hello,' Stella calls. She enjoys the rebelliousness,

proving she can do something he cannot. It feels good. 'How are you, I hope you are enjoying your holidays, there is much to see …'

The tourists grin in delight and tell her they are fine, loving their holiday, and something about a ticket to the theatre at *Epidavros* being lost. Stella smiles all the way through their sad tale, told in a strange accent. She understands most of what they say, but she is more interested in being seen to understand by both the farmers and by Vasso, who is looking on with wide eyes.

It feels good to impress people.

She walks a little taller, and less painfully, as she continues on to the shop, which she is surprised to find closed and the car gone.

The smells from the sandwich shop beckon her over to buy a *bougatsa* for breakfast. The vanilla cream-filled pastry is fresh and Stella is hungry.

'Did you see Stavros leave with the car?' she asks.

The girl says she saw Stavros loading something in the back of the car and a little later drive off towards town with the blonde girl in the short white shorts.

They are short, Stella reflects. Maybe that is ok in her country. It seems to be what all the celebrities wear in the summer, but Stella does not find it wholly appropriate for a young girl in an *ouzeri*, especially around Stavros. She sniffs.

She leaves with her breakfast in her hand.

The village taxi is parked by the square, the air above the bonnet shimmering with the heat. She can see Nikos relishing a coffee at the kafenio, his car keys on the table. The empty room rings with men's laughter, banter and the clack of backgammon pieces slammed down with force, the roar of the good throw of the dice as they play. The high ceiling and blank walls create echoes, layers of sound.

Stella doesn't feel comfortable going in, with so many men, so she hovers, hoping to catch Nikos' attention.

Eventually a man, sitting, leaning on a crook, looking out at the world, asks what she wants. The whisper passes to the back that someone is waiting for Nikos. It is a common event, he is a taxi driver.

Word reaches him and he looks out, spots her and lifts a finger in acknowledgement.

Stella knows she must now wait for him to finish his coffee. The front of the kafenio is baking in the sun. Stella thinks to move under the palm tree's shade. Normally this would be a good time to chat to Vasso. She checks the sleeves and hem of her dress to make sure they are covering the pictures of her marriage. She is not sure she has the emotional energy to cope with Vasso, her kindness, her strong opinions.

The memory of Vasso stopping her reaching Mitsos floods to her, Vasso's restraining hand on her outstretched arm.

Stella quickly looks at the ground. What does Vasso know? How can she know? Stella is not even sure she knows herself.

That's a lie, she knows.

'*Ela,*' Nikos brushes past her, telling her to 'come'.

Stella sits in the back, something she normally doesn't do. Her skirt will ride up when she sits down and she doesn't want a conversation about her private life.

She tells him to head into town and they banter for a while, raising their voices over the engine. The polished leather of the seats and the smell of various sprays Nikos perpetually uses to keep his Mercedes pristine delights Stella. There's no chip fat here. The seats do, however, make the turns in the road a sliding affair. Gripping on to the door causes her ribs to ache. She is glad when they arrive.

'Whereabouts?' Nikos asks as they cruise into

town.

'Here will do.' Stella slithers out and pays him through the window. As he drives away the warmth is already burning her, the sun in her eyes. Someone walks past, trailing a scent of coconut suntan cream.

Winding her way slowly between cars and across streets, away from the shops, she makes her way into back roads which are flanked by offices and apartments

The four-storey-high blocks were built before she was born, preserved only by careful cleaning and constant maintenance as the concrete crumbles. They are decaying, but slowly. A discrete white plaque marks '*Kleftis and Pseftis*', the lawyers who helped Stella organise her mother's affairs when she died.

She presses the bell and is buzzed into the building's gloomy stairwell. The buzzer continues after she enters. The antiquated, mirrored lift takes her to the unlit, windowless second floor, where she feels her way to the light switch. She depresses a large button which illuminates the hall, the button slowly extruding to click the bare bulb off after a short time. It is just long enough for her to find and ring the bell outside a lacquered, peeling wooden door. The smell of cooking drifts down the stairs from the floor above; the aromas of everyday living, tomatoes, onions, garlic.

The door is opened and the light is welcome. The office is enthusiastically air-conditioned. Stella feels a shiver run down her spine. The secretary has on a light jumper.

'Hello, Stella, how have you been? What, seven, nearly eight years? Everything ok?' Mr Kleftis shakes her warmly by the hand.

'Yes, well no …' She looks at the secretary and Mr Kleftis opens the door into his private office, follows her in and tucks his suit jacket flat around as he sits behind his desk. He bridges his fingers, elbows on his cluttered desk, and asks in a baritone voice, 'What can I do for you?'

'I need to know the lie of the land.'

'What?' He seems bemused. He is right of course, the phrase does not translate into Greek well.

'I need to know how things are legally with the *ouzeri* and the house and everything.'

'From what point of view?' he asks, dropping his chin and looking over his glasses at her. He picks up a pen and distracts himself, signing a document on his desk before reinstating his serious gaze.

'If me and Stavros … If I … If he …'

'Ahh, I see. Now, from my memory …' He

stands up and goes to the far wall which is stacked floor to ceiling with box files. He takes one out. Opening it, he sits back down behind his desk. A rummage through the contents produces a thin, dog-eared cardboard folder from which he draws out some papers. 'Yes, I remember now. Your father left a very clear will. Well, not really your father, but you know what I mean.' He reads.

Stella sits bolt upright. 'What? What do you mean?'

'The will, it was very clear.'

'No, what you said about my father?'

'Oh. Ah. Yes, of course, well, long time ago, doesn't matter now. So you and Stavros ...'

'What doesn't matter?' Stella's voice is raised, her stomach tight, she feels cold.

'It's nothing. Just a little point of law, if you like ...' He pauses, hoping this is enough, but when he sees it isn't he adds, '... that potentially made your inheritance a little difficult, but we dealt with it well.' He dismisses it with a wave of his hand.

'Dealt with what well?' Stella can feel the tension in her stomach increasing and a dull roaring in her ears. Her mouth feels dry.

'You knew about your mother, of course? I mean that she was a gypsy?' Stella can see small beads of sweat forming above his eyebrows.

'What has that got to do with anything?' Stella's eyes widen; she feels slightly sick. The last time she can remember feelings like this was when she had heard the rumours about Stavros and the teenage girl after they were married.

'No, quite, let's move on.' He flicks through the papers.

'No. What did you mean "not really my father"?'

He visibly sinks into the chair, deflated and wrinkly like an old balloon, his face collapsing like a candle in the sun. He exhales and interlocks his fingers across his chest. He sighs, takes off his glasses, puts them on the desk, rubs his eyes and then crosses his fingers across his chest once more.

'Stella, I am sorry, I didn't mean to blurt that out.' He waits, but Stella just stares at him, swallowing hard. 'Your father, and he was clearly a good father, judging by the provisions he made for you and your mother, was, well, by blood, not really, umm, you know, well, your father.' He stammers and picks up his glasses again.

Stella doesn't move. Her face remains still, her back upright. The ground opens beneath her. If she moves she will fall.

'I am terribly sorry to have told you in this way …'

He drones on, but Stella is six again, walking with her Baba to the top of the hill, the sudden view of the plain across the valley and the sea coming upon them, and her Baba bending his knees to be her height and saying, 'You see the world? Anything is possible, Stella. Anything. All you have to do is see the world from up here, like a game, a map. Just play the game well, without doubts. Once you are down there, among the people, you will find that your fears, your beliefs will hold you back. But up here, Stella, you realise anything is possible. No matter who you are.'

He said the words to her every time they climbed that hill. Even when she walked up there once with him, with an engagement ring on her finger, he repeated that monologue. By then, the words had become a mantra and she said them with him: 'Play the game well, without fear and don't let your belief hold you back. No matter who you are.' And Stella had added, 'If in doubt, look down,' and laughed.

That last time they had laughed together a long time and he had told her he loved her and put his arm around her and said what a lucky man Stavros was and he hoped that he knew it.

'So all I can say is, sorry for my clumsiness,' Mr Kleftis concludes.

Stella looks down. The carpet needs vacuuming. Now she understands why her father had added on, 'No matter who you are.'

'So who is he?' she asks, still looking at the floor. The swirling patterns become the sea and the plain of the valley.

'I believe, and I am very sorry to say this, but I believe your mother had no choice, it was some cousin.'

'A gypsy!' Stella's head shoots up.

Mr Kleftis swallows hard and blinks rapidly before slowly nodding his head.

Stella quickly looks back at the carpet.

Mr Kleftis looks at his watch.

Stella is silent and unmoving.

Mr Kleftis clears his throat.

'So, er, what can I do for you today, with regards to you and Stavros?' He stammers.

'I want him out!' Stella says loudly, and then shuts her mouth, frightened of what else might come out.

'I see.' He looks through the papers. 'Well, there is nothing legally binding about anything. No. You bought the "*aera*", the goodwill, if you like, but now the lease on the shop has expired and I presume you haven't signed a new one.' He looks up and catches Stella shaking her head. 'You just pay the rent each month, with a verbal agreement, and the same with the house. Neither of you are bound, or for that matter have real claim.'

'But it was my inherited money that paid the goodwill and deposits on them both, and the first two months' rent before we started to make an income. That must stand for something!' Stella rubs her forehead, and sucks on her dry mouth. The rest of the money from selling her father's house had paid off Stavros' debts. He had taken more than his share. The shop and house should be hers.

'Well, yes, you could use that as an argument if it went to court, but do you want to go down that route?' He says this with excitement, almost to the point of glee.

The swirls of the carpet are now very definitely the sea and the plain. Her father – and he was her father, no matter what any bit of paper says – holds her hand and she stands and walks out, leaving Mr Kleftis scraping his chair back to get to his feet.

'Er, I also forgot to give you this when we sorted out the will.' He hands her a folded sheet of paper which she snatches, he trots behind to escort her from the premises, but all too late as she closes the door behind her.

Stella wanders to the park to be under the shade of the pine trees. The heat is oppressive, the sun high in the sky, her long skirt sticking around her legs as she walks. A mangy-looking cat meanders by, unhurried, sniffing at the bins.

The weekly market along the play-area's edge is coming to its close and the sellers are packing up, vans reversed next to stalls with the rear doors open, boxes upon boxes ready to be loaded, discarded fruit thrown in a pile. There are numerous gypsy vans and trucks parked under the trees, whole families standing around in their bright colours and long floating skirts.

Thoughts of her father not being her blood tear at her chest. The foundation on which she had built her perception of herself falls away, leaving her teetering. One wrong move and she will collapse inwardly like a house of cards, leaving nothing but a remnant of herself. Her terror increases her breathing, and tears run down her face. She slumps onto a bench.

Some children shriek and run past her, barefoot, with uncombed hair, flattened at the back from sleep.

Her father was a gypsy cousin. Was he one of those who had emptied the house? The one who slapped her mother, perhaps? Stella is repulsed by the idea and gags. Is he still alive? She doesn't care. She hates him, whoever he was.

She is all gypsy. That cannot be changed. She cries openly.

The school taunting, the second-class feeling, rush in on her, a gust of humiliation. Another breath, another thought, and she will come undone and she has no idea what will happen then.

'Why are you sad?'

Stella looks up but sees only tears.

'Here, lady.'

Stella wipes the tears, to focus on a lollipop.

'Go on. It's nice, stop you being sad.' The child, with a dark tanned face, smears of dirt on her forehead and round her mouth, thrusts the sucked sweet at her.

Stella forms a sentence in her mind and opens her mouth to speak. A large woman, in a blue and black ankle-length skirt and her hair in a plait to her waist, grabs the child by the wrist and pulls her away. She raps the girl's head with her knuckles and speaks harshly to her. The girl does not cry. She listens.

'Gypsies do not mix with non-gypsies,' the flamboyant mother says.

The girl looks back at Stella, bewildered, and puts the lollipop in her own mouth.

Stella, engrossed in the drama, doesn't notice another gypsy girl, slightly older, who approaches, hand outstretched, palm upwards, until she hears the muttering, a whining, falsely pitiful, begging voice. The only word intelligible is 'money'.

Stella is about to fall into her usual habit of telling the child to go away when it occurs to her that the girl does not see her as another gypsy.

'I'm gypsy.' Stella tries the word out. It feels like a lie. The girl looks blank and continues her whining noise, the final word *"psila"* - loose change.

'Gypsy.' Stella taps her fist to her chest, and cries openly, looking the girl in the eyes.

The big woman with the plait marches towards her. Heels firmly first, the dark bare toes curling and splaying as she walks. Her pace slows as she nears, falters when she sees the tears.

'What are you saying, lady? You are no gypsy. You dress like a *Balami*. You do not speak like a *gifti*.' Her tone is soft but her movements sharp. She flicks her head, a well-practised movement, and her plait writhes like a snake and lands down her back as she takes hold of the wrist of the second child. 'Gypsy is in here!' the woman says, as she puts her hand on her heart, shifting her weight to turn.

'What would you know?' Stella sits straight, tears lost to tight withheld anger.

The gypsy's head tilts to one side, the child holding her hand looks from Stella and back to her mother.

'What do you mean?' She steps closer, sits next to Stella and pulls the child onto her knee, but the girl squirms off to run free.

'My mother is *gifti* and today I find out my father is also *gifti*. Stella twists her hands together, her eyebrows drawn low, her eyes brim with tears, the lump in her throat cutting off her breath.

'Why do you cry?' The gypsy's rough hand covers her own, 'to be a gypsy is only a good thing.'

The knot in Stella's throat will not allow her to answer. The younger child runs over and squeezes between her mother's knees and settles to see her mother's hand on Stella's, soothing comforting. She places her own little hand on top and copies the movements, her big eyes on Stella.

'I do not understand your sadness. You mother is

a gypsy - good! Your father is a gypsy - better! I watch the *Balamoi*, with their clothes and their cars and houses, and I watch how much they throw away. These same *Balamoi* that have so much to put in the rubbish, they turn my children away, who have nothing.' She points to her child's bare feet, tiny next to her own leathered feet, black with dirt. 'Their clothes, no longer fashion so they throw them away. Their children grow, they no longer fit their clothes so they throw the clothes away.' She pulls at her daughter's skirt as if to indicate its origin. 'If the woman sees a new cushion she likes, she throws the old one away. They appreciate nothing and waste everything. It is better to be a gypsy.' the woman takes her hand back but the child now leans against Stella, sucking her lollipop and observing the exchange with a serious expression.

'But you throw your waste by the roadside, paper and cardboard and empty water bottles,' Stella says, thinking of the mess by the way from the town to the village.

'Why do you think that is us?' The woman tries to run a hand through her daughter's hair, to untangle a knot or two. 'I watch, I see the *Balamoi* throwing what they don't want out of their car windows, to keep their lives clean. Then you blame us.'

'And how do you know they are not gypsy? The people in the cars?' Stella's father had driven them so many times into town to the market. 'We are not automatically *Balamoi* just because you don't know us!'

'And Gypsies are not dirty just because you don't know us,' the woman replies, but without malice. There is an awkward silence, but neither woman seems prepared to leave.

'My father is a gypsy.' Stella tries again, it feels less of a lie. 'And my mother.'

'Yes,' she gypsy states, her hands back in her lap, having given up on her daughter's hair.

'Yes,' Stella replies, she looks beyond the gypsy, past what is left of the market towards the hills. 'My grandmother moved into a village. As a help in a cheese factory,' Stella qualifies still looking beyond her immediate world. She is about to continue but the gypsy woman interrupts her.

'How could she do this?' Quick, eager. Stella raises her eyebrows, her focus returns to the park. The child runs off to play.

'Would you? I mean, settle down in a village?' She looks behind the gypsy at the vans with open sides and mattresses inside, televisions angled from the metal ceilings. A breeze drifts through the pines, blowing the needles across the compact earth. The children run, shrieking, in circles trying to catch an empty crisp packet caught in the wind.

'Ha! No village would have us. So how did your grandmother do this?' The gypsy straightens her back, her blouse has several stains down the front and as she raises her arm to adjust it Stella sees there are holes under the arms where the seams have given.

'I think it was because she was on her own.' Stella replies. Behind the gypsy another van pulls in and a group of children explode from the back, with cooped-up energy to spend. 'People feel afraid when you are in big families.' The man gets out of the driver's side, stretches and takes out a cigarette and lights it before running his hand over his wet-looking long hair.

The gypsy woman turns to see who has arrived, nods a welcome to the group. 'It keeps you from pushing us around,' she answers Stella. There is a hint of sadness in her voice.

Stella stretches her legs and stands, and the gypsy, coincidentally, also stands. The gypsy looks down at her. She could flick Stella across the park with her little finger, she is an Amazon, where Stella is a nymph.

'Would you settle down if you could?' Stella asks.

'I have children. You think I want them growing up in blanket houses, not going to school, being treated like they are dirt?'

Stella's mouth opens but no words came out for a second until, 'Why don't you then? Break away, do it.'

The woman looks around her, checking where her family is, but remains standing beside Stella. 'How? Even if we are one family, when we stay, people move us on. We send our children to school and they close the doors.'

Stella swallows. 'I know what it is like to be a *gifti* at school.'

The woman gives her a sympathetic look.

'They stoned me, the other children.' Stella swallows.

The gypsy lifts her hands and lets them drop into the sides of her skirts as if this was inevitable. With unblinking eyes that say more than words she looks at Stella for a long time. 'So you know, you understand, you have lived the life of a *giftisa*. How can we settle, how can my children learn? I cannot teach them, I know nothing.'

'Can your husband not get a job in a village and then you can stay?' Stella suggests. She watches the children, they have sticks now and are batting the crisp bag up into the breeze, batting again before it touches the ground.

'Him?' And she bursts into laughter, a rich, contagious, kind sound, her silky clothes shimmering with the vibration. 'He will never stop travelling, he does not think how it is to cook and clean. He does not think how to keep the children clean. He does not think of their learning. He wants them to be like him.'

She sneers in his direction.

'What does your husband do?' She asks.

"Not much. I run an *ouzeri* in a village. It was a shop that was empty for years so we got cheap rent, now we make a living, or we would if ...' The sentence does not feel worth finishing.

'But you do all the work. The same in my life.' She looks over to her husband. 'But he feels like a man, in charge, and he is happy.' She concludes, her hands on her hips.

'Our lives are not so different.' Stella looks across to the man, who has a big round stomach.

'Can you give me ten euros, then?' the gypsy asks. 'For nappies ...'

Stella transfers her weight onto her back foot.

'Why do you think I am in a position to give you ten euros?' Stella asks.

'You are *Balami* with an *ouzeri*, *Balamoi* has money.'

Stella stares hard at her. 'I am gypsy.'

'If you are gypsy then you must be proud, you have done much!' She turns on her heel and struts back to camp, the smaller child running to her. She hoists the smaller child onto her hip; the bigger one nuzzles into her skirts, under her arm.

Stella has only ever met her mother's gypsy relations. These people are different. They seem less rough, more of a family, cleaner, softer, prouder.

She watches them, until they notice, and then she looks away.

Stella's preconceived maps of her world tumble and spin away, perceptions switching, concepts fizzling, stone tablets cracking. Gypsies are not the bad breed her mother's family had led her to believe, and the '*Balamoi*', as the gypsy calls them, the non-gypsies, are not the clean decent civilised people she had always presumed them to be. Now that it has been mentioned she can remember numerous times she has seen village folk and town people throw rubbish from their car windows, but whenever the accumulated mess is discussed the blame is always on the gypsies and their camps. How many more of her beliefs are skewed like this? Safe has become unsafe; sure, unsure;

trustworthy, untrustworthy. Love has become hatred; friendship, love. Her world spins. Her hands reach up to her head and she looks up into the pine trees, searching for a fixed point.

She pauses to thinks of Mitsos, her rock, unchanging in all the years she has known him. She heard with relief, from Nikos, that he is ok, up and about. He has broken ribs and is in need of rest. She wishes she could go and see him but can think of no seemly pretence. She wonders if he has become close with Marina. Stella decides she will be his friend if that is all she can be, as long as she is near him, the rest of her life.

The word 'love' does not need to be voiced. The feelings are even deeper than that.

'Soul mates,' Stella breathes.

How has that happened, anyway? She liked him, she knew; she enjoyed his company. But for that to jump to more? He has shown her only kindness, not a hint of anything greater. She tries to squeeze him into a father-figure role in her mind but he won't fit. There is something about his square jaw and ample mouth that puts her feelings into the 'unsuitable' category for any sort of family relation. She snorts at the ridiculousness of her situation, quickly turning her head from the gypsies.

It is hot even under the trees. Not ready to face the village, or anything else for that matter, Stella wanders across to where the stall-holders are sweeping up. The aroma of fish lingers. She tiptoes between squashed tomatoes, plastic bags, empty boxes and soft onions. The men sweeping up have little energy left to put vigour in their work. Their days begin before it is light, some of them come from Corinth, others up from Kalamata, it's a long day.

She walks along the line of shops opposite, trying to decide whether her father not being her blood alters the way she feels about him, who he is to her and she to him. He took on a child, a child that was not his, a gypsy. That takes courage, guts. She feels proud of him. He was the hero, and he had picked her out of the ashes and the dirt of her family's heritage. But not so dirty it seems, well, not all of them. The gypsy woman had dignity, a confidence in who she was; she impressed Stella.

How did her Baba see the gypsies? He chose her, and her mother, despite the possible social consequences for him. She takes a deep breath, the tears no longer need to fall. He would not want her despairing. He would expect her to fight, fight her restricting beliefs, fight her fear. Fight Stavros. The pavement turns a corner. She is now walking up March Twenty-Fifth Street, named after Greek Independence Day, when Turkish rule was overthrown.

It feels somehow appropriate.

Somewhere inside Stella feels she has a strange freedom. It is not a happy one, it is too unknown, but nor is it unhappy. Her heart cannot be wrenched any more, and she is surviving. That gives a peculiar freedom. What she had believed to be true – about her father, about Stavros, the ownership of her shop, even about gypsies – all changed. It is twisted and distorted into something else. It could not be twisted further. Yet she is still here, still breathing. It is an odd liberation, a curious letting go.

She stops outside a glass-fronted shop, number thirteen, the inside aglow with pink striped walls. The colours lift her spirits. Not only the colours; she looks further, there is a dressmaker's dummy with an apron on standing by one wall, see-through green Perspex chairs around a shiny table on the other side. It's fun. But best of all, on the clean white open shelves in the window sit the most amazing little cakes Stella thinks, in that moment, she has ever seen. Like tiny works of art.

She does not have a sweet tooth but she is drawn by the aura of success about the business. This is her dream: not a fast-food shop in a village with rocky old tables, sticky floors and nothing but chicken and *giro* on the menu.

The whole place is bright and inviting.

'You want to try one?' A man walks from the counter to the open door. He wears a purple T-shirt with 'Real Men Eat Cupcakes' splashed on the front. Stella has never seen a man in a purple T-shirt before. He has an open countenance, friendly eyes.

Stella is drawn by his positive attitude and steps inside. The shop smells of warm sugar and fresh coffee.

'I am Alex', he states. 'The shop is named after my wife Liz. Liz's Cupcakes.'

All her disturbing thoughts swim away. She blinks. She is drawn by the brightness, of the place and Alex himself, the feel of cleanliness and of success. She is hungry to absorb it all.

Alex is easy to talk to. Liz comes out from the kitchen at the back wiping her hands on a tea-towel. To Stella's delight, she is English.

'Timer's on for fifteen minutes. Oh hello!' she smiles at Stella.

Within seconds the conversation grows animated, Alex's humour makes Stella laugh as she enquires about the business

'So we had weekends here and loved it, but I was training to be an architect and Athens was our home,' Alex relates as he fiddles with a camera he has set on a tripod on the counter. 'Smile.' He puts his eye to the camera. Stella grins, thinks of the gypsy lady and holds her head high.

'What do you do with the picture?' She asks.

'Facebook, if you don't mind, or just here on the wall.' He points to one wall which is covered with pictures of smiling faces and cupcake cases with goodwill messages written on them.

'You opened the shop instead of being an architect?' Stella asks.

'No, well, yes, I had this kind of shop in my mind as a dream,' Liz says. 'So when the economy turned bad and there was no work to be had in Athens we followed our dreams - make or break, do or die.' Liz turns to Alex who grins.

Stella feels slightly jealous at the way they smile at each other. She thinks of Mitsos. Even on a bad day, when he needs his crook to walk, she still relishes the sight of him. It makes no sense.

Liz takes out a magnificent lemon-coloured cupcake from the glass counter and offers it to Stella. It looks delicious, rich, creamy, beautifully presented in its own little bun case. 'Hand-made this morning,' Liz adds. Stella shakes her head. Her stomach is still churning, upset with the earlier emotions. She says how lovely it is to look at and orders a coffee. They all sit on the transparent green perspex chairs. Stella feels she has entered another world, a world of clean and shine, a modern world.

'Yup, these desperate times have called for desperate measures, and so we came here. We had nothing to lose.' Alex jumps at the sound of an alarm and trots into the kitchen. When he comes out he greets a new customer.

Liz looks around and gives the new customer a warm smile.

'Make or break,' Stella mulls over the words until she understands. She pauses and sips her coffee. 'But to be selling cakes in this time when people have no money, how you do this?' she asks.

'With energy and enthusiasm. Facebook, Twitter, and getting into the press.' Liz smiles as if it were the easiest thing in the world. Stella wonders what Twitter is. Behind Liz on the wall are photographs of press releases, pictures of Liz in glossy magazines and Greek newspapers.

She soaks up the atmosphere and Liz's words, like blotting paper. This is what she wants to do. If Liz and Alex can put this small town on the world map with energy and enthusiasm then she can make a restaurant in the village known in the town. That would be enough, for now.

Her secret dream of an international business

comes unbidden. She pushes it away, an unreachable fantasy. She takes the last sip of her coffee and tells herself not to be so ridiculous. If she hasn't got an international business at the age of forty-six it isn't likely she ever will. But the restaurant, she could do something there.

The immovable Stavros hovers into her thoughts.

Liz is tidying the shelves of books provided for customers to read.

'Did you have big, er, *embothia*?' Stella asks Liz in English.

'Obstacles?' Alex translates, smiling as he gives the change to his customer.

'Oh yes, many,' Liz finishes, neatening the books.

'What did you do?' Stella wants to hear a solution.

'We went round them, through them, over them or under them.' Alex wipes down the counter top. The place is spotless.

'They are only obstacles if you focus on them. Keep your eyes on the goals and they are just part of the path, no big deal. Just kept focused, didn't we, Alex?' Liz stands and reties her apron.

Ideas pop into Stella's head for the *ouzeri*. Abby's idea of fairy lights round the tree outside does not sound too crazy sitting here with Alex and Liz. She begins to fidget with her napkin.

A girl bursts into the shop, laughing and greeting everyone, and orders a coffee and a cupcake. She sits opposite Stella and says hello. She too is full of energy. The place seems to generate positivity. She came on her bicycle, wearing a huge yellow helmet, and a pair of Doc Martin boots. She chatters to Alex and Liz, switching from Greek to English and back as the conversation demands. Stella feels transported and excited, she can follow all the conversation and speak as an equal. The girl with the yellow helmet is telling of a film she has seen about Bulgarian gypsies and their Romany music, the wailing clarinets and excited violins. Before Stella has thought she speaks.

'Oh, I am gypsy.'

'Really, how fantastic!' The girl with the yellow helmet says. 'Gypsies have been recycling things a long time before it ever became fashionable, in fact I think the gypsies are the only people who are doing any large scale recycling in Greece these days, collecting scrap metal and so on. Something to be proud of.' She smiles openly. 'And I love your music.'

Stella shuffles in her seat. Being proud to be a gypsy has not ever been a consideration before, but all three of them look at her with admiration.

The conversation drifts to other subjects, each one discussed as energetically and positively as the last, and Stella feels recharged.

The shop is still mesmerising her. If someone else has done it then she can too. She will put lights on the tree, open the second door, have tables on the pavement. Her energy rises within her, she bids them all farewell and promises to return. She knows she will, if for no other reason to charge her batteries, stay connected with the modern world.

She is a little way down the street when Alex catches up with her. She has forgotten the folded paper Mr Kleftis gave her. She thanks him and renews her promises to visit soon.

The gypsies are still under the pine trees. The woman who she spoke to earlier is walking towards one of the vans, her back straight, her head high.

Stella smiles to herself.

In the back of a taxi, on the way back to the village, she looks at the paper.

It is a surprise but it fills a missing piece. Her Baba had left her a goat shed up behind the hill top, she has a vague recollection of its mention when the will was read. It must be the place she remembers, behind the bushes somewhere. It will all be fallen in by now. She scans for the size of the plot. Too small to build: there are laws about land outside the town limits. It must be over a certain size to qualify for planning permission. This plot is far too small and she has no need of a goat shed, in any condition. There is no land with it; it is on forestry land, scrub land. It is worthless. No wonder the lawyer overlooked it.

Maybe the shed would be useful to Mitsos, if he still has his goats.

Chapter 16

The taxi paid, Stella waves at Vasso, who looks up from a book, chewing the end of the pen she is holding. She appears to be really struggling with her accounts. Stella continues to the *ouzeri*. Through the window she can see the outline of Stavros, and her smile disappears. He is talking to someone.

At least he is back from wherever he spent the night, and the shop is open. She moves toward the glass and sees he is talking to is Abby. Stella exhales, her shoulders relax, she looks forward to Abby's company for the rest of the day, she will find the time to talk to her, explain. She checks her sleeves and the hem of her dress to make sure the bruises are covered. Abby will not understand everything, she is too young. She looks through the window again. Abby is in new clothes from head to foot. Stella knows she did not bring them with her, which means they are bought. Is that why Stavros took her into town? A fury passes through her. Their money spent, by him, on her. Stavros raises his hand. It is an odd movement and Stella pauses to watch. The hand moves slowly towards Abby. Stella's heart stops. The hand momentarily strokes Abby's hair, goes behind her head to her neck and he pulls her towards him roughly, his lips meeting hers, his belly pressing against her slender frame.

Stella pulls away. Her vision blurs, ringing in her ears. Her world silently implodes and the implications spread into the past and future, colouring all she knows with an acrid hue. She takes a breath and tries to clear her head but the image of them remains. Until now she had a choice, she could ignore his general behaviour or demand he leave. Now that choice has been taken away. He has already left her.

It had all felt a bit unreal until this moment, too big to be true, the shaking, the fight. Only the bruises kept it from slipping into a fantasy. Hovering in the world of half-truth, Stella had not felt the weight of the reality. She felt she still had a choice, some power. His actions towards her could have been a mistake. He might have apologised, begged for forgiveness, become a new man. The trip to the lawyer could have been an overreaction.

Her world splinters into shards of pain; her heart heaves and her throat closes. The misguided love that remains for Stavros billows with the possibility of its loss until there is only the Stavros of the past, her Adonis, the man who saved her from the village teasing, the bullying.

The true Stavros, the overweight, neglectful, disrespectful slob, fades from her reality in the pain of rejection.

Another breath brings her relationship with Abby to the forefront; the betrayal, the hurt. It is beyond her understanding that people could deliver such pain to a supposed friend just out of … out of what? Is she angry, is this payback? Does she think he would just up and leave with her, erasing twenty-five years of marriage to walk into an unknown world with no job and no money? Or worse, does she expect her, Stella, to be cast out into the world, a woman of an uncertain age with no skills and no savings, into the unstable Greek economy where youth employment is at fifty per cent and anybody over thirty stands no chance of getting any job anywhere if they become unemployed?

Does Abby wish this upon her, is this what she deserves or is this just unthinking youth? Or is she not what she appeared to be, has Stella been deceived? Maybe the British live that way. Maybe the language alone is not enough to understand these people. Maybe in the British culture this is an expected and acceptable way to behave. Maybe they are a cruel and selfish nation.

Well, not in her world! She has spent too long working hard to make the shop work, overcome personal fears of ridicule and torment to be the life and soul - the hub of the farmers' social world - to give it away without a fight, to her or to him.

But what if Stavros wants a fight too, what if he wants her gone, to be alone with Abby? What then? She has no rights over the shop. As his wife, the social pressure is to do as he says. She will be an outcast.

She stands rigid by the wall between window and door, hidden to those inside.

Stella battles with her feelings, then, with steady steps, she quietly enters the shop. She hears the sounds of a table leg being scraped against the floor. She imagines the worst, the lovers splayed over the furniture. Then she hears a squeal. Stella's cheeks colour. There is a second noise. She cannot go through, face the humiliation. But then, the noises, they don't sound quite right.

Without warning Stavros storms out of the back room and pushes past Stella onto the street.

Stella looks from him to the room he has come from, her mouth slightly ajar. She looks out at Stavros who stands lighting a cigarette, before she looks back inside again. Abby appears, her hair messy, her mascara run.

Stavros strides back into the shop and stops short when he sees them standing opposite one another.

He throws an apron at Abby and points her to behind the grill. His movements are brisk, strong. He brings a new sack of potatoes in, which he dumps at

Stella's feet before going outside for a smoke.

Stella looks from the sack, to Abby retreating behind the grill, to Stavros smoking. His shoulders are up, tense, his smoking rapid.

A farmer bustles in and asks Stella how soon his lunch will be ready. She looks at him unhearing.

'You are cooking sausages today? I haven't come into the chemist's by mistake, have I?' He laughs, pulling his loose, dirty, trousers up and running his hands around the waistband so it will straighten.

'Oh, er, yes sorry. I mean no. Sausages, yes, should be ready in …' she turns to look at the grill. 'Now, they are done now. Eat in or take away?'

'You are not with it today, Stella. When do I ever have the time to eat in?'

Stella laughs a brittle laugh and puts four sausages between two pieces of thickly cut local bread. She reaches for the silver foil.

'Am I not to have sauce on today then?' the farmer teases.

Stella takes her eyes from the back of Stavros.

'Oh, sorry,' she says. She takes the top layer off, generously sauces the innards before closing the bread, squashing it flat and wrapping it in foil.

He pays and leaves.

Before Stella has a chance to look at Stavros again, a boy comes in and orders an iced coffee - frappé; the sandwich shop frappé whisk has broken. Stella slips into the familiar actions, her mouth saying the words, her heart dissolving, alone, unloved. The cupcake shop is an unreal dream. Her reality is grim, cold.

Abby stays behind the grill, washing and cleaning.

Stavros sits outside and smokes, his presence permeating inside.

Abby, behind the grill, is shaking, her hands trembling, a fine sweat on her brow. She nearly marched out on the spot but he still has her passport.

She wonders if Stella knows he has her passport.

If she were to leave now, how would she get it back?

What would happen if she couldn't?

She takes a step towards the sink, then stops. She throws the apron at the pots and takes a stiff step back out. She stops again. 'I can't,' she whispers, and faces the sink. She picks up the apron. Its tying ends are soggy, having fallen to the bottom of the sink where the water sits, stinking in the heat.

Surely holding her passport is illegal, but how can she tell anyone? If she does, and they confront him, he could say anything he likes: she wouldn't understand.

She rests on the edge of the sink. She has really screwed up. How can she tell Dad? He will be furious. He might even want to come and get her, which would be a serious failure. He would never trust her, maybe never allow her out again.

But this is scary stuff. Perhaps it would be best if he came to get her. Even going back and not doing her A levels would be better than this.

She starts to cry but holds back any noise. If Stella hears her she will have to explain, tell her what sort of husband she has. Stella might blame her, say she was leading him on. Stella might believe him.

The tears come stronger. She reaches in her bag and brings out her keyring and rubs the teddy's soft body against her face. She should have gone to Saros as soon as she had the money.

She can hear the rhythmical noise of Stella peeling potatoes in the next room.

If she calls Dad and he decides to come and fetch her, what will Sonia say? Dad wouldn't want her to know because of the stress it will cause, the impact on the baby. If anything happens to the baby they will always feel it was because of her. Ringing Dad is not a good option.

She needs some tissue and looks around for the roll of kitchen paper. There is none.

She tries to walk casually from behind the grill. There is no kitchen paper on the counter either. Stavros is sitting smoking outside, his back to the shop. She starts to shake and the tears flow. She puts her hand over her mouth to stifle the noise and backs towards the room with the tables. She turns. Stella looks directly at her, hands paused over the bowl of potatoes, her long sleeves trailing in the cast-off skins, her eyes wide.

Abby looks to the floor hurries past to the toilet where she noisily blows her nose and sits on the lid to think.

She waits. She can think of nothing else to do.

Stella calls something, but not to her. It is in Greek.

It sounds like Stavros' voice from outside answering.

She hears a car door opening, creaking on rusty hinges. The engine coughs, pebbles under the tyres grind, and the sounds heighten then recede as it drives away. Abby breathes out and relaxes her head into her hands, her elbows resting on thighs. All is quiet outside the toilet door. She waits; there is not a sound.

She washes her tear-stained face and, as quietly as she can, she unbolts the door and walks out.

Stella is sitting facing her. No potatoes. No knife. Just sitting.

Abby is rigid. She waits.

Stella looks at Abby from head to foot, her eyes resting here and there, and then she rolls up her sleeves.

Abby watches her eyes.

Still sitting, Stella slowly pulls up the hem of her skirt. Abby blinks. Then sees. Her legs. And her arms. The bruises.

Abby wraps her right hand around her left arm, where it throbs, where Stella's gaze had paused.

Stella stands. Abby takes her hand from her own arm to show Stella the bruise but Stella is nodding her head, she knows. She holds out her arms and, sobbing, Abby runs into them. Her head rests on Stella's shoulder. She is easily the taller, but, at the moment, the smaller of the two.

Abby sobs. She doesn't want to let go. Stella smells safe, feels safe.

Chapter 17

After moments that stretch into hours and back into moments again, Stella gently releases Abby.

She looks behind her and outside.

'He may come back. It is best if you don't see him again.'

Abby sniffs and wipes her nose, running her hand up it from fingertips to palm. Stella, without thought, pulls some kitchen roll from under the counter and tears off a strip and hands it to her.

'Come on, get your things.' With nimble fingers Stella turns off the chip fryer and moves all the food from the top of the grill into a dish. Abby has her bag and stands waiting.

'What are you doing?' Her gaze follows Stella's rapid movements.

'Making sure it's safe to leave.' Stella checks out of the window before she opens the till and takes what money is there.

'You are leaving too?' Abby asks. 'But this is your shop.'

'Your safety, my safety, he has done this twice now, there is nothing to stop him ...' She doesn't bother to finish her sentence as she hurries her habitual closing-up jobs.

The street glare is blinding. The sun bounces off everything white. Stella closes the double doors to the takeaway, locks them and pockets the key. The two of them march through the square and turn as if to go home.

'Is your home a good idea?' Abby asks as she looks behind them, trotting to keep up with Stella's pace.

'We are not going home.' Stella's direction turns towards the church, but on seeing the doors closed she changes direction again and heads out of the village.

'Where are we going?' Abby is panting, her thin muslin trousers sticking to her with the sweat the brisk pace is producing.

'This morning someone reminded me of a place I thought was a dream.' She turns up the track. 'We will be safe there while I think and figure out what we must do.'

'Could we go to the police?' Abby's eyes are wide, her breath is fast.

'Stavros' best friend is a policeman.' Stella

hesitates before her next sentence, which comes out more quietly. 'They would not believe what a gypsy says over what he says.'

'What about my word?' Abby stops walking.

Stella stops too and turns to her.

'I am afraid with those short white shorts you had on they would say you had encouraged him.'

'But they are designer, everyone is wearing them.'

'But not in the village, and not when they are trying to convince the police that someone else has done wrong.' Stella begins to walk again, but not as fast. 'I met a girl some years ago in town. She was just sitting having a coffee. She looked sad so I was nice to her. She was half Greek, half English. I did not speak English then.' Stella lets out a brief laugh but there is little joy in it. 'She said she was chased by a man who tried to grab at her, on a beach that was far away from people. When she went to the police they asked her if she had been sunbathing without a top on. She said no but she had been under the water without a top, which was why she had gone to a beach so far away. "Ah," said the policeman. "So you lead him on, what do you expect?" and that was that.'

Abby gasps. 'That is so sexist!'

'But this is Greece.'

The track steepens and Stella puffs as she tries to maintain her pace. As always, the exertion gives her the illusion of power. She stops to let Abby catch up.

'Do you not do any sport at school?' Stella notices her labouring. Abby smiles and pushes on her knees as she climbs. Her breathing eases as the way levels slightly. The two of them turn with the path, from the gully, up the spine of the hill, onwards until they are at the top.

The panorama lifts Stella's spirits.

'Wow. Awesome. Wouldn't you love to live up here?' Abby rubs one of the bruises on her arm.

The whole of the plain is laid out in one big expanse. The village is a small cluster of red and burnt-umber roofs at their feet, the orange trees neatly lined up in field enclosures. Field, after field, after field, to the towns dotted around the coast, to the blue mountains, the fruit dominates.

Abby brushes off an upturned wooden crate by the track's edge.

'Handy,' she remarks, and sits on it.

'The goat herders have brought it up for exactly that purpose,' Stella replies. She is no longer looking at the view. She has found a stick and is beating at some bushes.

'What are you doing?' Abby stands.

'Looking for a track to take us to those bushes over there behind that rocky bit.' She points to a small summit further on.

'Well, there's one there that leads down.' Abby stands to investigate. 'Look, it goes back up further on, behind those bushes, but then it disappears.'

In Stella's mind the forgotten pictures are like yesterday, her legs moving fast down the hill, running with excitement, ahead of her father; her shoelace undone, her father calling to her, him bending down and, with the greatest of care, tying up her laces, slowly, so she can watch and learn, until one day she does it by herself without being shown. Her mother had thought it was a miracle.

'I remember! I have always looked to go straight across to the rocks from here, but now I remember.'

Abby is transfixed looking at Stella: her eyes are shining, her tense facial muscles relaxing, her brow lifting. She looks like a different person. Like herself but ten years younger.

'Where are we going?' Abby asks as Stella follows the track.

'My Baba would bring me up here.' Her tone hardens just a little, but she continues. 'I was reminded of it this morning. It is an old goat shed, but my Baba had no goats. He would come up here and make candles and soap.' Stella is ahead of Abby and stops while she catches up. 'The candles were just for use in the home. He had a metal table with holes in so he could make a few at a time. The soap smelt so lovely, lemon mostly.'

'Why up here?'

'I don't know. Most men go to the kafenio, but he used to come here. Not often, once, twice a year, for a few days in a row, and he come home smelling of wax, honey and lemons.'

The track peters out. They have reached the rocky outcrop and there is nothing but bushes. The track has released old memories in Stella.

'We go around the back,' she says.

Abby takes the lead and circumnavigates the bushes that grow up against the rocks.

'Oh, look here.' Abby ducks into an opening just the height of a goat. Stella remembers the entrance being higher, an arch of green, her Baba had not crouched. But that had been years ago, there are many more bushes grown since then.

286

She hears a squeal and pushes through the last bit of growth to where Abby stands upright in front of a lean-to shed. Stella remembers the slope of the roof, hanging onto the rocks at its top, pushing back the bushes near the ground.

The door has a rock in front of it to secure it.

Stella pushes it away with her foot and enters her dream. It smells of goats.

Abby waits at the door until the goat smell is not so strong to her. Stella moves, but slowly, memories giving everything significance and importance.

The sloping window in the roof creates a lozenge of light on the floor. Goat droppings form a carpet. They hadn't been there back then. The candle table has been moved, but it is still there, up against the opposite wall now, the soap frames still hanging from the beams above.

'It is all more, how you say in English, not made by factory …' She looks to Abby.

'Hand-made? Rustic?' Abby is looking at the candle-making table.

'"Hand-made" I think sounds right, this "rustic" I do not know.' Stella picks up the melting pot. She remembers it being much bigger. 'More "hand-made" than I remembered.' She outlines with her finger a patch that is welded to the base of the pot.

'It's like walking back in time.' Abby examines everything in the room. There is a second table, a fireplace in the back wall. She looks up the chimney and sees the blue sky. There are heavy iron cauldrons stacked in a corner. 'This would be trashed in England,' she states.

'What is this "trashed"?' Stella has found a stool and sits leaning against the wall by the door, looking around this drab, dusty version of her dream. It does not hold the answers she thought it would. Her face muscles sag a little.

'You know, people would come in and break everything and spray-paint their names on the walls. There would be beer cans on the floor and it would smell of pee.'

'P? The letter "P"?'

'No, pee, piss, urine, wee.'

'Ah, ah, better it smells of goat,' Stella chuckles before frowning. 'Why would people do that, what for?'

'Not sure. What's this?' Abby holds up a heavy pair of scissors with half-moon blades. With a hand on each half she tries to open them but they are rusted closed.

'Oh, I remember those. My Baba would hold the candle and let me cut the candle string.'

'Wicks,' Abby helps, but Stella falls silent for several moments, time playing games, lost to the present before coming to and continuing.

'But they weren't for candle string, they were for cutting the candles themselves, make the bottoms flat. I didn't have the strength for that when I was a child.'

'When did your dad stop coming, then?'

'I am not sure. I don't really remember coming here as a teenager, only as a small child. But I did have gifts of soap still, on my name day, right until I left home, when I was twenty-two, when I married Stavros.'

Abby's right hand comes up to hold the bruise on her left arm. Stella moves a wooden box next to the wall, inviting her to sit.

'He has my passport, did you know?' Abby studies the floor, sitting very still.

Stella shrugs. 'Maybe it is best to tell the authorities you lost it.'

Abby begins to cry.

'*Ti? Ti einai*. What, what is it, do they hurt a lot?'

Stella puts a gentle hand on her bruises.

'My passport, they won't let me go home without my passport.' Abby gives in to her tears.

'Explain to them,' Stella replies, but moves her stool closer to Abby's and puts and arm around her.

'Do you have a passport?' Abby asks, looking up, surprise on her face.

'No. I never have a passport.' Stella strokes Abby's hair back to see her face.

'They cost a lot of money and take ages to get, and someone who has known you for seven years or something has to sign your photograph to show it is you, and I haven't know anyone in Greece for longer than four days which means I can't go home.' Abby takes in a big breath, and as she exhales she cries again in earnest.

'Shh, my little one, shh, not to cry. We will fix this. He is not so clever. Your passport will be in the car cupboard ...'

'Car cupboard? Oh! Glove compartment,' Abby chuckles through her tears.

'Car glove cupboard, in the drawer under the sink in the kitchen or in his back pocket. He puts things nowhere else. We will get it back.' She pauses. 'Glove cupboard like gloves for the hands?'

'Yes.' Abby's tears are subsiding, Stella fishes a napkin from her ample pocket and hands it to her. 'Bastard.' Abby expletes before taking the tissue.

'What is this "bars-tard?"' Stella asks as she takes from her same pocket a mini bottle of ouzo. She takes a nip before offering it to Abby, who shakes her head as she blows her nose.

'It means he is a twat but worse, meaner, nastier.' Abby looks at Stella, no longer crying but her eyes liquid with tears.

'Ah ha,' Stella says slowly, but she has no idea what "twat" means either, although she can guess the general idea.

'What are we going to do?' Abby says, looking around.

Stella looks at the candle-making table. 'My Baba brought me up here. This was his private dream. I think he liked the quiet and the steady work. But before we got here we would look at the view and he would say that I could do whatever I wanted to do.' Stella sighs. 'So I thought here I would find an answer. But all I find is memories. Which hurt.' She takes another breath. 'He was not my father.'

'Sorry?' Abby looks at Stella, puzzled.

'I am not half gypsy, I am all gypsy. "Dirty gypsy",' She quotes, her lips thin, tight. 'I went to the lawyer to see "how the land lies" with the shop and the house and he told me by accident. My Baba is not my father, a gypsy is my father'.

A silence follows until Abby says, 'Wow, harsh. Are you ok?' She wipes the last traces of tears from her eyes.

'I was very upset, but then I met some gypsies.' Stella takes out the ouzo bottle again and has another nip and sits, legs outstretched, her hand holding the bottle, resting on her knee.

'What happened?' Abby asks.

'They didn't see me as a gypsy.' Abby continues to look at her, waiting for more. Stella jolts from her stare to turn to her. 'They are proud people the gypsies, not all rough and "bars-tards" like my family.' She offers Abby the bottle again. Abby shakes her head but continues to look at her. 'The woman gypsy tells me that to be a gypsy must be in your heart. So I think what is in my heart. My Baba, my real Baba, he is in my heart.' She looks around the room and then taps her chest. 'He is in here, and so is the shop.' She looks at Abby, whose eyes are swimming with tears again. 'And you are there.' She smiles and takes her hand. 'And I have found Mitsos is there.'

'Mitsos? The old farmer with one arm?' Abby cannot keep the surprise from her voice.

'Yes, the old farmer with one arm,' she says deliberately.

'Oh. Yes, ok, I can see it. He is very kind.' Abby backtracks.

'He is kind and thoughtful and he has lovely eyes, and he is tall and broad and not all his hair is grey.' Stella screws the top onto the mini ouzo bottle and puts it back in her pocket. 'And if he is in my heart and part of who I am then I am not a bad person. But I will tell you who is not there - Stavros.'

Abby's face tenses.

'Do not worry, my little one. In this searching of my heart when I found Mitsos and you and Vasso, I discovered something. There is a difference between love and, how you say, when you have many thanks for something?'

'Gratitude?' Abby suggests.

'Yes, I will learn this word,' Stella says quite loudly. 'A difference between love and gratitude. For Stavros I never felt anything except gratitude and maybe a little bit of "eros", how you say "sex", when we were younger. But not love. He has never given me reason to love him.'

'Gratitude for what?' Abby has taken Stella's hand in both of hers and is playing with her fingers.

'I think he stopped the teasing for me being gypsy, when I married him. But now I am not so sure. When I saw the gypsy, so proud, you could not tease her. So now I am thinking that the teasing stopped because I had pride, because I walk with my head up after I married him.' Stella sighs and sits silently for a second. 'I think the teasing at school was just kids, but because I let my head drop the children they did it more and it became how it was.' She pauses. 'From my Mama,' she clarifies, 'she always walked with her head dropped. She never looked anyone in the eye.' Again she pauses. 'Because of her family, they were not nice.' She takes a big breath and pushes herself back on the stool to straighten her back, still holding tightly to Abby's hand. 'And here I was about to follow the same thing with Stavros, watching my head drop year after year with how he treats me! I thought I wanted everything to stay the same. And then you came. You came and changed everything.' She pats Abby's hand.

'Me?' Abby swallows.

'Yes, you. If you had not come along none of this would have happened, it would just have continued,' Stella says.

'Oh, I am so sorry …' Abby begins. A tear forms but does not fall.

'Sorry? Why sorry? You are not understanding. You came and took the curtains down so I could see. I am very sorry that you have the bruises but now it is open we can all see. Now we make the changes.' Stella disentangles her fingers from Abby's to embrace her. As she holds her tight, her eyes glaze over with bliss. Her hold becomes more fierce until a new kind of tears fall from her eyes. They finally, gently separate.

'I think this is how I would feel if I had a child,' Stella says. Her face is open and relaxed.

Abby's cheeks redden. She does not say anything, looking to the floor.

'You know what I think?' Stella asks. Abby shakes her head. 'I think that if I had a child things would have been so different. I mean of course they would have been different, but I think that I would have been thinking of the child and not myself. I would not have been thinking what people thought of me being gypsy. I would have held my head up with pride in my child. I think I would have talked to other mothers and forgotten my birth. I would be a mother, not a gypsy. I wonder how long I would have put up with Stavros' way of talking if I had a child?' She looks around the room. 'So!' Stella's voice has energy. 'What will we do?'

'I need my passport,' Abby replies

'Oh yes, ok, we get your passport, and then?'

'Maybe I need to go home, I feel alone here. The only person who speaks English is you.'

'Ok, we can fix that now, come. Enough of this dirty shed.'

Chapter 18

Juliet makes more tea and takes it outside on a tray with another box of tissues.

'So Sonia met him online?' she clarifies.

'Sort of, well yes. She was a friend of a friend on Facebook. Dad found her comments funny and they friended,' Abby says. She looks at the pomegranate trees, their black trunks starkly silhouetted against the whitewashed wall, flowers planted underneath in the shade, pinks, purples and white.

Stella sits silently, her head turning to look at Juliet or Abby as they speak. Occasionally she looks up to the view of the hills beyond the garden wall. The craggy summits call out to be climbed.

'Turned out that she lived in Bradford too,' Abby adds, looking across the patio at the plants in pots. One tall pot's neck glistens, filled with water. A wasp hovers in the cool over the surface. One of the cats slinks towards the earthenware urn and, in one elegant move, places its front feet up on the rim and elongates its neck to drink.

'Bradford! Is that where you come from? I grew up there.' Juliet smiles, the sober mood held on pause.

'No?' Abby's face brightens a little and she turns to look at Juliet, re-assesses her, looking for familiar traits in her face.

'Yes, first seven years of my life. You don't have an accent?' Juliet says.

'Neither do you. I was born in Kent, then we went to live in Warwick. We've only been in Bradford since Dad got the job there, four years.'

'Small world. Stella, more tea? I think it will have brewed now.'

'Yes please Juliet, milk no sugar.' Stella speaks carefully, forcing an English accent. Both Juliet and Abby smile, hanging on to the chance to keep the mood lighter.

They focus on the tea tray, their faces grow stern again.

'So what's the problem - you don't like Sonia?' Juliet's voice falls back into a lower cadence.

'She tries to act as my mum, and then, other times, she acts like a friend, which she's not. But mostly it's Dad.' Abby's voice holds anger, her face fierce.

'Sugar?' Juliet asks. Abby nods and holds up her index finger.

'He says it would be more useful if I stay at home to help with the baby. He says there is no point in doing A levels.'

'Education is never wasted.' Juliet emphasizes her words with the baton of a delicate silver teaspoon, the residual drops of tea falling to the tiled floor, creating dark spots.

'But he sees A levels as what you do to get into university, and seeing as university is not a possibility I may as well stay at home and help Sonia look after the baby.' Abby's eyes are on the fallen tea-drops which widen as they soak in.

'Not possible because you have to pay now, you mean?' Juliet asks. Abby nods before looking up to say, 'That's why I came to Greece. A friend of mine told me about this bar and I emailed the guy. I thought if I could show Dad how I could earn money in the summer to pay for my uni fees he might let me stay on to do A levels.'

'Ah. This is the job that you were trying to get to Saros for, but ended up here instead,' Juliet clarifies. Both Stella and Abby nod. Juliet sits drinking her tea, her eyes not focused on anything outward.

'So, is your dad adamant that you will not stay at school?' Juliet asks.

'It was the way he said it, that it would be better

if I helped Sonia look after the baby. Like I should not think of myself any more,' Abby says. 'I grew up with no mum. When I was tiny Dad looked after me but as I grew it became more even. I did jobs around the house, made breakfast, washed up. I can remember, when I turned thirteen, thinking that I was a teenager and that I must learn to cook properly. So I did. That year I took on the cooking, not just the breakfast, and also the clothes washing. I even took on organising the money, paying the bills and stuff 'cause I am good at maths.' Stella looks at Abby sharply at this comment. 'Dad and I were very close.' Abby stops to drink some tea. Stella opens her mouth to speak but Juliet, almost imperceptibly, purses her lips and raises her eyebrows in a Greek 'no'. Stella closes her mouth and responds with an equally imperceptible nod of agreement.

'Then he started to say I should go out with my friends, find a boyfriend, have more fun. I thought I must have upset him so I worked harder at school to please him and did more at home. But it still seemed like he wasn't pleased with me. So I worked harder still. Then he seemed to relax a little and it was like old times.' Abby grabs for a tissue, pre-empting her next response. 'Then I found out about Sonia and it all fitted. His relaxedness, his happiness was not from me working harder but because he had met her.' She dabs at her eyes.

'And that is how it has been ever since. Sonia

first, me forgotten.' The tears come with noise, and both Juliet and Stella lay comforting hands on her back as she sobs.

'That is hard.' Juliet's voice is soft and kind. 'It sounds as if you feel you have lost him to her.'

'Yes, yes, that is exactly it!' Abby's voice, through her tears, excited to be understood. Juliet strokes Abby's hair until the initial tears subside to a snivel.

Juliet takes a breath and says, in a very measured tone, 'Let's just say you did go to uni, you would make lots of friends ...' She pauses to allow the words space to become real. 'Even if you went to Bradford uni the chances are you would spend all your time either in lectures, in the library studying or hanging out with friends.' She lets these thoughts dangle for a moment before adding, 'Staying overnight with friends, now and again perhaps.' There is a slight pause before she adds, 'There would be a pretty good chance you would meet someone, someone special.' Juliet waits.

Abby looks up at her, curiosity on her face.

'Do you think that all sounds possible?' Juliet asks her.

Abby nods.

'If you met someone special you would probably

want to spend all your free time with them. That's usually how it goes.' She smiles kindly.

Abby's wet eyes are held fixed on Juliet's as she continues to predict the future.

'So with you in lectures and the library all day, and with friends, and maybe someone special, the rest of the time you may make it home just to do your washing or sleeping, unless you bunk on someone's floor.'

'Bunk,' Stella repeats, testing the word. The finality of her pronunciation indicates she has clearly understood its meaning and seems to enjoy the word.

Abby doesn't hear Stella, she is still staring at Juliet.

'If that person is special, who knows what may follow after university? But whether they are or not you could go on to do more education or you could take a job that follows on from your degree. That job could be at the other end of the country.' She takes another sip of tea before asking, 'Do you think that all sounds possible?' Abby nods. Juliet puts her cup down. Stella and Abby wait for what Juliet will say next. Juliet becomes aware of both of them.

'Well?' she asks and looks at them both. 'With no Sonia, where would your dad be when you, the love of his life, are doing all this?'

Abby's eyes widen, her lips part.

Stella sighs her understanding and nods sagely.

Juliet drinks her tea.

The cats bump heads and one begins to lick the other.

A donkey on some distant hill hee-haws his loneliness.

'But he hasn't just found Sonia as a convenience, he says he loves Sonia,' Abby says quietly. Her voice sounds younger than her years.

'We find what we need in life. He may not have known it clearly but he needed to find Sonia. Sonia, and the baby, are his future. You have yours.'

Stella grabs a tissue and dabs at her eyes.

Abby grabs a tissue and blows her nose.

Juliet picks up a cat and strokes it.

'When I started doing my GCSEs I got different teachers that year. It was suddenly all changed.' Abby looks for somewhere to throw her now-scrunched tissue, but finding nowhere continues to hold it. 'Because I began to do so much at home I related more to the teachers.' She smiles and gives a short laugh. 'I swapped cooking tips with my maths teacher and I even gave my drama teacher advice on how to unblock his sink. I felt different from the other kids, but different from the teachers too. Neither one nor the other.

'This was at the same time that Dad first got together with Sonia, and I would see him, he would act one way with her and then another way with me. I accused him of being two-faced but a part of me saw he was in the same position as I was at school.' Abby looks out towards the far mountains. 'But I was … too angry … or selfish perhaps, to admit it.'

With no warning she begins to cry loudly. Stella shuffles closer to her and gathers her in her arms, rocking her, kissing her hair. Juliet puts a hand on Abby's back and pats her.

'And I just left him,' Abby blurts between sobs. 'I told myself I was coming to Greece to prove I could work my way through uni, which is sort of true but … oh Daddy, I came to hurt him. To show him how painful it would be if he pushed me out, if I was gone.' She sobs anew. Stella grabs some more tissues and blows her own nose while still holding Abby.

'I need to call him,' Abby says, sitting upright and breaking free of Stella's comfort.

'Yes, it would be a good idea,' Juliet agrees.

Abby looks expectantly at her. Stella glances

inside.

'But … here's a thought,' Juliet says slowly. 'If you call him now, of course he would be delighted to hear from you, but you are calling him upset and in a tough spot, as they say.'

Abby and Stella look at Juliet as if she is about to predict the future again.

'What if we could sort out the tough spot, and maybe then you could call offering only good news?'

'You have an idea?' Stella asks. Abby holds her breath.

'Oh no, no, not at all.' Juliet's eyes widen. She waves her hands in front of her to dispel any misunderstanding.

'Oh. You sounded like you had thought of something.' Stella sounds disappointed.

'I don't know.' Juliet rubs her forehead. 'I was kind of thinking of the whole thing. Abby needing funding, you needing something to fall back on depending on what happens with Stavros.'

Abby looks up at his name. Stella holds her protectively. 'Let him try!' Stella hisses. 'Oh Juliet, listen.' She adds, 'I learn a new word. He is bars-tard.'

Juliet shakes her head and her eyebrows raise in the middle. 'Well I guess it is a word used often by English people, but I wouldn't use it if I were you.'

'He is bars-tard, even if I don't say it.' She hugs Abby to her. 'Anyway, what you were saying?' Stella urges Juliet on.

'I was thinking of your dad's place. I am glad you have found it, by the way. You have mentioned that memory a few times so I am glad it is a real place.'

'What about my Baba's place?' Stella pushes.

'It was also the look that you gave Abby when she said she was good at maths and did the family bills. You were going to say something?'

'I was going to ask her if she would do my numbers for the shop.'

'Accounts,' Juliet prompts.

'Yes, accounts, but now is not the time to be talking such things.'

Juliet is still frowning. She stands up and goes inside. She is gone for some minutes.

'It's easy, look,' she shouts from inside.

Stella gets up and Abby follows her. Juliet is sitting at the kitchen table with her laptop.

'What's easy?' Stella asks looking over her shoulder at the screen. 'Oh that's like the table for the candles up at my Baba's *apothiki*.'

'"Hut",' Juliet corrects, but Stella does not hear her as she watches the video of a man doing what she remembers her baba doing.

'I love YouTube,' Abby murmurs. The two-minute film comes to an end. Stella sniffs.

'Baba did that,' she says sadly.

Juliet types and presses return, another video. They watch for a moment in silence.

'Yes, look, he will take the frame off and cut the soap now. It used to smell so good.' Stella is almost bouncing on the balls of her feet. Abby smiles at her animation. The film comes to an end.

'We should do it!' Abby says. Juliet smiles at her.

'Do what?' Stella asks. She looks from Abby to Juliet for the answer but it takes her by surprise when it comes from inside herself.

'*Panayia*!' she crosses herself, but as quickly as she is animated she slumps again. 'Who would buy? I can make all the soap and candles in the world, but if no one buys …'

They all stare at the now-still screen. Eventually Abby wanders back outside. She shields her eyes against the sun and wonders how the cats manage in their furry coats.

'*Yia sou, Yia*?' a woman's voice shouts from the lane. Abby cannot see her for Juliet's car but she recognises Vasso's voice.

'*Yia sou* Vasso,' Abby says, using the only Greek vocabulary she feels confident with.

'Abby? *Yiati eisai edo*?' Abby hears the intonation and understands she is asking a question but she is lost as to the meaning.

'Juliet, Vasso's here,' Abby calls indoors.

'Vasso? Really? Oh, I am coming.' The sound of a wooden chair scraping across rough tiles is followed by Juliet's light step.

'*Vasso. Ti kanis*?' Juliet says. Abby looks at Stella who has also come out.

'She asks how she is,' Stella translates over the top of Vasso's talk. 'Ah, it is nothing, some letters have arrived for Juliet, and Cosmas, the postman, has left them at the kiosk.'

'*Yia sou* Stella,' Vasso greets Stella. '*Ti ginetai edo*?'

308

'I love that about the Greeks,' Juliet says to Abby. 'They want to be involved, know what is going on. In England I always feel it would be impolite to ask why someone is somewhere or what's going on.'

Stella speaks for some time to Vasso in Greek.

'Is she telling her about Stavros?' Abby asks Juliet

'She hasn't yet. She is talking about her dad's place and the idea of getting it running.'

'Tea, *Tsai?*' Juliet invites. Both Abby and Stella shake their head.

'Nero,' Vasso requests, and Juliet goes inside to get her some water as Vasso talks to Stella some more. Abby hears the name 'Stavros' and watches a range of fleeting expressions pass over Vasso's face as she is updated. Vasso mutters some words that sound harsh.

'She's telling him the rumours about Stavros when they were first married.' Juliet reappears with a glass of water for Vasso who is now looking at Abby. 'Now she is asking your age.'

The conversation continues. It grows increasingly serious in tone and Vasso begins to raise her voice. Stella calms her down and then suddenly they both laugh.

Juliet doesn't join in or translate. Abby watches the two friends talking. Juliet leans her head back, her face in the sun, apparently in her own world until she exclaims, 'Oh my goodness! Vasso's right. There are more Greeks living abroad than in Greece.'

'So?' Abby asks.

'Well, as Stella said, you can make candles and soap till it comes out of your ears but if you have no one to buy them what's the point? They say tourism's down over thirty per cent. Judging by what you see in the town, I would say more.

'But Greeks abroad are very nostalgic, and Australia is not in recession. There are more Greeks there than anywhere. Stella, do you remember my friend who helped me clear the garden?'

'The illegal Pakistani?' Stella almost sneers.

'Yes, Aaman.' Juliet gives Stella quite a hard look and sits up straight. 'He went back to Pakistan and got a job there writing web sites. Well, he has just emailed me to say he has got a job offer in England. Didn't I tell you?' She turns to Abby, who shrugs. 'Guess where? Bradford! A business somewhere up behind the university.'

'Am I meant to understand something?' Stella asks.

'Vasso's right. More Greeks outside Greece than in, all missing home,' Juliet states.

'Sell to them,' Abby concludes, 'through a web site. I can do accounts and manage the site. I could do it from here or England.' She jiggles in her seat.

'*Ti, ti lei?*' Vasso wants to know what Abby is saying. Stella translates. Vasso replies with a grin and then laughs.

'What?' Abby asks, smiling at Vasso's laughter.

'She has just joined our merry team by offering her olives for the oil for the soap, and apparently she has bees, which I didn't know.' Juliet listens to Vasso for a moment. 'Ah, she says her son had the bees but when he went to Athens some cousin offered to look after them. Huh, in other words they are his now, but Vasso says she has no shame in asking for them back, he has only had them a month.'

'Does she know how to look after bees? Besides, wouldn't we need, like, loads of them for enough wax?'

'No idea, but we can find all this out.' Juliet sounds calm, assured.

Vasso addresses Abby. Abby looks to Stella and Juliet, who both start to translate at the same time, Stella allowing Juliet to finish.

'She says Stella says you are good at adding numbers.' Vasso speaks further and Juliet translates. 'She says if this is true you have a job every year doing her books if you want, she cannot get the hang of it.' Juliet smiles at Vasso.

'And mine?' Stella adds. 'We will pay you, but not as much as the numbers man …'

'Accountant,' Juliet interjects.

'… in town charges,' Stella concludes, ignoring the correction.

'Oh, wow, yeah, that would be so cool. As well as the candle soap thing, you mean, not instead?' Abby says. Stella nods. 'Would I need to speak Greek to anybody to do the accounts?'

'I don't see why,' Juliet says.

Abby smiles as she looks from one face to another.

'You wanted to be like the women in the films, Stella, and run an international business. Bet you never thought it would be in candles and soap.' Abby cannot hide her joy. 'This is like your dream.'

Juliet leans in to Vasso and translates.

'And like your dream,' Stella replies. 'If we do

this and make money you can go to university.'

Juliet mutters to Vasso. Vasso mutters back.

'Vasso says it is like her dream. Someone else to do the books, the olives and the bees, and make enough money to get some help in the kiosk.'

'And your dream, Juliet?' Stella asks. 'Is it your dream?'

Juliet laughs a gentle, pealing sound. She looks across the mountains, she looks around her garden, she looks at the cats and she looks at her friends.

'I am living my dream already.' She smiles, the sun highlighting the red flecks in her blonde hair.

Chapter 19

'The thing is, if it was this easy people would have done it already, wouldn't they?' Abby asks Juliet. Vasso has returned to the kiosk so as not to lose too many customers. Stella sits with her legs tucked under her on the sofa outside, her head leaning back, soaking up the sun, eyes closed. Abby is just inside the doors, in the shade enough to be able to see the screen of the laptop. Juliet is cutting bread to go with the Greek salad she has made. Through the small window in the back door a block of sun spotlights her golden hair. On the dresser behind her is a photograph of two young men standing either side of a pretty girl. One boy has his arm jealously around the girl's shoulder, the other boy has a wider smile, a carefree look. They both look like Juliet. Next to that is another photograph of an Indian-looking man with a kind face and a petite woman holding a new-born baby, the silver frame bright in the shaft of sunlight.

'That was a game I used to play when I still lived in England.' Juliet arranges the bread on a plate. 'When I used to go to the pub with Mick - ex-husband,' she doesn't smile, 'he would be droning on about nothing new so I would listen to all the plans of all the people around me. Pubs seemed to be the place to plan

314

back then.' She tears kitchen roll off in sheets and folds the rectangles diagonally and places one on each of the three plates she has laid out. 'Everyone seemed to have a five-year plan, or a ten-year plan, and they would brag: "Oh, me and Stacey are out of here in five. Gonna live in Thailand. Stacey's been training in Thai massage. We gonna open a salon on the beach. Cheap out there, we will live like kings" or, "Oh we will visit you, me and Kaitlyn are going to open a kennels out in the country. Just need to pay off a bit more mortgage, another five years should do it and then we will sell up and move to the country. Our time will be our own."'

Abby laughs at Juliet's impersonations.

'No recession then. Everyone dreamed. But ...' Juliet bends her knees to reach into the back of a cupboard. 'All these dreamers never did anything. I went to the same pub five years later, and there I was doing the same thing, listening to Mick whining, and there were all these planners, still planning. The five-year plans were still five-year plans, not four or three or two, no countdown. Stella, you want to eat?' Juliet calls as she puts the oil and vinegar on the table and looks over all she has laid out to see if anything is missing.

'Yes, but you did do something, you moved here,' Abby says, standing as Stella languidly walks in.

'And that's what we have in common.' Juliet sits.

315

Abby has hold of the back of her own chair but is looking at Juliet, waiting for more. 'You, you came here too, you didn't just talk about earning a living in the summers to pay for Uni, you actually booked a ticket and got on a plane and ...'

'And made the mistake of getting on the wrong boat to end up in the wrong place.'

'No such thing as accidents.' Juliet offers Stella the salad bowl.

'Course there are. If a man walks out of a building and a piano falls on his head, is that not an accident?' Abby laughs. Stella passes her the bowl.

'No, I mean the ones we do to ourselves. Like ...' She looks across the sitting room. 'OK, like Mick. I caught him kissing someone. Was it an accident I caught him? No, he wanted out of the marriage. We had a party. People started leaving. I felt unwell so I went to bed and let Mick finish up, see the last people out. Later I woke up, no Mick next to me, the house was quiet, but too quiet. So I got up. I was silent. I could have fumbled my slippers on and stomped down the hall, that would have been usual, but I didn't, I glided to the landing, I hovered down the stairs and I went through the kitchen to the sitting room so I didn't have to open any creaking doors and there he was.'

'Harsh,' Abby says quietly.

'Couldn't give a monkey's.' Juliet takes the salad bowl from Stella who is saying, 'What are these monkeys?' to herself. 'But the point is, he could have taken her outside, to her house, even into the dining room which you had to open a door to get into, which would have given him warning. I could have been noisy, coughed, opened a door. If either of us wanted for things to remain the same we could have made that happen. We didn't, we chose that he would be caught, that I would "accidentally" find him, and then things had to change. All subconsciously, of course.'

'So, taking the wrong boat by accident and coming here?' Abby takes a piece of bread, warm from the oven.

'You didn't want the bar job, perhaps?' Juliet says. Stella nods.

'Why are you nodding?" Abby laughs at Stella, whose mouth is full of bread.

'You, in a bar.' She laughs, spraying breadcrumbs.

'What's funny?' Abby's face flits between smiling and frowning.

'I think she is casting a comment on your character.'

'What is this "casting a comment"?' Stella asks, swallowing her bread.

'Cast, casting, throw out a line, like in fishing,' Juliet clarifies.

'I am not fishing, I want nothing back.' Stella stabs a piece of cucumber.

'What about my character?' Abby puts down her fork.

'I don't understand this fishing, but I think that you are a nice girl and like quiet and peace and reading,' Stella says and pops the cucumber into her mouth.

'I like fun, too.' Abby's tone is indignant.

'Would you, though, night after night, drunk English tourist and techno music on full blast so your ears hurt in the morning?' Juliet asks.

Abby shrugs and picks up her fork. 'But I didn't know that there was a job here, so that was an accident.'

'There was no job.' Stella dips her bread into the tomato juice of her salad.

'What?' Abby asks, putting her fork down again.

'Stavros said he wanted a foreign girl to work but

I think he wanted me to catch him kissing like Mick.'
Stella puts her own fork down and sighs. 'But I said
no. Maybe I was not ready to catch him kissing. Then
you are here, and Vasso had heard Stavros talk.' There
is no joy in Stella's voice and Juliet gives her a sad
smile. 'Vasso sent you over and I try to make you
leave.'

'Oh my God, yes, you were hot and cold. I
thought you were just a bit nuts.'

'Nuts? Like pistachio?' Stella asks.

'No, like mad,' Abby says.

'Mad, nuts, ok. Crazy language.' Stella mulls and
presses a large lettuce leaf into her mouth.

'So how come you let me stay?' Abby asks.

'I like you, and I didn't think you would be
kissing him.'

'Argg.' Abby shakes her head at the memory.

'I am sorry, Abby, I should have told you to
leave at the beginning.' Stella puts her hand on Abby's
arm.

'You tried.' Abby laughs.

'But not enough,' Juliet interjects, 'and now you
caught Stavros out and you and Abby will start a

business together which fulfils both your dreams, which you have to do now to prove that my theory is right and there are no such things as accidents.' Juliet raise her water glass. '*Yia mas.*'

'*Yia mas,*' Stella replies.

'Cheers,' Abby says.

They eat in silence for a while.

'So to make the business happen, if it was that easy why doesn't everyone do it?' Stella asks.

Juliet and Abby laugh.

'I just asked that when you were outside,' Abby says. 'Juliet pointed out that if you just get on and do things they change from plans to being real. That's what most people don't do.'

'Like Onassis,' Juliet says. 'Suppose Onassis was the born the same year as Stavros and they discussed shipping plans way back when they were both young. What would have happened?'

Stella laughs at the thought. 'Stavros would have drunk another ouzo and fallen asleep dreaming and Onassis would have gone out and bought his first rowing boat.'

'Exactly!' Juliet puts her fork down and leans

back in her chair, which she edges out of the sun that streams through the back door.

'Ok, so we do it.' Stella drops her chin onto her chest. 'But what of Stavros and my *ouzeri*?'

'What about my passport?' Abby ask.

'What about your passport?' Juliet says.

'Stavros has it,' Stella replies.

'He said he needed it, I presumed for something official so I could work for him. I haven't seen it since.' Abby pushes her plate away from her and looks away from the table, swallowing with difficulty.

'I told you, it will either be in his back pocket, in the glove cupboard in the car or in the drawer under the sink at home.'

'Right.' Juliet stands. Stella's mouth drops open. Abby looks up, her eyes wet and frightened. 'For goodness' sake, there are three of us.' Juliet states 'We will start at your home, Stella. If it is not there we will check the car and only as a last resort will we confront him. OK?' Stella looks at Abby.

'We'll go, Juliet. Abby can stay here.' Abby visibly relaxes. A cat jumps on her knee.

'I could clear the table and wash up,' she

suggests.

Juliet slips on her flip flops. 'Come on, Stella.' She marches towards the gate. Stella hurries after her. They turn to close the metal gate, which neither latches nor locks but gives a vague sense of security, when Abby comes running towards them.

'Wait, I'm coming.' She squeezes through the opening and they leave the gate ajar. Juliet winks at her and smiles.

'Good for you, Abby. Don't be scared ...'

'... of the bars-tard.' Stella finishes the sentence. Abby giggles and they walk in silence.

As they approach the square Stella sees, from a distance, Mitsos shuffling in the direction of her takeaway. She gasps. Juliet turns to her.

'You ok?' She follows Stella's gaze and sees the man with the cane and the slight stoop. 'Is that Mitsos? I am glad to see him up and about. You know he came to see me the other day, to get something translated. Nice man, old fashioned.' Stella does not answer. Juliet looks back to Stella's face. The focus of her eyes betrays the content of her heart. 'You are kidding me,' Juliet states as she reads Stella's features. Stella breaks her stare.

'Kidding, like kid, like goat, or like child?' Stella

is not focusing on Juliet. She is looking at the empty square where Mitsos was.

'Kidding, teasing, joking.' Juliet is still searching Stella's face. 'But you aren't, are you?'

'He is very kind to her,' Abby interjects. Stella glares at Abby. 'Well, he is.' Abby stands her ground.

'Well I …' Juliet begins. 'He seems a very nice man indeed,' she concludes, and after a small hesitation adds, 'and you deserve a nice man.'

They agree to nip up a side street that takes them on the smallest of detours to avoid the front of the kafenio which abuts the tiny cheese factory. At the back there are two small windows.

'That is the window of my grandma's room,' Stella says as they pass. She lifts her head a little higher and her back becomes a little straighter. 'My gypsy blood,' she says in a quiet but strong voice. 'We have good music and do lots of recycling,' she states.

The detour turns back to the square. They hurry past the rubble of the shop on the corner, hoping that Stavros is not sitting in his thronal position in the window surrounded by the farming men. None of them looks back to check until they are hidden by the corner wall of Marina's house. Juliet is the bravest and the first to look.

'No,' she says in a flat tone, 'He's not there,' and they hurry on to turn down Stella's lane, past Vasso's house. Stella takes Abby's hand to reassure her. She lets go when she sees Stavros' battered car is not there, although as he sometimes leaves it outside the *ouzeri* its absence is no guarantee that he is not at the house. She stops walking, Abby just behind her.

Juliet puts a hand up to shield her eyes from the sun as she looks at them. 'He is not going to do anything if we are all here together. If he is in there we will just walk out again, ok? No confrontation. Just turn and walk away. We will get the passport some other time. Agreed?'

Stella and Abby nod. Stella takes Abby's hand again and pats it with her other hand before they walk on. Stella only reaches Abby's shoulder.

The porch is as it has always been, but for Stella it seems different, cold, empty, unknown.

Juliet pushes open the door.

'*Yia*?' she calls into the shaded darkness. There is no response.

Stella looks round the kitchen. There are no signs of the horrors that now arc between her and Stavros. The static of their silence. The room strangely echoing, with one half of the double bed on its side, the thin mattress hanging over it.

'I'll wait outside,' Abby says, and turns to sit on the porch step in the blazing sun.

Juliet opens the drawer under the sink. She pulls out a ball of string, several screwdrivers, a pack of cards, a hammer, some receipts. She pushes her hand into the back of the drawer and pulls what's left forward.

'No, not here.' She bundles everything back into the drawer and pushes it shut. A screwdriver handle jams it from closing but she is walking away and does not go back.

'Where else?' Juliet asks.

Stella is standing by the fridge, having taken down a photograph in a frame that was displayed on its top. Juliet looks over her shoulder to see Stella looking childlike in a long white dress that is clearly a little on the big side for her, Stavros slim, standing tall, looking handsome by her side in a suit.

'Bars-stard.' Stella spits, the 'a's long and running into the 'r's.

'Try to really force the 'b', saying the "a's" as in slap, and cut the second syllable as short as you can - Bas - tad!' Juliet demonstrates in a strong Yorkshire accent.

'Blastad,' Stella shouts, and flings the photo of

her wedding on the floor and stamps on it with her thin sandals.

'Mind your feet.' Juliet pulls Stella's arm a little.

Stella kicks the remains under the fridge and crunches over the glass fragments to open the bedroom door, Juliet right behind her.

'Which is his?' Juliet waves her hands at the built-in wardrobe and the free-standing chest of drawers.

'He has the three drawers inside the wardrobe.' Stella opens the door. The wardrobe has hanging space next to the drawers. Above, as the built-in wardrobe is floor to ceiling, there are empty unreachable shelves.

Stella pulls out the drawers roughly and flings them, upturned on the bed. Boxer shorts, mixed with socks, familiar items that she has washed a hundred times now threatening her with their inanimate presence.

'What's up there?' Juliet points to the shelves above.

'Nothing.' Stella sighs. Juliet hurries into the kitchen and returns with a chair.

'What if he comes back? I think we should go,' Stella says in Greek.

'It doesn't matter, don't worry,' Juliet soothes in Stella's mother tongue as she pushes the chair up against the cupboard and climbs onto the seat.

'Oh! There's a shoe box.' Juliet reaches.

'Leave it,' Stella says.

'What?' Juliet pulls the box to the edge and takes it in both hands and climbs down from her pedestal.

'Guys!' Juliet jumps as Abby walks in the room. The box slips from her hands. Stella watches it fall but makes no attempt to catch it. As the corner hits the tiles Stella puts her hands over her face and turns away. Abby's jaw drops open. Juliet's hands scramble mid-air but do not manage to retrieve the box or lid. The lid slides from the top of the box as it falls and hits the floor to skid across and under the bed. The box splits on the corner it lands on, the weight of the contents spreading out of the sides, and the floor is filled with photographs.

Stella does not turn to look but begins to sob.

Abby's hand covers her mouth.

'Oh my goodness!' Juliet freezes for a second before turning to comfort Stella.

Abby reaches into the disgusting pile and retrieves her passport with finger and thumb and wipes it on her trousers, as if it is physically dirty, before putting it in a pocket.

'Did you know, Stella? Is that why you said leave it?' Juliet's voice has a small edge of hardness even though her hand is around Stella's shoulder.

'No!' Stella's voice is high-pitched. 'No,' she says again at a lower tone. 'Not until you told me there was a box. Then I knew.'

'You knew!' Abby's voice has tears behind it.

'No.' Stella repeats. 'I didn't know about the box. How could I? Even on a chair I cannot reach up there. But when Juliet said there was a box ...' She begins to shake before another round of tears takes away her control. It takes some minutes before her breathing steadies. Her words come out staccato, sobs in between, 'Part of me has always known. After we were married,' she pauses forcing the tears back, 'we lived in his village. In the beginning there were rumours,' she sniffs, Abby puts her arm around her, Stella looks up into her face 'a girl who was too young.' She bites her lip to hold back more tears. 'People looked at me with strangeness in their eyes.' Abby squeezes her and kisses her on top of her head. 'When I was introduced as his wife in the church that Sunday it was as if everyone breathed out, relaxed, and then I heard no more rumours, although I was asked several times my age.'

'It's ok to cry.' Juliet squeezes her shoulders.

'No, I will not give him tears, look.' She turns and faces the photographs on the floor. 'Look at that. Look at those children, who cries for them? We lock people like Stavros up but it does not stop these poor children from having memories. People seem pleased to lock people like Stavros up for ten, twenty, thirty years. But who cares, put them in a hole and leave them, the people should spend their energies to show these children that the world is not like this.' She kicks at the multi-coloured shining pile. Her legs lose strength and she sinks to the floor crying.

Both Abby and Juliet sink with her and hold her one on each side, all three heads close together, all three crying, until Juliet pulls away and shuffles the photographs into a smaller pile and turns the top ones over so they cannot see the faces.

Stavros' wheels grind against the kerb as he pulls in alongside the *ouzeri*.

On seeing the double doors closed and no movement within, the muscle under his eye twitches. His hands tremble slightly.

'Pacifying and grovelling to people over money.' He huffs at the steering wheel. 'Flirting gypsy.' The words expelled as he pulls the keys from the ignition.

'At least keep the place open!' He climbs out of the car. 'Useless foreign girl, where is she?' He surveys the street with a sweeping glance as he strides to the shop doors, ignoring the cluster of waiting customers.

'Hey, there you are.' One of a group of three farmers greets him. 'Thought we were not to have any lunch today.' He laughs easily and his friends smile.

Stavros does not speak but opens the double doors wide and hastens to poke at the grill, hoping it hasn't gone out. The sausages are warm on the end bars and the chickens are cooked, wrapped in silver foil to keep them warm. He flicks the chip fryer on and looks around for the chips. There is a bowl of half-peeled potatoes.

'*Panayia*, the lazy half-caste,' he mutters.

'Hello, chicken and chips for two, please.' Someone walks past into the restaurant. Stavros does not turn quickly enough to see who it is.

'Two *giros* with everything, please.' A boy's hand is visible, reaching over the counter with the money. 'Mama says I have to hurry because Grandpa gets grumpy when he hasn't eaten,' the hand enlightens.

'It'll be done when it's done,' Stavros snaps.

'Nektarios, is that you?' The words are called

from the restaurant. Stavros hears the light step of the boy's feet as he walks through to the speaker, and then the boy addresses the caller as 'Uncle'.

Someone else comes in. He can feel them hesitate, hear them scuffing their shoes as they balance their weight. He looks up from the peeling of the potatoes: it is that Mitsos. Mitsos leans his crook against the wall and stands tall to pull his trousers up. Stavros notices that they are not his working trousers. Is he done up like an Easter lamb for the baptism or for seeing Stella? The twitch under Stavros' eye intensifies and he picks up the poker.

'She's not here,' he snaps. Mitsos straightens quickly from his adjustments and begins to shuffle away. 'Take the dirty gypsy,' Stavros mutters under his breath. He notices Mitsos has forgotten his crook. 'She's only good for a cripple,' he adds. The courage to say it loud enough for anyone to hear eludes him, the words held tightly between clenched teeth, the meanings running inward, twisting his stomach.

A call from the inner eating area: 'Mitsos. Hey Mitsos, is it true that it is your nephew's baptism tomorrow?' But Mitsos is out of earshot, retreating to the kafenio as fast as his disconcerting balance will allow. Another farmer answers the questioner.

'Yup, and the whole village is invited, every man, woman and child. Food in the square. Which may well be served before my chicken and chips, eh Stavros?'

Stavros looks up.

'What? Everyone's invited?' Stavros asks. The farmer nods.

Stavros turns back to the peeling. If she has gone off to stay with one of her friends, he will wait and see tomorrow. She won't miss a baptism, flirting about, and the girl will not be leaving - he has her passport.

The chips hiss and spit as he throws them into the fryer.

Chapter 20

The baptism is in progress and Mitsos will be there.

Stella had not realised that she had been holding on to the thought of being with Mitsos at the baptism, maybe standing with him, cutting his food for him at the feast in the square. She wonders how close he has become to Marina in his convalescing. Maybe he has confessed his love to her. Maybe there is no room in his life for Stella now. But maybe there is. People change. He had not spoken to Marina for so long. What had her Baba said? 'Love is five per cent attraction and ninety-five per cent proximity.' Well, they had been nowhere near each other long enough for anyone's love to die. Stella will allow herself hope.

She brushes the last of the years of dirt out of the door.

'It's looking good,' Abby announces. Stella looks around her Baba's hut. It seems bigger than when they first discovered it. The crates and broken chairs they have stamped into firewood and piled by the chimney. The candle table sits centrally. Now only a light mist of dust dances in the shafts of light beaming through the roof window.

'You did a good job with the window.' Abby looks up at the clean glass.

'It will leak when it rains though, always did,' Stella answers, her tone flat.

'What's up?' Abby asks, moving nearer to Stella.

'Nothing.' Stella shrugs and leans the brush against the wall.

'Are you tired? I couldn't get to sleep for ages in Juliet's spare room.' Abby yawns.

'No, I slept well, the sofa was very comfortable,' Stella says.

'What do we need to do now?' Abby hugs herself as she looks around the room. Stella's forehead creases as she thinks.

'We cannot do anything. The bees don't give up their honey and wax until September and the olives stay on the trees until the same time, maybe later. We can't really start with the candles and soap until the end of the year.'

'Oh.' Abby sits heavily on one of the last intact wooden chairs. 'Is that why you sound a bit sad?' she asks. The room is all pale browns, with bare wooden walls, wooden workbenches and compacted earth floor. Stella's dress swirls with similar colours, her hair

334

the same darkness as the back of the fireplace which is built around a hollow in the rock that the shack leans against.

'No, I was thinking of the baptism.' Stella sits on an unbroken crate. 'We need more chairs,' she adds. Abby nods.

'Why does the thought of the baptism make you sad?' Abby stands, shakes her legs out. The colour of her blue wrap-around trousers is diffused in the interior light.

'I thought it would be good fun, to dance a little, spend time with people, with Mitsos,' Stella says.

'Ahh,' Abby replies knowingly.

'Well, we cannot sit here until September waiting for the bees,' Stella says with energy. 'We should go to the baptism party. Stavros will do nothing in front of the people.'

'If we cannot do anything until the end of the year, beginning of next year, what are you going to live on?' Abby asks.

'I was thinking this too. I need to get the *ouzeri*.'

'How?'

'I do not know.' Stella loses her smile.

'Maybe we could just be there, and when someone orders something put the money in our pockets instead of the till. Always be together, watch each other's backs until he sees there is no money for him,' Abby says as she opens the door and the sun brightens everything.

'I don't think he will give up that easily. But we will think of something. Come. Let's go to the party.' Stella jumps up from her crate and links arms with Abby, only to let go again as they cannot both get through the door at the same time.

Striding down the hill, gravity speeding their steps, they chatter about the business. It is decided that when Abby comes each summer that is when most of the candle and soap-making will be done. The more they talk the firmer Stella becomes that one way or another she will get her *ouzeri* back, it can fund the candles and soap making in the early years. They touch on the olive picking they will do and of pulling Mitsos in to advise them about bees - he is sure to know. Their voices grow strong with their planned future and their stride does not decrease as the hill gives way to the flat ground. Stella asks Abby to tell her again what she would do to improve the *ouzeri* and their ideas flow. Stella gets excited at the description of fairy lights wrapped around the tree outside the main door.

Stella holds Abby's arm a little tighter as they

enter the village. People are spilling out of the back of the church, but Stella guides Abby past the throng and into the square where Theo and some helpers are laying out tables under the shade of the palm tree. The drinks-fridges and ice-cream freezers of the kiosk are all closed with their metal shutters. There is nothing on display to be sold. But the window to the inside where the cigarettes are stored is open even though Vasso is not there.

'Vasso will still be at the baptism. She will sell a lot of cigarettes and cigars today,' Stella informs Abby as they walk on to the *ouzeri*.

'Won't he be there?' Abby asks, looking towards Stella's shop.

'No, who will buy chicken and chips when they can have roast lamb for free at the baptism?' Stella laughs and unlocks the door and leaves it ajar as they go inside. She opens the till, takes out all the money and gives Abby the two days' wages and the tips she would have earned had things been normal. Abby protests but Stella insists, they must start off on a good even footing. Stella pockets the little that is left.

She rolls up her sleeves, the bruises a dirty yellow now, and takes the chicken cleaver from the counter. 'Right, now we will do something!'

'What are you going to do?' Abby asks as she

puts her bag down on one of the rickety wooden tables and follows Stella into the restaurant part. Stella does not reply, but after drawing back the bolts on the restaurant door she runs the cleaver down the painted-over gap between door and frame that seals it shut.

Abby understands. She grabs the thin-ended poker from the grill and uses it to ease in the gap Stella is creating, once jammed in she uses her weight to lever at the door. The sound of paint cracking gives hope but the whole thing seems solid.

Stella stands back and sighs. Through the window she can see where Marina's corner shop once stood, the shop the widow had started and run by herself after her husband so tragically died. She wonders what Marina will do now, but she feels sure she will find something, she will not give up. Even if she is Mitsos' love, Marina's strength, determination and living as a single lady inspires her. Stella sets about the stuck door afresh. Her renewed vigour increases Abby's energy and together they hear more paint cracking.

'Even if it breaks!' Stella puffs, using all her weight on the meat-cleaver to jimmy the door. Abby wedges the poker in at the bottom of the door and together they force it as hard as they can. With a crack, it opens wide enough for them to get their fingers around the door's edge and the two pull, smiling at each other. The hinges object, but the pressure proves too much and it eventually gives, the door stands open, the sun lighting up the pale green interior and highlighting the layers of grease and dust. Abby and Stella grin at each other. Directly outside the door is the tree they intend to decorate with fairy lights, an area around it for tables by the road.

'*Panayia!*' Stella exclaims as she turns around to see inside the *ouzeri* in the sunlight.

'You had better call on all your saints and gods.' Both Stella and Abby jump at the sound of his bass grumble.

Stavros stands in front of the takeaway counter, hands on hips. He has a white shirt on with shiny white vertical stripes which only aid in accentuating his round stomach. Dark patches circle his armpits. Stella recognises it as his only good shirt and concludes that he has been to the baptism. She wonders why; he hates social gatherings.

Abby looks at Stella, but Stella seems to be lost for words.

'Get out!' Stavros barks.

'You are not having it!' Stella finds her voice and it is louder than she expects. She stands taller with the volume, and Abby stands by her side facing Stavros. His face turns a deep red and his eyes begin to bulge more than usual, their blue irises a harsh contrast against the bloodshot white of his eyes.

'It was my father's house we sold. You got your share paying off your debts. The *ouzeri* and the house are mine.' Stella can see the raised meat cleaver in her hand shaking. Part of her mind wonders whether it is with fear or rage.

'Stupid gypsy. Go live under a blanket. I am the man, you are only a wife, you do as I say. Now go, get out!' Stavros spits.

'*Esy fige*. You go!' Stella repeats the phrase, the second time in English out of spite, knowing he hates what he doesn't understand. Abby turns her head towards Stella momentarily at the surprise of hearing English. Her pride in Stella results in her taking a deep breath, her chest puffing out, her arms held out from her side, her grip on the poker firm. She faces Stavros, ready to defend her friend. But Stella does not stand sure. He is the man. She knows he will force her to leave. This time the stones being thrown are verbal but they hit with the same sting. She will be treated like her mother was, and her mother before her.

Stavros takes a step towards Stella. He raises his hand. Stella drops the meat cleaver. She is shaking all over.

His hand swipes at her face. Abby steps forward, the poker between Stella and Stavros. His blow catches the moving poker, knuckles taking the force, the skin tearing, the poker rebounding towards Abby who blocks it with her other arm.

'Stupid *Putana!*' he swears at Abby, his eyes on fire, white flecks of spittle gathering in the corner of his mouth as he turns back to Stella. 'What do you think is going to happen?' he shouts. He shakes with adrenaline and rage, his eyes black, dead like a shark's. 'With one word from me the farmers will no longer come, the business will stop. No man will side with a gypsy over someone who drinks coffee with them in the kafenio. Besides I have this.' He draws from his back pocket a folded piece of paper. He laughs.

'I saw the lawyer Kleftis today at the baptism, he told me you had gone to see him, you scheming minx, he also told me neither of us can claim the *ouzeri* because neither of us have a written lease.' He unfolds the paper, it looks like an invite to the baptism but it has writing on the reverse. 'Two rows back was our landlord, he was very happy to oblige, so the *ouzeri* is legally in my name, what, my dirty little gypsy, will you do now?'

Stella grabs for the meat cleaver, her anger flaring. She lunges towards him. But she is small, her reach is short. Stavros grabs her wrist and shakes the cleaver to the floor as if hers were the grip of a child. Abby raises her poker but she cannot bring herself to strike. Instead, she prods him hard in the stomach. He exhales and Abby takes his attention.

Stella stamps on his foot. He reaches out and grabs her by the hair. Abby prods him again, harder. He grabs the poker, twisting it from her grip, but she hangs on. He has Stella's hair in one hand, Abby attached to the poker held in the other.

For a second they are held in time. Stavros snorts with rage and exertion. Stella's hands prize between Stavros' fingers in her hair. Abby gazes into Stavros' eyes, refusing to let go of her end of the poker, afraid of what will happen if she does.

'Stop!' A voice from through the newly open door behind Stella and Abby breaks the standoff. Vasso enters, she is holding something above her head, waving it. Stella and Abby pause their struggle to look at her. Stavros releases Stella's hair. 'I think, Stavros, that perhaps you should leave and not come back - ever.' Vasso speaks clearly, but her voice wavers on the final word.

Stavros' sights are on the little maroon booklet Vasso holds above her head.

'Abby's passport,' Vasso says. Abby recognizes her name and the word '*diavatirio*'. She glances to her bag which lies open next to Vasso on a table.

Stavros' eyes grow wider, a glance of malice to Stella, the person who shares the wardrobe with him.

Stella looks back with a sneer of disgust. Stavros turns his shoulders to face her, his left eye twitching, the colour in his face deepening, his free hand clenching into a fist. He pulls the poker free of Abby's grasp, her weight pulled forward until she overbalances and grabs a table to stop herself falling. He lifts the poker and points the end at Vasso's face.

'You give that here!' he makes a little jab with the fire iron.

'She's under-age, Stavros!' Vasso shouts.

The poker lifts, ready to swing, rage in his face.

'If you had done the maths you would have realised,' Vasso says quickly, shrilly. There is a high-pitched edge of panic.

'What are you talking about?' He dismisses her with the curtness of his question but the poker is lowered slightly.

'This.' Vasso holds the booklet towards him, her finger pointing out a date next to the picture of Abby. Stella looks away from Stavros, interested in what Vasso has to say.

'Her date of birth. Stella, ask Abby if Stavros tried to kiss her or touch her.'

Stella relays the question in English. Stavros

watches in horror. Abby nods her head.

Stavros lowers the poker. He scowls at them all under his brow, guttural noises like a dog, the poker not lowered to the floor, still holding its menace.

'Under-age, Stavros. Fifteen years old.' Vasso sounds triumphant.

Stavros rocks back on his heels, his chin jerking upwards. Stella searches Abby's face, trying to reassess. 'And we have a few other items that we can call as evidence if Abby's word is not good enough. In fact I think it is time we called in the police.' Vasso feels through her pockets for her mobile phone.

Stavros lunges at her, a hand towards the passport. Stella grabs at Stavros' shirt sleeve to stop him, Abby grabs the shirt tail. But his momentum urges him forward toward Vasso.

Stella pulls harder, Abby makes a second grab, Vasso steps backwards and in the moment he twists in an unexpected way and falls on his face.

Mitsos stands in the doorway calmly pulling his shepherd's crook out from the tangle of Stavros' ankles.

'I just came back as I felt the need for my crook,' Mitsos says simply.

Stella grins at him. He puts the end of the crook in between the shoulder blades of the prone Stavros.

'Or I could not call the police, and leave Abby's father to do that when he arrives tomorrow. He flies out tonight, I believe?' Vasso looks to Abby for confirmation.

At the mention of a father Stavros twists his head and tries to look up at Abby.

'Abby, just nod your head,' Stella says, knowing that Abby will not understand a word of all that is being said in Greek. Abby nods, looking Stavros in the eye.

Vasso puts the passport down her blouse to nest in her ample bosom and takes her phone from her apron pocket and presses the button. 'I think it is time to call the police,' she says. Mitsos takes his crook from Stavros' back and picks up the folded piece of paper Stavros had brandished earlier.

Stavros, scrabbling to his feet, goes red, his eye bulge and he begins to back away.

'I suggest you go a long way away.' Vasso lowers the phone and holds it against her chest while she speaks. 'The police are always just a phone call away. When Abby's father arrives he will want to file the charges even if you have gone. You will be a wanted man.

'My advice would be to leave and go very very far away because round here they are going to look for you.' She turns her attention to the phone. 'Hello, yes, police. I would like to report an assault on a minor. He was in the village but I understand he has just left.'

Stavros glares at Stella, his rage expressed in his contorted features. He turns and faces Mitsos.

'Take the slut, she's only fit for a cripple,' he slurs into Mitsos' face, his nose almost touching Mitsos' in threat before he hurries outside and swings open the grating car door. Stavros jumps in, forces the ignition, rams his foot to the floor and the dust kicks up, hiding the world from view as he speeds from the village.

The shop seems suddenly silent, the four of them facing each other. Vasso puts her phone away.

In the quiet Stella turns to Abby and says in English, 'Fifteen?'

'What?' Abby replies.

Stella grabs the passport that Vasso is retrieving from her bosom and thrusts it at Abby. 'It says you are fifteen! Why did you lie to me?' Her voice cracking, she begins to shake.

'What are you saying?' Vasso asks in Greek, trying to lower Stella's arm which holds the passport up to Abby's face.

'I am asking her why she lied to me about her age,' Stella says quickly in Greek.

Vasso lets out a shriek of laughter.

'It is not Abby who lied, it is me.' Her shoulders shake as the laughter grips her. 'I knew Stavros would not have looked at the date of birth.' Stella turns the passport so she can read it for herself and she too begins to laugh.

'What's going on?' Abby says.

Mitsos watches Stella slowly cut up his food at the party in the square. Juliet is crying with laughter as Abby tells her what has happened. Abby has just got to the bit where Stella, Vasso, Mitsos and she had looked at the supposed lease Stavros had dropped, drawn up on the back of one of the baptism invites, to find it was nothing more than one of Theo's feast preparation lists. Juliet cannot catch her breath for laughing.

'So the bit about her father coming out to Greece, Vasso, was that a lie too?' Stella asks.

'Not only that, but my mobile has no battery, hasn't worked for weeks.' Vasso tips back a glass of wine and then gets up to trot over to her kiosk.

Someone is waiting to buy cigarettes, maybe cigars.

Mitsos asks Stella no questions about what has been going on. Stella asks no questions about Marina, who waves to them from another table. Mitsos takes the fork from Stella as she finishes cutting his food, their fingers intertwining briefly. Her eyes meet his and she smiles.

Chapter 21

The baptism feast is enjoyed by the whole village. The white tablecloths flutter in the slight breeze, children in their best Sunday clothes run between tables chasing one another. Theo hands out bottles of wine to each table to make sure no one runs dry. The butcher, who has set up a table inside the kafenio, carves endless slices of tender flesh from a roasted half pig, which are laid onto waiting plates. These are taken in turn and filled to overflowing with roast vegetables, beetroot with garlic sauce, peppers stuffed with feta.

A group of women in knee-length black skirts and black cardigans over black blouses natter away as they prepare bowl after bowl of tomato, cucumber, peppers, olives and feta, the olive oil poured liberally on top as local young men, turned waiters, hand them out along the trestle tables.

A man with a clarinet wanders around the square playing music from the mountains. His friend, seated with a bouzouki, accompanies him.

A stray dog sidles hopefully between tables and chairs. The only dog being fed belongs to one of the shepherds. The animal lies at his feet, licking from the floor any morsel his pack leader allows to drop.

As the food settles, the children begin to run and spin, playing tag in the area cleared for dancing. The musicians soak up their energy and amuse the youngsters with familiar tunes. Young men strut to the open area, the music changes and they dance with their arms outstretched, their hearts on fire, pride in their eyes. Older men, with less wine in their veins, take their places, showing them how it is done; the younger men taking a rest, kneeling on one knee and clapping their encouragement to the rhythm of the song.

A new music comes from the bouzouki player and the women give little shrieks, several of them take to the floor and dance with swaying hips, outstretched arms and circling wrists.

Abby is transfixed by all she sees, her heart full of the joy of her life and the people she has met, she feels she is home and yet …

'Stella?' She shouts over the music. 'Can I use the phone in the takeaway to ring my dad?'

'Yes, of course.' Stella has one hand resting on Mitsos' shoulder. She is singing to the music and waving her wine glass around.

'I'll pay,' Abby assures her, but Stella pulls a face.

The green walls look almost blue in the festive illuminations, the light dancing on the surfaces like underwater reflections, enchanting, cosy. The sound of the clarinet trails down from the square, haunting in the emptiness. It is hard to believe that only hours earlier she had been frightened for her life, right here, on this spot.

Abby draws the toe of her sandal across the boards she had stood on, terrified for her safety but too afraid to even hurt Stavros. She had been shocked by her own timidity - fancy poking him like that. She giggles in the quiet but tears prick her eyes; she had been very scared.

The fear when Stavros tried to kiss her had been different; flavoured with indignation, shock, horror, but he had not been violent enough for her to fear for her life, just bruises to her arms with his grip. Scary none the less.

She will not tell Dad any of this. Nor will she tell him of the wind, when the ferry could not leave and all her money spent on the ticket. That was a different fear, but still it was about her survival, and had felt bleak. She rubs her eyes with the tips of her fingers, recalling the memory of sitting on the bollard, the expanse of the sea stretching out before her, the enormity of the world behind her, alone and scared. Abby wonders what she would have done had the baker not turned up.

Perhaps the only thing she can tell Dad without him losing his cool would be about the tree falling on the shop. She has just seen Marina at the baptism party, and didn't even notice the cast on her leg at first, but she seemed in good spirits. She could tell Dad about that ... maybe.

The push-buttons of the phone are stiff, dirt clogging their depression.

She dials the number but there is silence and Abby is about to put the receiver down and try again when the tone turns to an intermittent purr.

She swallows. It will be nice to hear his voice. But what if he hasn't received the postcards? He will be furious. He'll probably be furious anyway. Abby takes the phone from her ear ready to replace it in the cradle; she can't handle Dad being cross. But then again him being cross is nothing compared to some of the things she has been through since she arrived in Greece. She puts the receiver back to her ear. She will let him know she is safe.

Imagine if her friends got to hear.

If she were to go home now and tell her friends all that has happened in the days she has been away they would be drooling at the height of emotion of it all, real soap opera stuff. Before she came away she had been just like that, wishing for some drama to ease the boredom, something exciting to happen to mark the day. Now it has happened she would gladly give it away - and spend the sun-filled days reading a book and peeling potatoes.

'Hello?' It is Sonia. Abby has not prepared herself for the possibility that Sonia might answer the phone.

'Abby is that you? Oh my goodness, we have been worried out of our minds, are you ok?'

This is exactly what she hadn't wanted. This was why she hadn't rung earlier. She ignores what Sonia says and asks again for Dad.

'Sorry, he's not here.' Sonia sounds softer than Abby remembers, more real somehow. She can picture her sitting in the hall, the dog probably looking up at her with his big eyes. She misses Rockie. His tail will be banging on the floor, his head to one side.

'You still there? You ok?' Sonia asks, 'We got your cards, it seems you have found a nice place.' But Abby can hear the tremor in her voice, suppressed emotion. Probably what Sonia really wants to do is shout about how she has worried them, stressed Dad out, been selfish. But her voice is gentle, caring, as if she is going to cry.

'Yes.' Abby pulls a serviette from the counter. 'It's been a bit of a roller-coaster ride but I am ok.' She surprises herself with the openness of her response. She rubs the tissue across her eyes.

'We sort of gather from your postcards that it hasn't been all straight forward.' Abby tries to remember what she has told them and what she has not, but so much has happened she cannot remember how discreet she has been. Sonia is saying something more, Abby tunes in again. 'But don't worry, I think he is anxious more than cross.'

'Is he there?' Abby asks, she wants to get this over with now. The clarinet is calling, her friends waiting, maybe this was not such a good idea.

'Abby, darling, you know what a fusser your Dad is, after the first postcard he was all for rushing out there to bring you home. I managed to persuade him that perhaps that wasn't the best thing to do, which was just as well as we both thought you were with Jackie on Soros, he would have ended up at the wrong place.' She lets out a short laugh, 'But when we got another postcard the next day, and it was clear that you had ended up somewhere entirely different, I couldn't stop him.'

'What? What do you mean couldn't stop him?' Abby's eyes widen.

'You didn't really expect ...'

'Sonia where is he?' Abby's voice sounds so in

control, so adult, she shocks herself.

'Look, your dad is your dad and always will be. You are his first-born, first love and all that, why else would he fly out there to be with you?' Sonia asks

'Flown here you mean? When?' Abby jumps up from the chair which falls over backwards, she looks out of the *ouzeri* window almost expecting to see him there in the street.

'Abby, hang on before you get all uppity. Listen, I am a bit worried for him to be honest. I am not worried for you. You are one of life's survivors.'

'When will he be here?' Abby is not sure if she is concerned, pleased or cross.

'Are you listening to me? I am worried about your dad. He stresses too much, over me, over you, the baby. Look at all that fuss he made about your A levels, what nonsense.'

'Sorry?' Sonia has Abby's attention now.

'Your dad with your A levels, of course you should do them, why on earth not? I think your education is paramount at this point in your life, don't you?'

'Really?' Abby picks up the chair and sits before she takes a tooth pick and begins digging out the dirt around the buttons on the telephone.

'Yes. Look Abby, I have had quite a strong word with him about school. Let him blow off some steam when he arrives if he needs to, and he probably will need too, but let's you and I agree you will be going back to do your A levels and I'll deal him later if we need to, ok?' Sonia sounds so kind, 'Don't be shouting back at him, raising his blood pressure, it's pointless. Oh, I need to pee again, no morning sickness, just a constant need to pee.'

Abby can hear her struggling to get out of the hall chair.

'You still there Abby?'

'Yes.'

'Ok so we are agreed, yes?'

'Ok.' She hears Rockie yap.

'Look I have to go to the loo. Will you do me a favour and persuade him to stay a few days, take a break, unwind, stop fussing. Give me a break too! Get him to swim in the sea, float a bit. Will you?'

'Um, Ok, I'll suggest it.'

They say quite a warm goodbye. Abby wonders how big Sonia's stomach is now and if she can feel the baby kicking yet. It feels funny that she is so far away.

Abby replaces the receiver and sits in the dark, listening to the party in the square, the laughter and the dancing. It's getting late. The dogs around the village stop their endless barking, the last cockerel gives his final salute. There is the occasional wooden creak of shutters being pulled on old hinges and the slam as they close: Abby finds it all so alien, all so familiar.

She is conscious of her happiness. A happiness that will be short-lived, Dad will be here soon, tomorrow, the next day?

He is going to make such a fuss when he gets here. What if he is rude to the villagers, ignoring them as he focuses on her? It will be humiliating. He'd better not dare to shout at her. He will ignore what she has to say, thinking he is right, that his way is the only way. Why are all grownups like that? She wonders where he is now. Athens airport, in a hotel somewhere?

She closes the *ouzeri* doors and wanders slowly back to the square. She will deal with Dad when he gets here. She can see Stella dancing, the 'sirtaki', the 'ten minute dance', because that's how long it took Abby to learn it. Step - step - kick, step - step - step - kick … Stella is arm in arm with her neighbours, the one on her left with his head bent forward, following Stella's steps, feet clumsy. His white shirt is striped

357

and for a moment his familiarity transforms him into Stavros, and Abby catches her breath. But Stella is laughing, the man is almost bent over following her steps. It cannot be Stavros, and besides, this man is not obese. He straightens, stands upright. Daddy! How can that be, she has only just got off the phone to Sonia? But then Sonia never said when he left ...

Abby's first instinct is to run and hug him, a rock in all this roller-coaster world she is part of. But her second impulse is to hide, avoid him, why can he not leave her be, let her have her own life, stop fussing? How does Sonia stand him?

Her feet continue unbidden until she is on the edge of the circle of dancers. Dad looks past her, he is laughing, he looks a little drunk. How long has he been here?

'Ah Abby, look who introduced himself to me!' Stella has no understanding of how or why he is here and a look of inquiry flits over her face replacing a dance of emotions. Abby notices Stella's big hoop earrings, like a gypsy's, they suit her floaty dress.

Dad turns, still smiling, but when he sees her he frowns and looks her up and down.

'Abby? Abby!' He says.

Abby marches off to the other side of the kiosk, hiding from view of her friends. Whatever he wants to say it will not be in public. Dad follows her.

'Abby darling …'

'Stop Dad, before you say anything I have talked to Sonia and it has all been agreed …'

'Hang on, what? Aren't you going to even say hello to your old man after I have flown all this way?' He opens his arms out, inviting her to hug him.

'Sure, hello.' Abby folds her arms and looks away.

There is a moment of tense silence.

'I hardly recognized you, you look, well, amazing. I love your trousers, very retro.' Abby doubts he knows what retro even means. 'Do you know I saw you earlier from a distance but I didn't recognize you at all, you look so, well, er, grown up.'

'It's hardly likely that I have changed in these few days, Dad.' Her tone sarcastic, 'How long have you been here?' She didn't mean to sound so sharp.

'Well, when I arrived it was odd, the village was empty and then some bells rang and all these people swarmed out of the church up here.' He turns to point. Abby decides that he is definitely tipsy, 'Someone pulled me with them and told me to drink, little shot glasses, all the men around me cheering and shouting something. It felt rude to refuse.' He giggles, Abby feels her cheeks colouring, it's so embarrassing, 'Then they invited me to eat. How amazing is that! I was starving but I tried to explain that I was looking for you, but they just brought me food and more wine and then that woman made me dance ...' He trails off.

'That's Stella. Dad, what are you doing here?' Abby meets his eye, defiant.

'Oh darling, did you think I wouldn't come? How could I not come? You must have been so cross at me to make such a big display of running away like this.' He puts his hand, tentatively, on her shoulder.

'It is not a display, and I have not run away,' Abby say and pulls her shoulder away from his hand with a twist from her waist, 'I am laying down some foundations so I can go to university, I am getting on with my life. I suggest you do the same.'

'Yes exactly, yes darling. I have been so taken up with the baby and everything that perhaps I didn't explain myself very well about your schooling. Of course you will do your A levels next year, of course my dear, I have talked with Sonia and she agrees, and then we will just have to see about university when we get to that bridge.'

Abby looks him up and down, he no longer frightens her. When did he suddenly become so annoying? But he clearly only means well. He would never treat Sonia like Stavros treated Stella, he is not bad in that way. But he does suffocate her, with his views, his superior knowledge. Look at his opinions on university - because he has never been he thinks there is no value in it, he thinks making a mark in the world is more important. Just because she does not have a laid out path he thinks that road does not exist.

He lives in a different world to her. A world where a job is a job for life, a trade a guaranteed income. Well that is not her world.

Greece has shown her something different. Something she never 'got' in any of her classes in school. For one thing she had never realised just how big the world is - or how small it is, lots of little places all linked together. More excitingly how the world is just lying there open for whoever wants to discover it and at every place she stops there seem to be so many paths that lead on from there. Well Dad, some are easy walking, like your job for life, guaranteed income path. Some are a bit more of a struggle, but she knows, in her life, there will always be a choice of direction and what matters most will be how she handles each step.

She smiles to herself.

Taking the wrong boat and ending up here, in this tiny village in the middle of nowhere, has taught her that if she grasps what's on offer with both hands she can create the best out of any circumstance.

Dad is smiling back at her, uncertainly.

She has also learnt, directly from Stavros, if she pokes at things in her way timidly it will not have much effect and the fear will seem insurmountable.

She unfolds her arms, she looks up at the stars. '*Stella*', apparently is the Greek word for star. Or is that Latin? It doesn't really matter …

Everything is made bearable with the right people around her, no matter what the path. People with whom she chooses to surround herself, not the random selection Dad has found himself involved in with his job. She steps from behind the kiosk so she can see her table of friends. Vasso is miming something for Juliet who is laughing. Stella is dancing, Strong women. Mitsos watching, tapping his crook against the table leg in time to the music. Impressive people.

Dad tentatively reaches out for her attention.

'Actually Dad, you are right,' Abby says. His smiles grow confident, but then his eyebrows arch as he senses there is more to come.

'I will be doing my A levels and I will go to university,' she takes a breath before adding, '… at some point.' She enunciates clearly. Dad frowns, his mouth hangs open a little. He has a piece of spinach between his teeth, Abby doesn't want to see and looks past him to the party. 'But right now what is most important is to get this business going with these friends I have made.' She pauses but Dad says nothing, he continues to stare at her. 'That comes first and then, my guess is, life will take care of the rest.' She edges out from the shield of the kiosk, Dad following her lead.

'You may not have physically grown since you have been here, but you sound like a different person.' He straightens his back and looks her in the eye, they are the same height. He seems surprised, as if he has only just noticed. Abby feels taller than him.

'Dad, will you do something for me?' She takes another couple of steps towards her friends, away from him.

'Yes, what do you need?' His back softens immediately, he tries to keep in step to look at her. Abby notices he has one or two grey hairs at his temple. She taps her own teeth with her finger and looks him in the mouth.

'Thank you,' he mutters and takes a hanky from his pocket and rubs it against his mouth.

'Will you stay a few days, give Sonia a rest from your fussing and yourself a rest from your stressing?"

His first expression is shock, then he smiles and

shrugs before considering and then he nods. They have reached Abby's friends.

'So you must be Abby's dad?'

'Bernard' He says.

'Hello. I am Juliet.' She holds out her hand and shakes his vigorously. 'Now take hold of this', she passes him and Abby each a little shot glass, she holds another out to Vasso, and picks two more up for Stella and Mitsos. When they are all gathered around Juliet continues.

'Bernard, there are two very important words you must learn, they mean "to your health", but they also mean more than that, they mean here's to life, here's to seizing the day, squeezing the joy out of living. *"Yia Mas",'* she shouts.

They all chink glasses. *"Yia mas,"* they shout, which is responded to by those on the neighbouring table, the call of *"yia mas"* ripples out from the centre, through a sea of smiling faces.

Bernard puts his arm around Abby and pulls her close, she leans into him, just perceptibly, and smiles.

As Mitsos stands he whispers, 'My beautiful Gypsy, my dream,' and gives Stella a small bow as he takes hold of his crook to leave the square and amble his way home. Stella responds with a grin which breaks into a laugh.

Vasso links her arms with Stella and Juliet stands, holding firmly to the back of her chair.

'See you tomorrow,' Mitsos says with a wink, and begins to head towards the road to his home and then suddenly changes direction and makes his way over to his brother to wish him and the baby well.

Stella watches the back-slapping and the laughter. Mitsos' younger brother, who is not so young now, has the same nose but his eyes are not as kind. He takes something from his top pocket and presses it into Mitsos' hand. Mitsos seems to be refusing but his brother is insistent. New drinks are brought to the table, and while his sibling is distracted Mitsos quietly walks away.

Stella loves this about him, his humility, never one to push himself on anyone. She leans against Vasso, gazing at his retreating back, which slightly curves as the crook takes his weight.

'For goodness sake, you are like a soppy teenager. Get a grip, woman.' Vasso smiles.

'No, enjoy Stella, enjoy,' Juliet's speech is slurred.

'Ok, who's for a little night cap?' Stella turns her eyes to her three friends and then sees Bernard. 'Ah, Bur-nards, a drink to your wonderful daughter.' she laughs.

'Don't mind if I do.' he raises his glass. '*Yia mas!*'